The Blue Haired Girl

ADAM HAYES

Copyright 2019 Adam Hayes

All rights reserved.

ISBN: 9781071163672

DEDICATION

On August 23, 2017, I was diagnosed with a deadly cancer known as Hodgkin's Lymphoma and nearly died from the disease.

Therefore, I would like to dedicate this book to:

Dr. Edward Brooks
Dr. Muthanna Kettana
Dr. Howard Roy Gilbert
Dr. Willie Jay Pewarchuk
Dr. Marilyn Vanderputten

And all the rest of the hard-working medical staff of British Columbia whose combined efforts saved my life. It is because of them that I am alive today to write this book.

On behalf of myself and all other cancer survivors, I would like to recognize them for their tireless efforts.

You are all my heroes.

Thank you,

Sincerely,

Adam Hayes

ACKNOWLEDGMENTS

Erica Orloff – Editor
http://www.editingforauthors.com

Paisley Prophet – Proofreader
https://www.fiverr.com/p_prophet/edit-and-proofread-your-
ebook-in-72-hours?ref_ctx_id=4b8c017c-85d8-4cb8-aa37-
367daa1eb713

Oliviaprodesign - Cover Design
https://www.fiverr.com/oliviaprodesign/design-professional-
book-covers?ref_ctx_id=01ae7f2b-a71e-405d-89cd-
1914f871dc4d

- CHAPTER 1 -
The Missing Gemstone

"Keep looking, rat! It's here somewhere!" hissed Mareitsia menacingly as she threw Anni to the ground beside the wagon.

There was a loud cracking sound as the end of Mareitsia's whip found the small of Anni's back.

An all-too-familiar pain shot through the slave girl's torso as she crawled on the earth before her owner.

"I'm looking, Mistress!" whimpered Anni as she dove under the wagon to search the dry, brown grass. "But I don't remember ever seeing a stone like that."

"Don't be foolish! It's worth more than you are! Find that stone!"

Anni pawed through the grass, a pair of cursed black

THE BLUE HAIRED GIRL

bracelets dangling from her wrists as she searched for the lost gemstone. They hadn't seen a person, let alone a customer, in more than a week, and they had been heading further east for hours each day, so the missing gemstone was probably long gone.

There was another loud crack of the whip from outside the wagon. Anni pulled herself further under the shelter of the carriage, running her hands across the bent grass, searching for the stone and hiding from her mistress.

Mareitsia, Anni's owner, was a busty, middle-aged, mean-spirited drunk. She was a fortune-teller in a one-woman show, who worked and conned along the borderlands between Golairia and Yuspiereia. Anni had long since figured out that her mistress was a fraud, as she made the same predictions over and over again, no matter whose fortune she was telling. Plus, real fortune-tellers usually don't have slaves steal from the pockets of their customers.

Slavery was not uncommon along the borderlands, as slaves were cheap and generally easy to attain. Slavery was officially outlawed in Yuspiereia, but it was rarely enforced along the fluid borderlands, as few would dare risk accidentally stumbling into Golairia.

The vast open region bordering Yuspiereia and Golairia was known as the "goatlands" to the locals, and it was where Mareitsia ran her business. The land had earned its name from a combination of the word "grassland" and the favorite euphemism

12

THE MISSING GEMSTONE

"fit for a goat," meaning not worthy of humans.

The goatlands could be best described as a land of nothing.

Other than a few villages of thieves, cutthroats, and slavers, the goatlands were just an empty expanse of endless rolling hills and tall, brown, windswept grass that went for thousands of miles in every direction. Anni had lived with Mareitsia on the vast emptiness of the goatlands for her entire life. Mareitsia had bought Anni from a slave market when she was too young to remember.

Mareitsia's business model was simple. She entertained the customers with fake seances and spirit readings, and sold overpriced talismans and other assorted junk. It was Anni's job to keep the place clean and occasionally steal from the customer's pockets whenever she got the chance.

The only thing Anni had ever known was a life of scrubbing pots, washing clothes, and occasional thievery for her mistress.

"Where is that stone!? Dwarf! I order you to find that stone, now!"

"We'll find your damned stone!" barked Kolten.

Kolten was a short, bulky, bald-headed dwarf. He was Mareitsia's only other slave, and his job was more laborious than Anni's: cutting firewood, mending the wagon, hauling heavy loads, basically anything that required good hands and a strong

THE BLUE HAIRED GIRL

back. He, too, pawed across the ground, searching for the lost gemstone.

"It's here somewhere! Anni, any luck?"

"It's not down here," Anni replied, crawling out from under the battered, old wagon, her blue hair dusty and covered in dry grass.

Another loud crack pierced the air, and Anni collapsed to the ground from the force of Mareitsia's whip.

"What's it look like?" asked Kolten.

"You're a dwarf!" snapped Mareitsia. "It's a gemstone! Should be easy for you!"

"I'm not a miner!" he replied through gritted teeth at this rather crude stereotype. "What's it look like?!"

"It looks like a gemstone! Are you deaf and ugly? Find it now! I order you!"

"I'm looking, you old—" but Kolten's insult was cut off by a sharp intake of breath, as if someone had just jabbed him with a sharp object.

"I don't want you looking! I want you to find it! I need it, now!"

Anni kept crawling around on her hands and knees, poking and prodding through the tall grass. She found Mareitsia's sudden need to find the stone to be bordering on the insane. Even if they found it, what possible use would Mareitsia have for a gemstone out here?

THE MISSING GEMSTONE

There was no store or shop anywhere nearby to spend it at, and as far as Anni knew, the only thing Mareitsia ever bought was wine.

"Rat! Are you looking?!" she barked at her slave.

"Yes, Mistress!" said Anni quickly. "It's not over here!"

"Then why are you looking over there?! Look somewhere else!"

Anni knew what was coming. Mareitsia had a violent temper, and beatings would soon follow.

"I found it!" shouted Kolten. "No, wait; it's just a rock."

Mareitsia let out a scream of fury, and a threatening crack of her whip pierced the air, along with a stream of muffled swear words.

There was only one thing for it: Anni needed to act before Mareitsia's temper boiled over. She had just one card to play, and it was risky, but it was the only chance either of them had to avoid the beating to come.

"Mistress," said Anni, looking up from the ground, "why don't you rest and have a drink while me and Kolten keep looking for it? It can't be far. I'll fetch your wineskin from the wagon."

There was a brief silence as Anni prayed, holding her breath.

"Well, don't just sit there, rat! It's in the food locker!

THE BLUE HAIRED GIRL

Go on!"

Anni sighed in relief as she sprinted across the campsite, before Mareitsia could change her mind.

Anni knew her mistress well enough to know she had already been drinking. She liked to keep some extra wine hidden in her bed in the wagon. Although, judging by her foul mood, it was likely that whatever secret stash she had was gone. There wasn't much point in hiding it, as neither Anni nor Kolten could touch it, even if they wanted to.

Anni pulled open the food locker at the rear of the wagon beside the tool chest.

As Anni opened the locker, she noticed that they were entirely out of food. This was not altogether surprising, as neither Anni nor Kolten had eaten anything in days. Mareitsia must have finished the last of the food herself earlier today, and the water barrel wasn't far behind.

Food was not only scarce on the goatlands, other than the few villages scattered around, it was practically nonexistent. It was an awful place that Mareitsia had chosen to run her business, but she risked capture anywhere closer to civilization.

But there was no time to worry about the food situation now.

Mareitsia's wineskin hung inside the empty food locker, and Anni grabbed it.

Right away, she noticed that, while it wasn't empty, it

16

THE MISSING GEMSTONE

was nowhere near full. Still, she hoped it would be enough to render her mistress unconscious for the evening.

Mareitsia snatched the wineskin from Anni and took a long, deep swig of the cheap wine, and Anni returned to her fruitless search, waiting for the drink to have its desired effect.

Even with her mistress's back to her, Anni had no choice but to continue to crawl through the tall grass, searching for the missing gem.

It was ironic that the grass in this part of the goatlands was so high. If only Anni could duck and crawl just like she was doing but *away* from the wagon, she could escape, and Mareitsia would likely never notice until it was too late. Anni would have loved nothing more than to start running, but this was impossible. The hoop-like bracelets around Anni's wrists shifted as she scoured the grass.

After close to an hour of fruitless searching, she and Kolten had both turned up nothing. The sun was starting to dip behind the highest rolling hills to the west, casting shadows in the two parallel wheel tracks the wagon had left in the grasses behind them. The lines snaked over the endless hills and seemed to go on well past forever.

When the sun finally fell below the horizon, leaving the goatlands in the dim shadow of early nightfall, Mareitsia called Anni and Kolten over to her.

Their mistress's wineskin lay on the ground. It was

THE BLUE HAIRED GIRL

missing its stopper, and the container was flat with emptiness.

Cursing her bad luck, Anni obeyed and approached her mistress, who sat hiccupping next to the campfire.

The woman stared into the fire and spoke to Anni and Kolten with a cold, disdaining voice, her tone a product of wine, hunger, and her sheer loathing for her two slaves.

"You don't believe me, do you?" she said in a slightly shaky voice.

"Mistress?" said Kolten, with a look over at Anni.

"Y-You don't think I can find it?" she said, with a slight burp on the last word.

"Mistress, we've been looking for your gem…" started Anni, not knowing what to say.

"I'm not talking about the gem, you stupid, blue-haired rat!" she spat.

Anni opened her mouth and closed it again, before touching her hair instinctively.

"You don't like me, do you?" she slurred.

Neither Anni nor Kolten dared to speak.

"I know you're just here cuz a those," she said, indicating the black, hoop-like bracelets that covered all four of her slaves' wrists.

Their shackles, called darkwrists, were deceptively simple-looking, small, black, bangle-like bracelets imbued with evil magic. They were the absolute bane of Anni and Kolten's

18

THE MISSING GEMSTONE

existence, far worse than Mareitsia's whip.

Darkwrists were designed to cause pain to slaves and keep them from acting against their masters. They would punish and torture the wearers by tightening, burning, or cutting into their wrists without any of the usual constrictions of iron chains. The wearers could carry out their masters' bidding without their owners fearing their slaves' escape, making them the perfect tool to keep slaves in check.

Darkwrists were illegal in most of the civilized world, including Yuspiereia, and just owning a pair carried a severe punishment. But the isolation of the goatlands kept them beyond the reach of the Yuspiereian government, rendering the borders mostly lawless. So Mareitsia had never been caught, nor was she likely to be anytime soon.

Of course, Mareitsia was wrong about one thing. It wasn't that they didn't like her. They hated her.

They had endured years of beatings, starvation, abuse, and occasional sadistic torture at the hands of their mistress. If it weren't for the darkwrists, Anni and Kolten would have abandoned Mareitsia years ago, and Kolten probably would have killed her.

Mareitsia picked up the empty wineskin. She bent her head back, facing the sky to allow the last drops of liquid to fall into her mouth. When not a single tear fell from the hopelessly empty wineskin, she angrily tossed it into the fire.

19

THE BLUE HAIRED GIRL

The campfire surged for a moment as the alcohol-soaked vessel caught fire. Within moments, it had dissolved, consumed by the flames.

"I own you, you know," she said to both of them.

"Yes, Mistress, you do," said Anni in a defeated tone.

"Right!" she thundered, with an exaggerated and unsteady gesture toward Anni. "I can make you do whatever I want, right, dwarf?" she added, turning to Kolten.

Kolten's look was cold and full of the purest loathing, but he remained quiet and slowly nodded.

"Right," she said as she shook her head left and right, as if trying to ward off some unseen insect.

"Now, where's the gemstone?!" she demanded.

Anni's heart sank.

"We don't know where it is," said Kolten.

"Yes, we do! Go get it!"

Kolten didn't move, and his darkwrists didn't react. There was a weakness in the magic that gave them the occasional reprieve. The darkwrists could only force them to follow her instructions when it was possible to do so.

Anni was quite convinced that the stone didn't exist, but they had made a genuine effort to find it.

"Get me that gem!"

The darkwrists did nothing. They were limited to enforcing orders that were possible for the slaves to carry out.

20

THE MISSING GEMSTONE

This was a critical loophole that Mareitsia occasionally missed, especially when she was drinking.

Still, even if the darkwrists wouldn't force them to find the stone, Mareitsia's whip was still by her hand.

"I ordered you to find it!"

"And we couldn't," said Kolten.

"You stole it, didn't you?!"

"No," said Anni automatically.

"You would love to have it all to yourself, wouldn't you? You filthy rat!"

"No, Mistress," said Anni, knowing it was too late. Her faint hope that Mareitsia would pass out before their beating had failed.

"You both will pay for this!" she sneered as she forced herself unsteadily to her feet. "Don't move!"

The darkwrists held them firmly in place, as if cemented in midair. Mareitsia took a few moments to steady herself as she picked up the whip from the ground, with a look of drunken malice across her face.

- CHAPTER 2 -
Lost

"Thief!" screamed Mareitsia as she drew back the whip and struck Anni in the small of her back, the smell of cheap wine clinging to her breath.

"*It wasn't my fault! I didn't steal anything!*" wailed Anni as the whip struck her bare back, leaving a deep red scar to match the others. The magic shackles on her wrists held her firmly in place.

"Liar!" she replied as the whip found its mark again. "That gem was worth more than you!"

"It wasn't her fault!" protested Kolten. "There...there must have been a hole in the bag!" said the dwarf.

"Silence, dwarf!" she sneered, as she drew back the whip

22

LOST

and struck Kolten for good measure.

The dwarf gritted his teeth and said nothing more.

"I should sell you both for this!"

With each additional blow, Anni grew steadily fainter, and she was already tired from the lack of food. She had hoped that encouraging Mareitsia to get drunk would help them escape her violent temper. Unfortunately, they didn't seem to have enough wine. As cruel as Mareitsia could be when sober, when she was somewhere between drunk and unconscious, she was downright terrifying. Trying to get the alcoholic gypsy to drink was a high-risk gamble that had paid off in the past, but tonight fate was not on their side.

"I'm sorry!" Anni sobbed as another blow came cracking against her side, sending a wave of pain up her torso.

Anni's eyes were full of tears, and her wrists were bloody and scarred from the magical shackles binding her solidly in place. Her naturally sky-blue hair was stained with filth and dried blood from the beating. It had been dirtied by her crawling around in the dry grass looking for the fictitious stone.

As the old gypsy drew back her whip once again, she suddenly lost her balance and collapsed to the ground beside the campfire. She fell asleep almost immediately. The whip's handle still in her hand, she snored loudly, the smell of cheap wine wafting through the air.

Mercifully, the darkwrists loosened their hold, and the

THE BLUE HAIRED GIRL

two could rest on the cold, grassy earth now that Mareitsia had finally passed out.

Anni dared to reach her hand around her back to touch the marks left by the blows. More pain shot through her side as her fingers felt wetness.

"One day…" panted Anni through gritted teeth, and she sat on her backside on the cold ground.

Kolten placed his hand on her shoulder lightly, avoiding the areas the whip had struck. The dwarf sighed, staring down at the magic shackles that had been the source of their years of torment.

"Anni…" said Kolten hopelessly.

Anni's face remained defiant as her shackles started to heat up magically; she ignored the burning pain on her already scarred and blistered wrists. She stared furiously at the whip lying in Mareitsia's unconscious hand only a few feet away. It may as well have been on the other side of the world. The darkwrists would never let her get anywhere near it.

"I hate—" but she was cut off by her darkwrists as they quickly grew spikes on the inside of their rings and ruptured her blisters. A small trickle of blood poured down her wrists and dripped off the tip of her finger, falling to the ground.

The campfire gave out a sudden crack as the last fragments of Mareitsia's wineskin vanished in flames. Anni wondered if Mareitsia would remember what she had done with

24

it in the morning. More than likely, she would blame her slaves for its disappearance, just as she had done with the gemstone.

"*Caw!*"

Anni sneered at the sound of the nearby bird. Blade, Mareitsia's nasty and clever raven, was perched high above their heads on top of the gypsy's wagon, looking down at the pair coldly. He had returned from feeding, his talons empty but stained with the blood of some poor rodent.

It was a pity that the bird had not bothered to bring his meal back with him. Anni was so hungry that she would have seriously considered wrestling the bird's meal away from him and taking whatever punishment the darkwrists or her mistress imposed. It seemed, however, that Blade had been smart enough to eat his fill before returning to camp.

"You know, one day, she's going to sell you to a butcher," spat Kolten at the nasty bird. Kolten twitched slightly and gave a sharp intake of breath, presumably as the darkwrists punished him for it.

Blade gave one final caw of insolence and flew over Kolten and Anni's heads. The bird circled above them a few times.

Suddenly, the raven dove at Kolten's face with its claws at the ready.

At the last second, the bird pulled up when Kolten tried to swat it away. The dwarf winced from the darkwrists, and

THE BLUE HAIRED GIRL

the bird cawed maniacally at the pain it had caused. Blade then landed and settled once more on top of the wagon.

Kolten picked up a twig from their dwindling pile of firewood and began to stoke the fire. The flames struggled as a gust of soft wind blew past and rustled the tall grass nearby. They always kept the fires small. A few wayward coals could quickly start a brush fire on the dry, open fields, fed by the constant wind.

One of the unsettling things about the goatlands was the silence. The region's population was so sparse that days or even weeks could go by without a sound being heard from anything other than the constant wind and the gentle swaying of the grass.

The openness and stillness of the area always gave Anni a feeling of unease that she could never really get over. They were completely exposed and uncomfortably close to the Golairian border.

Tonight, however, the endless whispers of the wind on the tall grass and the crackling of the fire were broken by the occasional sound of Mareitsia's long, drunken snores.

Despite the beating, it was a beautiful night. The stars glowed brightly over the goatlands from one horizon to the other, but neither of Decareia's two moons was visible yet.

"Where are we going tomorrow?" asked Anni, looking over at Kolten.

LOST

"We'll keep heading east, I guess."

"What about the horses? You said…"

"I know, they are dying, the same as we are. There's not enough water for us, let alone for the horses, and I know that front wheel won't last another week."

"What will we do, then?"

"Same as we always do, take it as it comes."

The idea of trying to deal with Mareitsia's violent temper with a broken wagon wheel or lame horses was a terrible thought. The image of her and Kolten being forced to pull the cart themselves under Mareitsia's whip flashed through Anni's mind.

One of Kolten's duties was to keep the wagon working, and he had warned her in the past that it was falling apart, but one of the many things Mareitsia didn't do well was listen.

Things would be even worse now that the wine was gone, but they had no choice. The darkwrists kept them following Mareitsia's orders, even if it was to their deaths.

Despite that rather unhappy disaster looming just over the horizon and the new scars on her back, this was still the best part of the day. Mareitsia had passed out for the night, so she couldn't order them around. As long as they finished their duties, the darkwrists wouldn't bother them, and they could stay up as late as they wanted.

The dwarf Kolten Citrane was the only friend Anni had

THE BLUE HAIRED GIRL

ever had, and the closest thing she knew to a father. He had been a part of her life for as long as she could remember.

The dwarf had very kind, brown eyes, and a completely bald head. His brown beard reached down to his waist and hung under his chin like a cascading waterfall. Kolten was very good with his hands and could fix almost anything.

He was short like all dwarves, with huge, bulging muscles built for working in the forges and digging in the mines. His long, slightly crooked nose was somewhat birdlike. The dwarf's heavily tanned skin had many scars and bruises, covering his entire body from countless years of enslavement.

Anni had asked him before how old he was, but Kolten's enslavement had lasted for so long, he couldn't remember his age anymore. Still, a good guess was that he was well into his sixties, which is not overly old for a dwarf.

Despite his rough exterior, the dwarf had a soft spot for Anni. He had, on occasion, taken beatings for her by claiming responsibility for things that were her fault. And Anni had long since realized that if it weren't for the dwarf's help, it was unlikely she would have survived this long.

Anni herself, on the other hand, was very different from the rough-and-tumble dwarf. She was human—at least, she appeared to be—and was skinny from a lack of food. Kolten had counted eight winters since Mareitsia had bought her, so they guessed that Anni was about eleven years old.

28

LOST

Anni was about the same height as the dwarf, though nowhere near as muscular, having much more delicate features. Anni had never known where she was from, who her parents were, how she had wound up at the slave market all those years ago, or even if she had a last name. The only thing Anni knew about herself, for sure, was that she was the only person anywhere who seemed to have naturally blue hair.

Mareitsia always did her best to keep Anni hidden from her customers because they tended to find her blue hair distracting, so she always made sure Anni kept it covered when she was around anyone other than Kolten and Mareitsia herself.

Still, the odd time when someone did see her hair, it always came with the sideways glances, whispers, and looks of disapproval, as if it were blue on purpose.

Nothing in Anni's life was on purpose.

"How's your back?" Kolten asked as the goatlands' breeze passed through his beard.

Anni reached her hand around her back again, but before she touched the wounds, she retracted it as pain shot through her torso.

Suddenly, Mareitsia let out a particularly loud and drunken snore.

"All she does is sit around and sleep," muttered Anni coldly.

"What else is there to do?" asked Kolten.

29

THE BLUE HAIRED GIRL

"What do you mean?" she said, turning to the dwarf to find that he had cocked an eyebrow.

"Anni, we're lost."

"What?!"

Kolten took a deep breath.

"I've been stuck with that woman for longer than even she can remember, and we've never been this far east before. She has no idea where we are. I've tried telling her that, but she wouldn't listen."

Anni suspected from Kolten's tone that he had been wanting to tell her this for quite a while.

"There must be a village or a road or something somewhere around here."

Kolten sighed.

"It's possible, but we haven't seen a sign of anyone in ages. No smoke, no tracks, no buildings, not even garbage. Nothing."

"Maybe tomorrow we'll find someone..."

"Anni, I've seen maps of this area before; the goatlands stretch for thousands of miles to the east. Whatever Mareitsia thought we were heading toward, we've obviously missed it. She just keeps pushing us deeper and deeper into the goatlands, getting us more and more lost."

Anni wanted nothing more than to not believe it. Mareitsia had been talking about a village to the east for days now, but they had found nothing, and all signs of civilization had long since vanished.

She lay there on the cold dirt, looking up at the vast skies that stretched all around them. Kolten was right: no smoke, roads, buildings, or signs of habitation anywhere. The only light under the endless night sky was their small, crackling campfire. There was not so much as a candle anywhere to pierce the perpetual darkness in every direction.

They were well and truly lost.

The thought of an old, rotting wagon materialized in Anni's mind. She could visualize three dried, sunbaked skeletons lying by a rotten old wagon, all completely forgotten by everyone but the gentle goatlands breeze tugging at the tattered remains of their clothing.

It was not a pleasant thought.

"We're out of food, you know," said Anni abruptly.

"I know," Kolten grunted.

Then the raven took off from his perch atop the wagon. Once again, he circled over Anni and Kolten's heads as he had done before. This time, instead of diving at Kolten, he lifted his clawed feet and defecated on him.

The dwarf wiped the white, smelly goo from his beard as best he could with the back of his hand. He uttered a swear word at Blade as the raven returned to the wagon, where his cage was kept.

THE BLUE HAIRED GIRL

Anni crawled over to Kolten and lay down beside him; she felt the sharp stabbing pains in her back stinging anew. Mareitsia's whip had left such painful marks, she was forced to sleep on her front, and her wrists ached worse than usual, making it impossible to get comfortable. The painful marks in her back would make it difficult for her to work.

Anni couldn't help but think of what was coming tomorrow. They would be facing something far worse than a hungry or drunk mistress. In a few hours, Mareitsia would go from drunk to hungover, and that could be far worse.

Anni rested her head down in the dirt by the dying campfire, her back in pain, and her stomach growling from hunger.

Like many nights before this one, Anni cried herself to sleep.

- CHAPTER 3 -
The Crystal Ball

"Rat! Have you fixed breakfast yet?!" Mareitsia wailed as she sat up, her whip still in her hand.

If Mareitsia passed-out drunk was the best part of Anni's day, then the following morning was a strong competitor for the worst. Usually, Anni did her best to make sure her daily chores kept her well away from Mareitsia when she woke up after a night of heavy drinking.

Mareitsia was furious, hungover, and hungry. All Anni could do was hope that burying herself in her chores would help keep her out of her mistress's way.

Their pitiful campfire from the night before had gone out while they slept, and Kolten was busy looking around the tall

THE BLUE HAIRED GIRL

grass for something they could use as firewood. Although the grass itself was dry enough, it tended to burn far too quickly to make a useful fuel for sustained fire.

Without the heat of a campfire, Anni had no choice but to use a pot of cold water to wash Mareitsia's clothes. She stirred them with a large, wooden cooking spoon and beat them against the side of the container with her bare hands.

As Anni did the washing, she hoped that Mareitsia would leave her be, at least until her clothes were dry. If Mareitsia chose to beat her, it would risk getting her wet clothes dirty, and Anni would have to start all over again.

Other than Mareitsia's wine binge, none of them had eaten since the food had run out. Anni was not looking forward to reminding Mareitsia of that rather unpleasant fact.

Before Anni could think of an answer to Mareitsia's demand for food, Kolten spoke up.

"We're out of food, Mistress," he said from under the axle of the front wheel.

The dwarf was busy with his tools, working on one of the wagon wheels. He had a grim look on his face.

Fortunately, Mareitsia seemed to remember their lack of food suddenly, and perhaps the effort of wielding the whip didn't seem worth risking her hangover getting worse.

Instead of losing her temper again, Mareitsia got up from the ground and walked behind the wagon. There was the sound

THE CRYSTAL BALL

of splashing as Mareitsia squandered some of their precious water. She emerged from the back of the wagon, her face and clothes dripping wet, and entered the carriage presumably to rest.

Anni could make out the impression of their water barrel behind the wagon, lying on its side, its valuable content spilled all over the grass where Mareitsia had let it fall.

She quickly tried to get up to see how much they had lost, but the darkwrists held her firmly in place.

"That's the last of the water!" she protested, but the darkwrists did not let her move.

They didn't seem to care whether or not they were in danger, only that Anni was trying to stop doing her chores.

The pain in her wrists that followed forced her to continue to wash Mareitsia's clothes in her cooking pot that now contained the last remains of their drinking water. She watched in horror as her own hands were forced to dirty this now extremely precious resource to clean Mareitsia's clothing.

One by one, Mareitsia's ugly dresses, socks, and undergarments were dunked into the pot, scrubbed as clean as they could be. Each article of clothing rendered the last of their water evermore dark, filthy, and undrinkable.

A large piece of black cloth bubbled to the surface of the large pot. It was a triangular headscarf. Mareitsia had long since ordered Anni to wear it whenever they approached a village. It might have been that Mareitsia didn't appreciate Anni's hair

THE BLUE HAIRED GIRL

drawing attention away from her show.

Anni didn't much like the headscarf—it didn't breathe, it was hot and itchy—but compared to everything else in her life, wearing it was a minor annoyance.

Over the last few weeks, Anni had been allowed to wear the scarf less and less because they hadn't seen any people in ages.

When the last item of clothing was clean, the darkwrists even forced her to dump the pot of dirty water out on the grass and leave the pot upside-down to drain, as this was a regular part of the chore.

The dirty water disappeared into the brown grass and seeped into the dry soil.

It was official: they were entirely out of water.

She's going to beat me for this for sure, Anni thought.

There was no time to dwell on this, as the darkwrists reminded her that there were more chores to do. The lack of water and food meant Anni couldn't cook anything or clean very much, and the darkwrists seem to understand this.

The only task she could think of at the moment was polishing and organizing Mareitsia's charms, which sadly meant entering the wagon, where Mareitsia was resting.

Anni approached the wagon entrance and knocked on the door as she was supposed to.

"Go away, dwarf! I told you, I don't care about the damned wheel!" she called.

36

THE CRYSTAL BALL

"It's me, Mistress. I need to polish your charms,"

"Fine"—she snorted—"but keep it down."

Anni entered the small wagon, and the light from the morning sun illuminated the carriage.

The chipped and faded paint of Mareitsia's wagon was an ugly collection of primary colors, mostly reds, and yellows.

The front side of the wagon had a small, soft bed with a blanket that Mareitsia was lying in half-asleep, and beside it on the floor was her whip. Set over and beside the bed were a few shelves of things that Anni wasn't allowed to touch.

The sight of Mareitsia's whip on the floor made the marks on Anni's back start to sting anew, but she forced herself to ignore it.

Mounted on the wall opposite the door was a fold-up table. A small leather chest with a padded cover was next to it, where customers could sit when Mareitsia conducted her phony seances.

The only other furniture in the wagon was Blade's metal birdcage, which hung over the center of the room. The raven sat in it, eyeing Anni callously.

Anni took a quick look over at her mistress. Mareitsia lay facing the front of the wagon, with her back to Anni.

Anni bent down and opened the leather chest quietly, to not bother Mareitsia or cause Blade to rouse her.

The box contained her usual assortment of junk: a

37

THE BLUE HAIRED GIRL

jumble of tarot cards where every other one predicted death, and cheap costume jewelry she sold to ward off the disasters that her cards predicted. There was also a set of weighted dice, several "magic stones" that they had found on the side of the road, some wooden chicken bones for soothsaying, and near the bottom of the trunk was Anni's least favorite of Mareitsia's wares. Mareitsia sold the vials of fake yellow "potion" as everything from a love potion to a miracle cure-all for diseases.

The potions were just as fake as everything else Mareitsia sold. Anni already knew, all too well, what the smelly, yellow liquid was. Collecting it from the horses was one of Anni's chores, and on one occasion, she was even forced to produce the yellow liquid herself when the horses were unable to.

The thought made her shudder with disgust.

It was revolting to imagine one of Mareitsia's customers applying the disgusting liquid to an infected wound, or adding it to a drink in hopes of attracting a lover.

Anni began to organize Mareitsia's tarot cards when she was suddenly interrupted.

The sinister little bird had hopped down from his cage and perched atop the chest's open lid, staring at her. His beady little eyes looked up at her scornfully.

"Go away," muttered Anni. "I'm busy." She balanced the neatly organized tarot card deck on the corner of the chest. This way, she could put them away when she had finished assembling

THE CRYSTAL BALL

the rest of the odds and ends in the box.

Blade did not seem to appreciate being brushed off like this, especially by the slave that cleaned his cage. He gave Anni's blistered wrist a hard peck right under the darkwrists, sending a shot of pain up her arm.

The raven had long since figured out that the darkwrists caused them great pain, and prevented her from responding to his or Mareitsia's torments.

"*Caw!*" he cackled loudly, and Mareitsia stirred.

"Please…" Anni whispered. "Just let her sleep."

"*Caw!*" he cackled again.

"Rat! Stop bothering Blade," Mareitsia murmured from her bed.

Anni looked away from the bird and returned to the chest.

Blade sat there, still perched menacingly on the side of the open chest lid as Anni leaned forward into it.

"Ow!" said Anni as pain shot through her head.

A tuft of sky-blue hair was clasped in Blade's beak, and he looked very pleased with himself.

Anni touched the back of her head where the hair had been.

With gritted teeth, she returned to organizing Mareitsia's things. It was clear that the bird was rather enjoying himself.

Anni reached down into the chest and started counting

39

THE BLUE HAIRED GIRL

the number of faux magic stones, when Blade made a sudden move.

The bird flapped his wings quickly, and the stack of neatly piled tarot cards that Anni had just organized scattered across the floor.

"Caw! Caw! Caw!" he said in a laughing tone.

"Shut up!" Mareitsia shouted, and the blankets on the bed shifted.

Anni clenched her jaw and glared down at the raven, who almost seemed to smile at her. She started gathering up the cards that now littered the wagon floor and organizing them all over again.

Blade hopped into the chest and pulled out a vial of translucent yellow liquid. Perching atop one of the walls of the chest and grasping the bottle under one of his talons, he started working away at the stopper with his beak.

"No, please," Anni whispered. "She'll kill me!"

The bird stopped for a moment, glared at her, and then returned to his work.

Anni knew there was nothing she could do to stop him. In moments, the entire wagon was about to be drenched with warm horse urine, and they had no water to clean it.

All Anni could think of doing was to remove Mareitsia's belongings from the chest to keep them from getting damaged.

She started gathering up Mareitsia's belongings when her

40

THE CRYSTAL BALL

eyes fell upon an object in the bottom of the chest.

It was Mareitsia's old, scratched crystal ball. Anni couldn't remember the gypsy ever keeping it in here.

Quickly, Anni reached past the bird, who was starting to make progress on the stopper of the yellow vial. She reached into the chest and retrieved the glass sphere.

As she pulled the crystal ball from the chest, it suddenly began to glow.

Blade gave up his battle with the vial's cork for a moment, as both he and Anni stared at it in amazement.

The small sphere grasped in Anni's hand glowed as if it were a miniature sun. Anni had seen and helped Mareitsia run her show many times before, but she had never seen anything like this. This trick was far more impressive than any of Mareitsia's others.

The glowing sphere began to scream. It was a shrill, piercing shriek that sounded like a wounded animal.

Anni was so shocked that she dropped the crystal ball, and the moment it left her fingers, the screaming in her ears stopped. The crystal thudded to the floor, but thankfully, it didn't break.

She and Blade stared at each other for a moment. Anni wasn't sure if he had heard it too, but the bird did seem as dumbfounded as she was, like he had seen something impossible.

She didn't dare touch the crystal again, but she couldn't

THE BLUE HAIRED GIRL

leave it on the floor. Using her dress like an oven mitt, Anni bent
down to pick it up.

As the cloth from her dress wrapped around the crystal,
she felt something pressing on her back.

"Rat! You're not allowed to touch that!" yelled Mareitsia.

It was her mistress's foot, which held Anni to the floor.

Mareitsia reached over to retrieve her whip, but Anni
managed to wriggle free and slip out of the wagon. She was so
disheveled from the experience with the crystal ball that she
barely felt the pain from the darkwrists as she scrambled out of
the carriage.

Mareitsia shouted a few obscenities at Anni but did not
pursue her; likely, her hangover was still bothering her, and she
had returned to the wagon to rest.

Anni stood on the other side of the camp, where Kolten
was cutting a handful of thorns he had found into makeshift
firewood.

"You all right?" asked the dwarf.

Anni surveyed herself for a moment. Mareitsia hadn't
gotten to her whip in time. So, although shaken, Anni wasn't
hurt.

Usually, the crystal ball lived on the high shelf with
Mareitsia's other private belongings. Anni had specific orders
never to touch the things on the shelf. It seemed, however, that in
one of her drunken stupors, Mareitsia had inadvertently put it in

THE CRYSTAL BALL

the chest by mistake.

In the moments that followed, Anni thought about telling Kolten about what she had experienced, but she didn't dare try and speak of it.

Years of living in enslavement had taught her to err on the side of caution. It was unlikely the darkwrists would ever allow her to get even the first few words out, although technically, Anni hadn't done anything wrong. After all, her job was to organize the content of the chest, and she had done that. She hadn't known the crystal ball would be in there, and she certainly hadn't known what it would do if she touched it.

Still, telling Kolten about her experience in the carriage felt a little too much like pushing her luck, so she decided not to risk it, at least not yet.

Anni couldn't help but wonder if she had just fallen victim to one of Mareitsia's parlor tricks. Or perhaps Mareitsia was not entirely the fraud that Anni had always taken her for.

But one thing was for sure: if this was just another of her mistress's cons, it was a good one.

A really good one.

- CHAPTER 4 -
Crickets

Several hours had passed since Anni's experience with the crystal ball, and Mareitsia had not left the wagon since.

The sun was high in the sky now, so it was probably close to midday mealtime. Not that it mattered, as they had nothing to eat. Anni's stomach growled louder than ever.

Kolten was lying by the wagon with his head underneath the axle, examining the front wheel. His tools were spread out across the ground beside him in arm's reach. The dwarf had picked a long blade of grass and was chewing on it while he worked on the failing wheel.

This seemed like a good idea to Anni, and she mimicked him. She selected a long, thin blade of grass from beside the

CRICKETS

wagon and placed it in her mouth. The grass around here wasn't edible for anyone but the horses, and it did nothing to help the growing hunger pains in Anni's stomach. But it felt good to have something to chew.

Their only faint hope for staving off starvation was finding a village, wild edibles, or maybe an animal carcass they could scavenge.

But as bad as the food state of affairs was, the water situation was downright bleak. The goatlands were extremely dry this time of year. It was hard to imagine finding a river or lake anywhere nearby in the endless grasslands. At this point, even a dirty brown puddle would be a welcomed find.

If they were lucky, it might rain soon enough to stave off dying of thirst. But Anni had kept a sharp eye on the sky since she had first noticed the water barrel was getting low, and she had not seen a single cloud yet, let alone rain.

Without water, the horses would not survive another week, and without the horses, they were as good as dead.

An added difficulty with having no food or water was Anni found that she had very little to do. She suspected the darkwrists would not allow her to sit around idle, but it was hard to think of many chores that required neither food nor water.

After she finished working beside the carriage, scraping the dirt off the frame using her dress like a rag, Anni could think of nothing else to do. She was not so stupid as to risk a beating by

45

THE BLUE HAIRED GIRL

entering the wagon to ask a hungover Mareitsia what she should be doing.

As she stood up and brushed the dirt off her dress, Anni glanced down at the darkwrists. The bangle-like objects didn't stir. Perhaps they understood that Anni didn't know what she should be doing.

Suddenly, Anni heard something nearby that made her heart skip a beat.

It was a sound that made her smile, followed by a loud, painful rumble in her stomach.

Field crickets.

They usually were only heard at night or in the early morning, and often the constant goatlands winds would muffle their chirping.

But there was no mistaking it. Anni heard crickets, and she and Kolten and their mistress were all starving.

They even tasted good. Crunchy when eaten raw, and much like a nutty chicken when cooked. There was no way of knowing how many there were, but Anni's stomach demanded she investigate.

Anni took another look down at the darkwrists, as if to ask their permission. But they did not respond.

Cooking was one of Anni's main chores, so it only made sense that if they had no food, going to get some would fall under that umbrella, as long as she didn't stray too far.

46

CRICKETS

Anni took an exploratory paw through the grass, just as she had done the day before in the search for Mareitsia's gemstone.

"I'm looking for food that I can cook," Anni said to her darkwrists as she crawled along the ground.

As she had guessed, they made no effort to stop her. It seemed to Anni that as long as she cooked whatever she caught, there would be no need for the darkwrists to punish her. Thankfully, roasted crickets were easy to cook without water by skewering them on a blade of grass.

Anni followed the sound of the crickets to her left, running her hands along the shafts of the tall grass, but turned up nothing. Moments later, the sound of the chirping seemed to be coming from her right instead. Frustratingly, the chirps appeared to be coming from everywhere at once.

In addition to being hard to find, there was another aspect of her hunt that was deeply depressing. Mareitsia's camp had a firm pecking order. Whenever food was scarce, as it often was, Mareitsia always ate first; when she was full, then Blade would eat, and Anni and Kolten would get the table scraps. Considering how hungry they all were, it seemed unlikely that Anni would be able to catch enough of anything to earn herself a share. The darkwrists would see that any she found would go to Mareitsia.

Anni would likely need to catch close to a hundred

47

THE BLUE HAIRED GIRL

crickets to have any chance of getting any for herself. She would also have to cook, clean, and prepare the full meal for Mareitsia and her pet but would likely get none of it.

She remembered a time in the past when they had eaten a meal after Mareitsia and Blade had both eaten their fills. The raven had decided to roll around on the plate of leftovers and then defecate on them before leaving the food for Anni and Kolten. The sad image of Anni and Kolten trying to salvage the ruined leftovers as Blade cawed callously at them stuck out in Anni's mind.

Anni's stomach let out a violent growl, and pain shot through her abdomen. It had been so many days since she had had any food, she couldn't even remember what they had eaten last.

They had gone without eating for a day or two in the past, either from famine or Mareitsia choosing not to allow them food. But this was different; it had been far too long, and Anni was growing weaker by the day—they all were.

They may well have found themselves in one of the most remote parts of the goatlands. There was no way to know; even Kolten didn't remember being this far east, and he had been with Mareitsia since the beginning. It was entirely possible that the few crickets chirping all around were the only food anywhere for hundreds of miles.

Anni crawled around on the ground, searching for the

CRICKETS

untraceable chirping, but she found she kept having to double back on herself.

The distant sound of Blade's cawing came from somewhere overhead. If he roused Mareitsia, she would probably blame Anni for waking her.

Gods, I really hate that bird, thought Anni, looking skyward.

As if the bird had heard her thoughts, he swooped down toward her, his claws at the ready.

Before Anni could even duck, Blade shifted his course and dove into the tall grass to her right and disappeared.

A moment later, he emerged from the grass with an unusually large and succulent cricket grasped in his beak, looking quite pleased with himself.

Anni threw him a nasty glance and returned to her search.

Blade swallowed the cricket in a single gulp and retook to the air.

Moments later, the bird dove at the ground again, and once again emerged from the grass with a cricket in his beak, this one even larger and more delicious-looking than the last.

Can't you go look somewhere else? thought Anni as the bird gawked at her, savoring its meal. *You've got the whole field.*

Anni made several more attempts to catch a few crickets of her own, but she was no match for Blade's keen eyesight and

49

THE BLUE HAIRED GIRL

his ability to attack his prey from above, and he caught one after another. The miserable bird was incredibly selfish. He wasn't even starving. He could catch whole field mice out here, and Anni remembered the night before he had done precisely that.

Within a few short minutes, the sound of crickets had all but vanished, either from being driven underground by Anni's clumsy hunt for them or ending up in Blade's stomach.

Why couldn't Mareitsia have had a pet fish? thought Anni, sneering at the bird.

Anni guessed that his time living with Mareitsia had taught the bird to delight in creating misery. That would certainly explain why Mareitsia prized him as much as she did.

Then Anni's eyes fell on a single yellowish field cricket near the base of a blade of grass. It was smaller than any of the crickets Blade had caught, and its color was off, suggesting it was ill. It may well have carried some nasty parasites. But Anni had crippling stomach pains already, so it would be worth the risk.

Anni made a grab for it, and to her near astonishment, the insect didn't move.

She held it firmly in her tightly closed fist.

The cricket let out a defeated little chirp but did not attempt to escape.

Anni, having no pockets, held it firmly in her hand and returned to search the grasses for any more stragglers that had survived Blade's onslaught. She already knew it was no good. The

50

CRICKETS

chirping sound was gone, which could only mean the crickets
were all spent.

She had caught one.

One measly cricket.

In a way, one was worse than none. It would do nothing
to relieve Anni's hunger, as this one was sure to go to Mareitsia,
and she would probably receive a beating for having not found
enough. It wasn't even an option to let this one go, as Anni was
positive the darkwrists would never allow it. She was already
pushing her luck just being out here without express permission
in the first place.

As Anni contemplated her next move, there was a sudden
flutter of black feathers across her face.

Anni lost her balance and fell on to her backside.

Blade landed on the ground next to her and let out a
combative squawk.

"What?!" said Anni out loud.

Blade held out his wings aggressively and pecked at
Anni's leg.

"Ow!" She recoiled from the angry raven.

The blow hadn't drawn blood, but it had left a painful
sore on Anni's left leg.

The bird half flew, half jumped toward Anni's face with
his claws at the ready.

Anni instinctively shielded her face with her hands.

51

THE BLUE HAIRED GIRL

There was a sharp pain in her hand under her darkwrist, and Anni heard the bird return to the ground.

As she opened her eyes, she saw Blade swallow her lone cricket, and he let out a squawk that sounded a little like a burp.

There was a small cut in Anni's blistered left hand right under her darkwrist, where Blade had clawed at it to force her to drop the insect.

The contemptuous little bird wouldn't even let Anni have a single one.

Even though Anni knew she would never have gotten to eat the cricket, she found herself overwhelmed with hunger and emotion. Here she was, dying of hunger and thirst, and all Mareitsia's pet could think to do was harass her.

Tears began to fall down her cheeks like they had not done in months. Starving, thirsty, miserable, and constantly bullied and harassed by a bird. Anni fell backward, lying in the grass, and looked up at the blue sky through tear-filled eyes. She didn't care if the darkwrists punished her for not working; she didn't care if she died right here and now. Maybe death was preferable to the miserable life she lived.

"Why me?" sobbed Anni, not even bothering to wipe away her tears.

Anni couldn't feel the darkwrists. She was entirely numb to them right now. It was like she was floating.

Her eyes were sightless, and her ears were deaf, her skin

CRICKETS

without feeling.

There was nothingness all around her.

Then, slowly, feeling started to come back to Anni. The world began to return to normal. The blue sky above her came into view again, wreathed in a halo of shifting dry grass. The feeling of the rough ground under her back returned.

On her left side, Anni felt something pressing against her waist.

As her vision cleared, she saw it was Blade. He was resting his head on her side, looking up at her.

The bird was staring up at her with a strange look in his eyes—a look Anni had never seen before.

It was like he was offering her comfort—as if the bird had finally realized that he had gone too far and was looking to make amends for his misdeed.

Blade began to nuzzle her side.

Anni couldn't help herself. She reached out her hand to pet him.

Suddenly, the nuzzling became more and more violent, like the bird was having a seizure.

With a sudden, violent thrust of his head, the bird gave out an abrupt cough and vomited all over her.

A putrid mess of half-eaten crickets covered the tattered remains of Anni's only dress. The sick looked like every single cricket that Blade had eaten.

53

THE BLUE HAIRED GIRL

The bird let out a caw of laughter and hopped back toward the wagon, leaving Anni dripping in bird vomit to follow him.

- CHAPTER 5 -
The Discovery

"You smell worse than the dwarf!" snapped Mareitsia at the sight and smell of Anni's dress.

Kolten sneered with anger, but he said nothing to Mareitsia.

"What happened, rat?!"

Anni tried to explain about Blade, knowing perfectly well that Mareitsia would neither believe her nor care.

Anni's dress was long past it's prime; once pink in color, it had long since faded to an ugly reddish gray and was full of holes and patches. But now it was ruined entirely. Tiny pieces of half-eaten cricket stuck to Anni's dress like barnacles mixed with a thick, yellowish-brown, pus-like ooze from Blade's stomach.

THE BLUE HAIRED GIRL

The smell was so foul that it made Anni's eyes water.

Some kind of acid from the raven's stomach was mixed in with the muck and made Anni's skin itch and burn like poison oak.

Blade perched on top of the carriage, cawing with laughter-like squawks at the sight and smell of Anni's clothing.

Mareitsia had always resisted getting her slaves anything more to wear than was necessary, as it cut into her profits. It was a difficult game for a slave owner to play, as poorly outfitted slaves tended to die and needed replacing. Mareitsia managed to keep hers close to the edge of their endurance.

The only clothing Anni had right now was this one dress and the pair of open-toed sandals on her feet. Mareitsia had sold all her winter clothes months ago, just after the spring thaw.

Even Anni's summer sandals had seemed a luxury item to Mareitsia at one time. However, she had been forced to get a pair for Anni several summers ago when her feet wouldn't stop bleeding, making it impossible for her to work, even with the darkwrists' constant encouragement.

"You've ruined it!" said Mareitsia, stating the obvious.

"Then give her something to wear," replied Kolten.

"Silence! I decide what my slaves wear!" she snapped, her temper rising again.

"Actually, I think your bird decided that," Kolten shot back. "She can't walk around like that."

THE DISCOVERY

Anni wasn't sure if this was enough to constitute insubordination and draw the darkwrists' punishment, but Kolten wasn't wrong. They didn't have any choice in the matter, but if the darkwrists had inflicted pain, the dwarf hid it well.

"She must have done something to Blade! Rat, what did you do to him?!"

"Nothing," said Anni honestly. "I didn't do anything."

"Tell the truth!" she ordered.

"I did," replied Anni.

Her darkwrists did nothing, showing Mareitsia that she was, indeed, telling the truth.

"What did he eat?!"

"Crickets," said Anni, indicating the muck on her dress.

"Crickets?!" roared Mareitsia. *"Rat, how many times do I have to tell you!? Crickets make him sick!"*

Anni was at a loss for what to say. She was pretty sure that Mareitsia had *never* told her anything of the sort, nor was it her fault that Blade had eaten the crickets in the first place.

"Don't move a muscle!" Mareitsia ordered, and she turned back toward the carriage, where she kept her whip.

"Mistress…" said Kolten pleadingly.

"Silence!"

Moments later, Mareitsia emerged from the wagon with her long, black whip in her hand. Blade still sat upon the top of the carriage, watching with keen interest.

THE BLUE HAIRED GIRL

"Hold still, rat! Maybe this will help you remember next time!"

Kolten's bearded face was full of sympathy, but he could do nothing to help her, having long ago been given standing orders not to interfere.

Mareitsia towered over Anni, her old face cold and ruthless as she drew back her whip.

Anni instinctively backed away, raised her arms, and averted her eyes.

Nothing.

Anni opened her eyes.

Mareitsia was lying on her backside with her face buried in her hands. Her fingers were massaging her temples and eyes.

It seemed she was still not quite over the hangover from the night before and had lost her balance. She sat there a moment, gathering her breath, and then finally stood up.

"Pack up the camp! We push on to the next village. You will wear that!" she said, sneering at Anni's filthy dress. Without another word, Mareitsia returned to the wagon to rest; the whip was still in her hand.

Blade, looking as disappointed as a raven could look, followed her into the carriage.

Anni couldn't believe her luck. Mareitsia's hangover had made her unable to wield her whip effectively, and she had managed to escape the beating.

THE DISCOVERY

The two slaves looked at each other, and Kolten shrugged as the door to the wagon snapped shut behind Mareitsia.

As they packed up the camp, Anni noticed at the back of the wagon, the empty water barrel still lay on its side where Mareitsia had spilled it.

Despite being empty, they needed to keep it, should they be lucky enough to find some water or, gods willing, it rained.

Anni bent down to retrieve the barrel; even empty, she could hardly lift it. Luckily, the shelf where they kept it rode low to the ground.

It took all of her strength to shimmy the barrel onto the back of the wagon by herself. As she reached for the long rope that secured it, Anni saw in the bottom of the barrel was a small puddle of water.

It was less than a pint. When it had fallen over, the shape of the barrel had kept the last few drops from pouring out. It was barely a one-day supply of water for one of them, let alone three. Not enough to make much of a difference.

It seemed odd that the barrel had just been sitting there all morning. Anni really should have checked it sooner.

Wait a minute... thought Anni.

Anni's darkwrists should have punished her for not righting the barrel and putting it away, but they had not. The spilled barrel had been left there all morning, even when Anni

THE BLUE HAIRED GIRL

couldn't think of anything else to do. She had been so distracted by the crickets that she hadn't noticed.

Anni had made honest mistakes in the past, and the darkwrists had never hesitated to punish her before. Neither mercy nor honest mistakes were something the darkwrists seemed to understand. They had done nothing when Anni had forgotten about the water barrel.

Now that Anni thought about it, it had been quite a while since her darkwrists had done much of anything at all. They had been strangely silent since—

The crystal ball! Anni thought as her jaw dropped in shock, and all thoughts of hunger or thirst vanished in an instant.

The darkwrists usually punished her all day long. But they had done nothing since she was washing Mareitsia's laundry this morning. Had her contact with Mareitsia's crystal ball somehow interrupted the darkwrists?

It would make sense, considering Mareitsia always kept the crystal ball on the shelf with the belongings that Anni and Kolten weren't allowed to touch.

When Mareitsia was sleeping off her hangover, Anni had gone out to catch crickets without her permission, even when there was a job that needed doing. Anni had assumed that the darkwrists had allowed her to go as part of her cooking duties, but had they? Darkwrists could be temperamental.

It was only moments ago that Mareitsia had specifically

60

THE DISCOVERY

ordered Anni not to move a muscle. But she had managed to step away from her mistress, causing her to miss with the whip and fall over.

If the crystal ball had managed to break the darkwrists' spell, then Anni was free. She could walk away right now and leave this life behind her.

It sounded too good to be true.

Anni stood there, looking out at the rolling hills all around them. The windswept grasses all seemed to be gesturing her to join them in the breeze. They were like a million long fingers, curling and uncurling, beckoning her to follow them away toward the horizon. Freedom lay in every direction, and there would be nothing and no one that could stop her.

Mareitsia was getting old, and the horses were half-dead, so she would never be able to catch Anni if she ran. After all, they had no food or water, so even alone on the goatlands, her situation would be no worse off on her own. Not to mention, she would be free of Blade and Mareitsia's whip forever.

But there was one reason she couldn't leave. Leaving would mean abandoning Kolten. However much Anni hated Mareitsia, Kolten absolutely loathed her, and was the only friend Anni had ever had.

I can't leave him, thought Anni.

Kolten had finished tending to the front wheel, and he had a worried look on his face.

THE BLUE HAIRED GIRL

"It's not going to last," he muttered as he ascended the ladder and onto the top of the wagon.

When the camp was finally packed up, Anni climbed on top of the wagon to join Kolten in the driver's seat.

The dwarf picked up the reins from their hook on the driver's seat.

"Ready, Mistress?" he called down to her.

"Yes, yes, go. Remember, we turn east. There's a village less than a day from here if we hurry," Mareitsia barked from inside the wagon.

"Uh, right." Kolten scratched his bald head awkwardly. They had already been heading east for days now and had seen nothing all around them but grass and sky; still, Kolten obeyed her.

The dwarf made a clicking sound out of the side of his mouth.

One of the horses kicked at the wagon in protest, leading Mareitsia to shout obscenities at them.

Both horses were nearly exhausted from the weight of the wagon over the rough terrain. Anni had even given them the last drops of water she had found in the barrel. If the horses gave out, they would all die, stranded out here among the endless rolling hills.

Riding on top of the carriage left them entirely exposed to the elements. But Anni and Kolten were both used to the wind

62

THE DISCOVERY

and the occasional rain, as Mareitsia would never share her quarters with them. Not that they minded; it was nice being away from her during the long trips.

"Come on, fellas," said Kolten, with another clicking sound. "No other choice."

The horses slowly started to walk, heading eastward as they had done for many days.

From the driver's seat on top of the carriage, they could see for miles all around. In every direction, there was nothing but the low hills of the goatlands and a vast blue sky. The only landmarks anywhere were the tracks left behind the wagon.

Over the years, many of Mareitsia's past slaves had ended up as nothing more than garbage left in the tracks behind the wagon. After dying in her service, their bodies were left abandoned to rot in the grassy hills.

Anni could remember several times when she had sat atop the wagon, watching the corpses of dead slaves disappear over the crests of the hills. All without so much as a thank you for their years of service. Their only funeral was the sight of the wagon disappearing over the horizon.

Anni had often wondered if that fate would befall her one day.

But no longer.

Somehow, the goatlands looked different, as if the world was already telling Anni the darkwrists were genuinely dead, and

63

THE BLUE HAIRED GIRL

all Decareia was celebrating with her before she even knew for sure. The sky looked a more brilliant shade of blue, and the tall brown grass moved more rhythmically than before. Even the wind itself seemed to snicker in her ear, as it whistled past her and shifted her blue hair.

Anni sat quietly and waited until she could hear Mareitsia's snores coming from inside the wagon.

If this was true, there was only one way Anni could think of to test her darkwrists.

Luckily, Mareitsia had given Anni a very straightforward order before retreating into the wagon. An order that it would be very easy to disobey.

The disgusting, vomit-covered dress she was wearing was still making Anni's eyes water and her skin itch.

Anni stood up in front of her seat and reached down for the folds of her filthy dress. With a slight pull, she lifted it up over her head and let the putrid, stinking thing fall to her feet. Her naked body towered over the wagon, lit by the warm goatlands' sun.

Kolten's bearded jaw dropped, and he averted his gaze politely. She smiled broadly, standing there defiantly as her darkwrists hung off her hands uselessly, their magic utterly spent.

Anni was free, in every sense of the word.

- CHAPTER 6 -
The Ax Blade

"You're so lucky," said Kolten quietly, unable to hide the envy in his voice.

It was true, Anni was very lucky. The darkwrists still hung above her hands but had gone entirely silent, snuffed out by some magic from Mareitsia's crystal ball. The darkwrists looked normal; they just didn't do anything. So, as long as Mareitsia didn't examine them too carefully, she would have no idea that Anni was free.

Anni had been forced to wear the darkwrists for as long as she could remember. Now, she could say and think and plan and do anything she liked. If Anni wanted to, she could abandon the wagon and run right now, and there was nothing Mareitsia

THE BLUE HAIRED GIRL

could do about it.

Anni had taken off her disgusting dress and hung it off the back of the wagon to see if the wind could reduce the smell.

Kolten had taken off his shirt and given it to Anni to wear, and now sat bare-chested. His massive muscles were bulging and covered in scars. The dwarf's frame was so big that his shirt was many sizes too large for Anni, and it hung down well past her waist, though just barely concealing her privates. Every time the wind shifted, it exposed Anni's nakedness, but at least the shirt wasn't covered in bird vomit.

"Maybe we can get yours off in the same way," replied Anni, trying to downplay her incredible stroke of luck.

Kolten laughed in disbelief as he glanced down at the black, evil bracelets that decorated his wrists.

There was a brief silence, broken only by the sound of the wagon wheels on the rocky soil.

The sun was low in the sky, and nightfall would soon be upon them. If they didn't find Mareitsia's mythical village to the east soon, they would have no choice but to stop.

There wasn't much point in setting up camp, as they had no food, water, or firewood. But the horses would still need their rest, or they wouldn't live out the week.

"You can leave right now, you know," said Kolten with a flinch.

"What?"

"Take whatever you can carry, and you can run away

66

THE AX BLADE

right now and be free," he said, the last few words coming through gritted teeth as his hands started changing color.

"What about you?"

"I'll be fine." His arms twitched.

"I'm not leaving you with her."

"Anni…"

Any pride that Anni ever had was long since beaten out of her, but even so, she would never admit that she had, indeed, thought about running. Kolten was like a father to her, but life in the darkwrists was no life at all. Anni would do almost anything to never have to suffer them again. Anything, it seemed, except abandon her friend.

"No," said Anni in a tone she never knew she had.

There was a loud snort from the wagon below, followed by more long, deep snores.

Something about saying the word "no" out loud felt strangely satisfying to Anni; she had rarely had the chance to use the word before.

The decision to stay with Kolten until he was free was something Anni didn't take lightly. She could leave right now and never suffer the pain and indignity of a pair of darkwrists ever again. But no matter how much she hated them, Anni was determined to stay and help Kolten.

Suddenly, there was a loud crack, and the wagon tilted deeply to one side, followed by a series of loud curses and threats coming from inside the carriage.

THE BLUE HAIRED GIRL

"Aw, damn it," muttered Kolten.

Anni and Kolten climbed down off the wagon to survey the damage and let Mareitsia have her tantrum. It had finally happened; the front wheel had given way.

"What did you do to my wagon, dwarf?!" she shrieked. "Fix it!"

Kolten examined the damage to the front wheel.

"I can't," he said quickly.

"Why you—"

"Look at it!" said Kolten, pointing to the remains of the wheel.

The weight of the carriage on the rough terrain had finally crushed the old wheel. It lay in many pieces on the ground.

If the wheel had merely slipped off the axle or had broken a spoke or two, there might have been a chance of repairing it. But in this state, it was hopeless, and the other three wheels weren't far behind.

"Fix it!"

"I've been warning you about this for weeks! It's junk!"

"Then replace it!" she snapped.

"I can't; you sold the spare last month."

Over the last few months, in her frequent drunken stupors, Mareitsia had sold much of Kolten's equipment, including the spare wagon parts, despite his objections. Anni had suspected that most of the money raised from the sales had gone

68

THE AX BLADE

to keeping her wineskin full.

"Well then, make a new one!" she snapped.

"With what?!" retorted Kolten, placing his hand on one of his wrists.

This deep in the goatlands, there wasn't a single tree for a hundred miles. They had taken to burning mostly bushes and dry grass in the campfires for days now, so of course, there was no wood for building a new wagon wheel from scratch.

"We have to make it to the village by sundown!" she snapped at the dwarf; fortunately, she had left her whip in the wagon.

From where Anni was standing, she could tell that sundown was probably less than an hour away, and there was no sign of anyone, let alone a village, anywhere.

"What village, you miserable, old buzzard!?" roared Kolten, throwing his blood-soaked arms into the air, his temper boiling over. "We've been lost for weeks!"

Mareitsia's tyranny had dominated their lives for so long that they had all but given up. But it might have been something about Anni's newfound freedom that had reignited the desire to resist within the dwarf. As if something long since beaten into submission was now fighting its way to the surface.

"Why, you insolent, little toad! I know exactly where we are!" she spat at Kolten, who remained steely-eyed and defiant.

Mareitsia and Kolten were still screaming at each other, paying no attention to Anni, when she saw it.

THE BLUE HAIRED GIRL

The door to the wagon was open.

Anni could see it from where she was standing. Sitting on the high shelf beside Mareitsia's bed was the white crystal ball, the object that had set her free. The power of the mysterious object scared her, but it was the only possible way to free Kolten.

It was so close that Anni could almost feel its warm glow in her hand. She took a quick look back toward the front of the wagon, where she could see Kolten screaming in pain and defiance.

Anni stepped silently into the wagon and climbed up on to her mistress's bed. With her tongue gripped between her teeth, Anni reached out her hand toward the glass sphere.

Suddenly, there was a flutter of black feathers, and she found herself face to face with Blade. The raven perched on the crystal ball, his beady little eyes staring at her menacingly.

"Caw! Caw! Caw!" The bird snapped at her with his beak and flapped his wings threateningly.

Anni was sure that Mareitsia could hear him from just outside the wagon, even as she and Kolten shouted at each other. But as Anni looked at the nasty little bird, something inside her snapped. Great, hot, burning anger at everything to do with Mareitsia.

Anni hated the wagon. She hated the smell of cheap wine, the whip, the darkwrists—oh, how she hated the darkwrists. But even the darkwrists were nothing compared to Mareitsia herself, the miserable, cruel, deranged old drunk who

70

THE AX BLADE

regarded Anni as of less value than the pots she cleaned, or the money she had been forced to steal from countless head-bobbing, mouth-breathing, idiotic yokels who wouldn't know a con artist if they sat on one.

Resting on the shelf behind the squawking bird was the long, black whip. Mareitsia's personal instrument of torture. It had left deep, lifelong scars along Anni's back. There it was, just sitting there, looking harmless, like all the other useless junk the woman had acquired over the years.

Perched before her was not Blade, the raven; it became the squawking and flapping culmination of all the years of pent-up hatred she had ever had for Mareitsia and the life forced upon her.

"Move!" screamed Anni, all thought of staying quiet forgotten.

With a mighty swing of her arm, Anni sent the little bird sailing across the wagon, soaring out the open door. The bird collapsed in a twitching heap on the ground outside.

The crystal ball, nudged out of its resting place by Anni's assault, began to roll. Before she could stop it, it slid off the high shelf.

There was a loud crunch, and the crystal ball was nothing but glass shards covering the wagon floor.

Mareitsia reached the door of the carriage, looking murderous, her precious, injured pet held delicately under her arm.

THE BLUE HAIRED GIRL

"What have you done to Blade, you miserable, little rat!?"

Mareitsia grabbed at Anni's wrist with a look of pure hatred in her eyes.

Anni, thinking fast, scrambled out of the wagon's window just before Mareitsia could grab her.

Anni raced around the wagon and made a B-line straight for Kolten.

The dwarf was getting to his feet and clutching his wrists, which were bloody from defiance.

"Rat, what did you do to Blade?! You will die for this!" wailed Mareitsia from somewhere behind her.

Anni turned to see Mareitsia holding the whip in one hand and her raven in the other. She was coming straight for Anni, her face full of cold, hard fury.

But Kolten stood in her way.

Anni instinctively backed away, while Kolten stood between her and Mareitsia in a gesture of protection, looking the vile woman square in the eye.

Kolten took a quick look down at his battered, bloody, and scarred hands and the darkwrists that now hung uselessly upon them.

It seemed the shattering of Mareitsia's crystal had broken the curse upon him, at last. When the pain stopped, Kolten must have realized what had happened.

He massaged his wrists for a moment to survey the

THE AX BLADE

damage done by years of Mareitsia's torture.

For the first time since Anni had known him, Kolten's hands were his own.

The dwarf Kolten Citrane was finally free.

"Anni, you got the crystal?" asked Kolten, breathing very hard. His back was to Anni.

"It broke," she said, unable to see his face from her position.

"Out of my way, dwarf!" snapped Mareitsia, trying to push past him to get to Anni. As she did so, Mareitsia lifted her whip to strike Kolten with it.

Kolten reached out his hand and caught the whip before it found its mark. He held it quite still in his huge dwarven fist.

Anni still could not see Kolten's face from behind him, but she was not sure she wanted to.

"Leave. Anni. Alone," he said in a slow, deep, and challenging tone.

"Dwarf, how dare—" but her voice failed her as she saw the darkwrists hanging ineffectually off of the fist upon her whip.

A few drops of blood trickled down the dwarf's huge burned and scarred fist. Mareitsia made a few tries to wrench the whip from Kolten's grasp, but he held it firmly with a grip of stone.

Anni saw Mareitsia's eyes dart over to the wagon; a few pieces of the shattered crystal ball were visible through the wagon's open door. It seemed to take a moment for Mareitsia to

73

THE BLUE HAIRED GIRL

process what had happened.

"It's been…It's been…hell, I've forgotten how long," he said through gritted teeth, but this time it was not from any pain.

Mareitsia opened her mouth and closed it again several times.

"D-Dwarf…" said Mareitsia in an unusually soft tone.

"My! Name! Is! Kolten!" he spoke each word with the furious rage of an animal escaping the slaughter.

With a sudden thrust of his hand, Mareitsia was thrown several feet backward and landed on her backside in the tall grass. Never once looking away from Mareitsia, Kolten folded up the leather whip and tore it to pieces with his bare hands.

Although Kolten was smaller than Mareitsia, he was much stronger. Without her precious darkwrists, she was defenseless.

Mareitsia didn't move; her eyes looked oddly cold. Anni had seen the horrible woman angry, drunk, something resembling happy, hungover, and of course, she had seen her cruel almost daily. But Mareitsia had a look on her face that was entirely unfamiliar. Her eyes were wide, and her lips were quivering, and she was breathing very fast. There could be no mistaking it— Mareitsia was frightened. Anni could hardly blame her.

One feeling Anni knew all too well was fear. She had spent her entire life in utter terror of Mareitsia and her violent temper. And now it was Mareitsia's turn, and she was entirely at their mercy.

THE AX BLADE

In the few minutes since the wagon wheel had broken, their whole world had changed.

Kolten sneered and turned toward the rear of the wagon. The ground seemed to shake with each step he took as a free dwarf.

He ripped the lid of the tool chest clean off.

He turned back toward Mareitsia, holding the woodcutter's ax in his hands.

Anni looked into Kolten's eyes, and she saw a coldness that had never been there before. Something had been triggered in the dwarf—he had the look of a lion, about to devour its prey.

The woman held up her hands in front of her defensively and backed away from him, toward the front of the wagon.

It was hard to imagine her being able to talk her way out of this. It was impossible to justify a lifetime of enslavement under anyone, let alone someone so cruel.

"D-Don't forget...I-I feed and clothe you!" she said, pleading and backing away toward the horses.

"No more talking," he said coldly.

Mareitsia's back was now pinned up against the wagon hitch. Both horses were nervous, sensing something was amiss. The look on the dwarf's face had grown even more determined.

"Kolten, no!" screamed Anni, and she shut her eyes.

A dwarven battle cry echoed through the goatlands, followed by the distinct sound of an ax blade finding its

75

THE BLUE HAIRED GIRL

mark.

- CHAPTER 7 -
Freedom?

Anni opened her eyes into tiny slits and looked to see Kolten standing over Mareitsia, the ax still in his hands.

The blade was clean; the ax had severed the wagon tongue. It had left Mareitsia unharmed, while freeing the horses from their burden. The two animals moved away from the carriage instantly, as if fearing they would be hitched to the craft again if they lingered too long.

"We have our lives back, so should they," the dwarf muttered in disgust.

"K-Kolten…" sputtered Mareitsia.

This was the first time Anni had ever heard Mareitsia use his name. Something about hearing the contemptuous, old woman speak it aloud sounded out of place.

THE BLUE HAIRED GIRL

"You do deserve to die..." he said.

He said nothing more and turned away from her.

Mareitsia lay there in utter shock.

Kolten approached Anni. He was breathing hard, as if he had just run a mile, but otherwise, he appeared to be returning to normal.

"A-Are you okay?" he asked Anni.

Anni surveyed herself, and although shaken, she was unharmed. The dead darkwrists still hung from her wrists. They both had deep, painful cuts, burns, and scars on their wrists that would likely never fully heal. But hopefully, now that they were free, at least the healing process could begin.

Mareitsia herself lay on the ground and began to cry in loud wails, like a toddler in need of attention. The woman started to scream and sob and occasionally swear, but she did not address her former slaves. It was like the cruel, old crone had broken. She was crushed by the weight of her slaves' newfound freedom.

Kolten dropped the ax and looked down at Anni's darkwrists.

"We should see if we can get those off of you," said Kolten, indicating Anni's darkwrists.

Kolten stepped to the back of the wagon briefly and returned with a hammer and chisels.

Anni placed her hand on the broken tool chest lid, and Kolten began to work at the hoop on her left. It gave her no pain or resistance of any kind as Kolten tried to remove it. If Anni had

FREEDOM?

not known any better, she would have thought it just an ugly
piece of black jewelry.

Mareitsia let out a sobbing wail from the front of the
wagon.

"Shut up!" shouted Kolten over his shoulder.

With a steady application of force from his expert hands,
the hoop split under the chisel's blade, and Kolten bent it off
with ease.

Anni took a moment and surveyed the damage done to
her wrist by the years of enslavement. She had many dark red
scars and some fresh scabs from the darkwrists' most recent
assaults.

She couldn't help but smile as the other one came off
even easier than the first, breaking into pieces like glass under
tension.

Mareitsia sobbed louder, like a child having a temper
tantrum.

Kolten rounded the chisel on his own darkwrists and was
about to remove them, when he let out a scream of fury and
threw his tools to the ground.

"What is it?!" asked Anni.

"They won't let me," he snarled.

Anni looked at his darkwrists, and it was clear they were
still very much active, despite how dead they had looked just
moments ago.

Kolten stepped away from the wagon and picked up his

79

THE BLUE HAIRED GIRL

ax again, heading straight for Mareitsia.

Her sobbing stopped, and she looked up at him in fear again.

Kolten stood over her and raised the ax.

"Ahhhhh!" he screamed, and he dropped the blade, his darkwrists cutting into him again.

Mareitsia peered up at Kolten and started to gather herself up.

"You s-see? They won't let you hurt me. You're still mine!"

Kolten tried to pick up the ax again, but the darkwrists refused to let him.

"Now, kneel before me," she sniffed, her confidence returning.

Kolten didn't move; he merely stood there.

He examined his darkwrists curiously when they did not respond to his refusal to obey her order to kneel.

"What's going on?" demanded Kolten.

Mareitsia just stared at him with a blank look on her face.

The darkwrists seemed to be malfunctioning. They wouldn't force Kolten to take her orders, but he also couldn't remove them.

Suddenly, Kolten's face filled with understanding and his bearded jaw dropped.

"Anni…Try giving me an order," he said gravely.

80

FREEDOM?

"Kolten, pick up the ax," said Anni, hoping the dwarf was wrong.

Kolten hesitated, but soon the darkwrists reacted and forced him to comply with her instructions.

"Drop it!" ordered Mareitsia, but the darkwrists did not respond.

It seemed the breaking of their control crystal had caused the magic of the darkwrists to go haywire. Instead of releasing Kolten from bondage, they had transferred ownership of him to the last person to touch the crystal ball, and that was Anni.

Anni was Kolten's new mistress.

"You stupid, old hag!" he roared at Mareitsia, who he evidently held responsible.

The dwarf lifted the ax above his head, looking straight down at Mareitsia. This time, Anni was quite sure he was going to end her life.

"*Ahhhhh!*" he shrieked, and he was forced to lower the ax to his side.

"I don't understand," said Kolten, looking down at Mareitsia. "Why can't I hurt you?"

"Because I ordered you not to," said Anni as the realization dawned on her.

Before, when Anni thought Kolten was going to kill Mareitsia, she had begged him not to. The darkwrists must have considered that to be an order.

Suddenly, Anni had an idea.

THE BLUE HAIRED GIRL

"I order the darkwrists to come off."

They didn't move.

"They don't work like that," said Mareitsia. "You can only give orders to the slave, not to the darkwrists."

"Then I order Kolten to be free."

Still, the darkwrists didn't respond.

"How do we get them off?" demanded Kolten as he flinched again.

"I don't know."

"She's lying. Anni, let me hurt her! And I'll find out what she knows."

Anni didn't answer. She didn't want a slave, and certainly not her best friend.

"Tell us how to take them off," Anni said to Mareitsia.

"I don't know how. I never had to take them off before. They just fall off on their own when the slave dies."

Kolten looked murderous.

"Who does know?" asked Kolten through gritted teeth.

Mareitsia looked up at him with a hint of her usual contempt for the dwarf. She crossed her arms, looked up and away from them both, and she said nothing more.

"Kolten, make her talk," Anni commanded.

"Gladly." The dwarf grabbed Mareitsia by the front of her dress and lifted her off the ground, keeping her face close to his, and placed his other hand around her throat.

"The Republic of Zoltan," she gasped.

FREEDOM?

"The Republic – Across the Great Sea? They can help?" asked Kolten.

Kolten kept his hold on her throat for a moment, but Mareitsia still managed a nod.

"We need to get to the Republic," said Kolten, "or at least find someone from there that can help."

"You'll never make it," muttered Mareitsia coldly.

"Yeah, you did do a good job at getting us lost, didn't you, you ol' bitch?" sneered Kolten, looking around at the emptiness in every direction.

Mareitsia said nothing.

"We head north from here," said Anni firmly.

Both Kolten and Mareitsia looked at her.

"What makes you say that?" asked Mareitsia.

Anni did not have an answer. Although they were lost, Anni knew the Golairia-Yuspiereian border ran east to west, so if nothing else, heading north would at least get them away from Golairia.

"That's where we're going. We still have the horses," said Anni, pointing to the tired old animals, still hitched together.

"But what about my wagon?" asked Mareitsia.

"What do you mean, what about it?" asked Kolten. "You're sure as hell not coming with us…Wait, is she?" He turned to Anni cautiously.

Thanks to a strange turn of events, Anni was effectively in charge now. Without meaning to, she had suddenly found

THE BLUE HAIRED GIRL

herself in a position of great power. The darkwrists would see that Kolten would have to go along with whatever she decided. And even in his tired and hungry state, Kolten was still much stronger than Mareitsia. Whether or not Mareitsia came with them was effectively up to her.

"Well…"

"But you can't just leave me here," protested Mareitsia.

"Oh, yes, we can," replied Kolten with a half-smile. "You can look after yourself, for a change. By the way, watch that front wheel. I hear it's a little weak."

"B-But…" Mareitsia stammered. "You'll starve to death. You need me."

"Need you?!" Anni shouted in disbelief. "We've never needed you! You need *us*! I've been cooking and cleaning up after you since before I can remember. Me and Kolten can take care of ourselves."

The dwarf nodded with a proud smile hidden under his huge, bushy beard.

Mareitsia started to cry again from her spot on the ground.

It felt good, looking down at the vile and broken woman and watching her squirm. Even if Anni wouldn't let Kolten hurt her, Mareitsia was in a lot of trouble, and she knew it.

"I'll tell you what, you old hag," snapped Kolten. "Just keep right on pushing eastward to that imaginary village of yours. If you go that way long enough to hit the coast, keep right on

FREEDOM?

going and give my regards to the sea monsters."

She let out another sob.

"I-I know where there is food," pleaded Mareitsia.

"You don't even know where *we* are!" Anni snorted with derision. She knew Mareitsia far too well to fall for any of her cons.

Anni felt no sympathy for the awful woman, but even so, it was hard not to pity her a little. Mareitsia was pathetic: a woman in her fifties, cruel, vindictive, and full of nothing but hate for everyone around her, yet entirely dependent upon others for survival.

Mareitsia couldn't cook, she couldn't clean, couldn't fight; she had no useful skills, whatsoever. Her entire existence had revolved around taking money from stupid people, so she could get drunk and then do the whole thing all over again.

She was truly worthless.

"You know, Anni, I know where we can get something to eat," sneered Kolten, looking down at Mareitsia.

There was a stunned silence as Kolten reached down for Mareitsia.

"Kolten, no," said Anni quickly.

"Not *her*," he said in disgust. "She would probably poison us. I got a better idea."

Anni felt her stomach growl with anticipation as Kolten explained himself. It was not something that Anni had ever considered before, but it was an excellent idea.

THE BLUE HAIRED GIRL

The dwarf was nothing, if not resourceful.

Mareitsia screamed and wailed in protest as Anni gathered up the dry grass for a campfire.

Meanwhile, Kolten had been far more aggressive in their need for firewood. He had taken his ax to the wagon itself and chopped off several wooden planks. Out here, the carriage was useless with its broken wheel, and the horses had no strength left to pull it. At least as firewood, it could provide some limited, temporary use.

Soon, they had a modest campfire going.

As it hissed and crackled away, Kolten took the pieces of Mareitsia's whip and tossed them unceremoniously into the fire.

It would never hurt anyone again.

Mareitsia continued to sob like a child as the food hissed and sizzled over the campfire.

Anni even, somewhat spitefully, offered a share of the meal to Mareitsia. The gypsy refused sobbingly and cursed at her former slaves.

Although the meat was tough and slightly gamy, it was the most satisfying meal Anni could remember eating.

When they finished, the only leftovers were a few claws and a pile of torn, black raven feathers.

- CHAPTER 8 -
The Flight North

"You can't be serious!" shouted Kolten.

"We bring her with us."

Anni could hardly believe it herself, but she had made up her mind. Mareitsia was coming with them. The gypsy was still sobbing to herself on the ground by the campfire, looking up at Anni with a confused look on her tear-stricken face.

"After what she did to us?!" roared Kolten in disbelief. "What she did to you?!"

Anni truly loathed Mareitsia, but she was free now, and she would never have to serve her again. Something about leaving her out here, lost and alone on the borderlands with no food, water, or means of defending herself, seemed wrong.

Maybe bringing Mareitsia along wasn't the best idea—

THE BLUE HAIRED GIRL

Kolten certainly didn't want to—but as long as Kolten wore the darkwrists, it was Anni's decision, and she thought it best to take her with them. Out here in the goatlands, with Kolten under her control, Anni really could do whatever she wanted to Mareitsia. There was no point in denying it: abandoning the woman out in the goatlands was a slow death sentence that seemed a bit too harsh, even for her.

"Just until we find a village or something," clarified Anni. "Then she's on her own."

Kolten turned toward the horrible woman sitting by the campfire, leaned in close to her, and spat straight in her face, but he did not argue.

"Get up," Anni ordered her former mistress.

Mareitsia wiped the dwarf's saliva off her face and obeyed.

"You can stay with us until we find some help," said Anni, looking her straight in the eye. "But the moment we do, I never want to see you again…*ever!*"

Anni shouted the last word at her former mistress as if she were trying to deafen her.

Mareitsia nodded, her eyes wide with understanding.

"Kolten," Anni said, turning to the dwarf, "if she tries *anything*," she shouted the last word again, "you have my permission to pull her head off."

The dwarf nodded a little too enthusiastically, causing Mareitsia to take a step away from him.

THE FLIGHT NORTH

"From now on, you'll do what we say," said Anni.

Mareitsia nodded again.

Anni didn't say another word to the gypsy and turned her attention to the horses.

As it turned out, the animals were in a far worse state than Anni had realized. The moment Anni removed the wagon hitch, one of the animals collapsed. She had laid down on her side, and her breathing was labored. The sick animal refused to get up, no matter how they tried to coax her. Anni knew just by looking at her that she would never get up from that spot again.

She would be dead by nightfall.

The other horse was in a better state; although he was still weak, he was able to stay on his feet. The horse's ribs were visible under his skin, and his gait was unsteady, but he still had some strength left.

Even so, the horse would never be able to carry them for long. Instead, Anni and Kolten loaded him up with whatever they could salvage from the remains of Mareitsia's wagon.

Most of Mareitsia's things were junk, fake magic talismans, some ugly dresses, tarot cards, urine bottles, mostly trash. On the floor of the wagon were the shattered remains of the old crystal ball that had changed their lives forever; it, too, was useless now.

Still, Mareitsia had a few useful items. A blanket, sewing kit, a compass, Kolten's tools, the cooking equipment Anni used to feed her every day, and an old saddlebag that they used to pack

89

THE BLUE HAIRED GIRL

the items. Anni also took her headscarf and tucked it away in the saddlebag with the other items, in case she needed it. Traveling would be far more comfortable without the old wagon to slow them down.

Before leaving, Anni stepped behind the carriage with one of Mareitsia's ugly dresses and tore it down to size. She took off Kolten's shirt and put on the dress.

Mareitsia's old dress was an ugly shade of reddish-purple that clashed horribly with Anni's blue hair. Mareitsia's large bosom made the stretched out bust-line far too large for Anni's young, girlish figure, but it was better than the vomit-covered rag that still hung off the back of the carriage.

Mareitsia eyed her disapprovingly as Anni came out from behind the wagon, wearing her old dress, to return Kolten's shirt to him, but Mareitsia didn't dare protest.

By the time they left the wagon with the one surviving horse and Mareitsia's few possessions, the stars were coming out. Although they had a compass, Kolten had guided them by the stars many times through the borderlands in the past. All they had to do was find the South Twins, a pair of bright stars that always orbited around due south, and then go in the opposite direction to find north.

It was incredibly awkward to be free and yet to be walking mere feet from the woman who had whipped and tormented them for years. They were equals now; whatever happened to them from now on would be a future of Anni's

THE FLIGHT NORTH

choosing.

Both the moons of Decareia were visible that night. The larger was partially in shadow, but the smaller was full. They were both glowing brightly, and Anni was grateful for the light they provided, as they had no torches.

Golairia bordered on the goatlands, and it was widely known as the slave capital of the world. None of them wanted to risk enslavement, Mareitsia probably least of all, given how she had treated hers over the years.

"There's something behind us," said Mareitsia, looking over her shoulder after they had been walking for close to half an hour.

Anni turned to see a tiny, flickering light coming from the direction of their abandoned carriage.

"The wagon's on fire," muttered Kolten, his keen dwarf eyes piercing the darkness. The flatness of the goatlands would allow him to see for miles.

Although Anni couldn't see it clearly, there was nothing else the large, flickering object could be.

As they watched the flickering firelight, a low, deafening squeal echoed over the goatlands hills. It was the sound of a massive pig, followed by drunken laughter.

Anni had heard the sound before, and though she had never actually seen one close up, she knew what it was.

A Golairian raiding party, and they had a battle boar.

It seemed they were not quite as alone out here as Anni

THE BLUE HAIRED GIRL

had thought. It was a good thing her and Kolten had broken free of Mareitsia when they had, or raiders would have found them.

"We should move," said Kolten quickly. "Get up over the ridge-line before they see us."

Over the years, Mareitsia had at least been smart enough to pack up the wagon and leave when she suspected raiders were around.

One thing Anni had seen in the past was what was left of the villages after raiders had finished with them. More than once over the years, the wagon would approach a town to set up shop. But when they arrived, they found nothing but the smoldering remains of houses. The rotting, bloody corpses of men littering the ground, the women and children likely carried off to be sold.

If captured, they would probably murder Kolten and take turns raping Mareitsia and possibly Anni as well. If they survived, Anni would head right back to slavery.

Both of Decareia's moons were behind them, illuminating the trio, so if the raiders looked in their direction, they would likely spot them.

The sounds behind them didn't seem to be getting any louder, suggesting the raiders weren't following them.

They're probably still watching the wagon burn, thought Anni thankfully, as soon they would disappear into the night once they came to grasses tall enough to hide them.

Just as Anni started to think they might make a clean getaway, she noticed something odd.

THE FLIGHT NORTH

The smell of smoke wafted through the air, and the sound of a crackling fire joined the wind at their backs.

"Shit!" muttered Kolten. "The idiots let the grass catch fire!"

Anni thought back to all the campfires she had built for Mareitsia over the years. One of the first things her mistress had taught her was to always clear the brush away before lighting the fire this time of year. Lighting a fire too close to the grass would risk setting the whole region ablaze.

Anni coughed as the smoke grew thicker, and a flickering orange light began to close in on them, spurred on by the goatlands winds.

"Move!" said Mareitsia, louder than was wise.

They clambered down the other side of the hill as the sound, smell, and heat from the fire raced after them.

Their only remaining horse was still half-dead from exhaustion and could barely carry even one of them, let alone all three, especially with Kolten's heavy dwarven frame.

They hurried through the tall grass; a brisk walk was all they could manage with the horse laden with the equipment salvaged from Mareitsia's wagon, and Kolten's bulk was not built for speed.

Suddenly, Kolten let out an involuntary grunt, and he collapsed to the ground.

"Tripped," grunted the dwarf as Anni bent down to help him.

93

THE BLUE HAIRED GIRL

"He-yah!" yelled Mareitsia, followed by the sound of hooves. Anni saw in the darkness the shadowy figure of a woman riding away on their only horse, with all their supplies.

Cowardly, old hag! thought Anni silently.

Anni cursed at herself for ordering Kolten to spare Mareitsia's life. She had repaid Anni's mercy by abandoning them to save herself.

The fire was getting closer and had now reached the crest of the hill they had just descended. The flames would soon be upon them, and they couldn't outrun the blaze with the goatlands winds at its back.

"Over here!" called a voice from a ways ahead of them.

As the firelight got brighter and the heat reached the small of Anni's back, she saw a small child standing with three large, horse-like creatures.

"This way!" he shouted.

The child appeared to be a boy, but he was so tiny that he couldn't have been older than five years old. Where he had come from, Anni neither knew nor cared.

Anni and Kolten stumbled toward the boy and, more importantly, his steeds. One of the horses wore an odd-looking metal helmet on its head, with silvery horns.

The fire was closing in fast.

"Now!" shouted the boy.

The helmeted horse let out an odd sound, and there was a sudden flash of light.

THE FLIGHT NORTH

A bolt of lightning exploded from the animal's helmet. It tore across the landscape before them, and in seconds, their only escape route was ablaze as well.

"Shit!" Kolten bellowed as they reached the boy and his animals just as the fire encircled them completely.

Everywhere Anni looked, there was nothing but burning dry grass.

"What the hell did you do that for?! We're done!" bellowed Kolten, looking at the small boy.

The boy wasn't looking at Kolten. Instead, he was looking down at the fire the horse's bolt of lightning had created.

Anni looked all around her for a weak spot in the wall of fire but found none; it was as tall as she was in every direction.

There was nowhere to run.

The fire the boy had started raced across the ground like the one at their backs, burning the goatlands grasses to cinders.

The boy took hold of the reins of his steeds and started to walk them towards the fire he had just lit. They didn't run; they walked as if heading to the market or casually down a mountain road, and he gestured for Anni and Kolten to follow him.

As Anni approached him and stepped onto the charred ground, Kolten let out a hearty laugh and grinned widely.

The fire the boy had lit was in front of them and was moving away, forced in that direction by the constant goatlands winds. The flames burned away all the grasses as it went and,

95

THE BLUE HAIRED GIRL

leaving the fire at their backs without fuel, it started burning itself out.

"Fighting fire with fire," the boy chuckled as the tiny circle of flames around them grew.

"That's very clever," said Kolten.

"Knew we would never outrun it in this wind," he said. "Climb on."

In the dim moonlight and heavy smoke, Anni saw him gesture toward the odd-looking horses. Anni grabbed the reins of the helmeted animal that had started the fire that saved them and hoisted herself onto its back.

Kolten clambered on the next, and the child on the far one.

"Don't worry; they know the way. *He-yah!*" he shouted, with a whip of the reins, and they headed off, following the fast-moving flames northward.

Soon, the sight, sound, and smell of burning grass disappeared into the darkness.

- CHAPTER 9 -
The Brynywyn Folk

Anni and Kolten had been following their rescuer for almost two days, and the sun had just peeked over the horizon, signaling the dawn. Thankfully, they had not seen any sign of Mareitsia, the fire, or the raiders since the night before.

Although Anni hated Mareitsia with a passion, a small part of her still hoped that she had escaped as well. A very small part, but a part, nonetheless. Being burned to death would not be a pleasant way to die, even for Mareitsia.

The grass fire had long since burned itself out, and they had left the dry, smoldering, ash-covered goatlands far behind them. Although Anni hadn't actually seen the raiders who had set fire to the wagon, they had probably been killed by their own

THE BLUE HAIRED GIRL

stupidity of letting the grass catch fire.

For them, Anni had no sympathy whatsoever.

You would have to be an idiot to be out on the goatlands and let the grass catch fire, Anni thought.

For the first time in Anni's life, they had reached the edge of the seemingly endless goatlands. The rolling hills had yielded to low mountains, and the dry grasslands turned to brownish-green undergrowth and sparse trees.

Other than the odd village and occasional lake, Anni couldn't ever remember seeing anything but rolling grassy hills in every direction. This part of Yuspiereia was mostly foothills, and on the horizon, the mountains were covered in dense temperate forests. In the distance, at least one unusually tall mountain stood, its peak featuring what could only be a skiff of fresh snow, despite it being the middle of summer.

The grass didn't grow long here. It was only a few inches and reached just over the hooves of Anni's mount. The whole area felt strangely claustrophobic, as if the terrain were slowly closing in on her.

The air was not as dry here as it was on the goatlands; perhaps the moisture in the air was captured by the peaks of the mountains and found its way down to the valley floor.

What struck Anni as strangest about this region was the wind—there wasn't any. The tops of the few sparse trees moved very little in the still mountain air.

98

THE BRYNYWYN FOLK

The sound of the wind blowing past her ears and the tall grass was something Anni had become so accustomed to, it seemed odd not to hear it. The air was strangely silent. The only sounds Anni heard were that of their mounts' hooves on the rough terrain, and their voices as they spoke to one another. It made talking much easier, even though Anni's ears kept popping.

As they spoke to their rescuer, it became clear that he was not a small child, as Anni had previously thought.

He was very tiny, perhaps half the size of an adult human, but he had a thick, brown mustache, and his face had some early traces of wrinkles, like a man just entering middle age.

Tycron was his name, and he called himself a "brynywyn," whatever that was.

Anni's steed had slowed down from a trot to a walk.

Anni had rarely ever ridden a horse before, but one thing was clear. The mounts they rode on were definitely not horses.

The creatures were black and were built more like over-sized reindeer, but that wasn't what made them so strange. On the head of Anni's mount was not a horned helmet, as she had first thought, but actually a set of magnificent, metallic antlers. But they didn't look natural. They were long, silvery-looking things, as if someone had dipped the animals' antlers in molten metal and allowed them to cool.

Anni found, at one point during the night, that it was unwise to touch them. The moment her finger contacted the

THE BLUE HAIRED GIRL

antler, she felt a sudden, painful jolt like a static shock that made her hair stand on end, and the animal did not seem to like her doing that. It was evident that these animals had some magic about them that Anni didn't understand.

"*Thunder elk*," Tycron had explained when they were clear of the fire. "We herd them."

This didn't answer most of Anni's questions, but she was far too tired and hungry to press the issue.

Soon, they came to a small walled village with many streams of smoke billowing into the air from its many houses. A shallow trench and wooden palisade wall of sharpened stakes encircled the town. The posts were old and rotten, and a few were missing, as if some unknown person had removed them for their own purposes and never bothered to replace them.

One side of the wall leaned over dangerously, as if a strong wind might cause it to collapse entirely. The tops of many houses peeked up over the fence, and smoke emerged from the open holes in the roofs of all of them, despite the warm summer weather.

A small drawbridge made of wooden planks covered the trench and guarded the entrance to the village. The drawbridge had no ropes, and the planks had embedded themselves deep in the earth, indicating they had not moved in quite a while.

It seemed whoever lived here was not expecting an attack. The general disrepair of the village defenses suggested it

THE BRYNYWYN FOLK

had been many years since it had seen combat, if it ever had at all.

The only guard the village had was an ancient-looking, white-haired man of the same small stature as Tycron. He had long, white hair and the same bushy mustache as Tycron, except his was pure white and hid the deep wrinkles of a tired, old face. On his belt was a long hunting knife that he would have been able to wield like a sword. Anni suspected he had probably never drawn it.

He was also slumped over in a chair, fast asleep.

"*Oi!*" shouted Tycron. "*Ol' Shep!*"

The man stirred but continued to sleep.

Tycron rolled his eyes, clambered off his elk, and physically shook the man awake.

The old man fell off his chair and landed on his backside.

"Damn it! Can't a man get some shuteye around— Tycron, what do you want?" he shouted, annoyed.

"Good to see you're keeping alert, Sheppard," he said with a smile. "We have guests."

The old man turned to Kolten and Anni, who were still astride their elk.

With his hand on his knife, he surveyed Anni and Kolten.

His eyes widened slightly at the sight of Anni's hair, but he said nothing. Instead, he poked and prodded at the saddle that Anni sat on and tugged at her dress; what he was searching for,

THE BLUE HAIRED GIRL

Anni didn't know. She was even pretty sure she also saw his nostrils flare, as if he were sniffing the air.

Soon, he finished his examination of Anni, but Anni had nothing for him to find. Everything they had salvaged from the wagon had disappeared with the horse when Mareitsia had abandoned them.

The old man's eyes fell on Kolten's darkwrists, and his jaw dropped.

"Contraband!" he snapped. "Those are not permitted! Slavery is banned in the village! Sound the alarm! Sound the alarm!"

Judging by the complete lack of commotion from inside the village, it was likely that no one cared what Sheppard was going on about.

"We're trying to get them off," explained Anni. "I want Kolten to be free."

"How do I know that?" asked Sheppard suspiciously. "Maybe you're trying to fool me."

"We're trying to get to the Republic of Zoltan," said Kolten.

"Oh-ho! Foreign spies, are you? I knew it!"

"Come off it, Shep," replied Tycron, rolling his eyes again. "If I'd known you would be making this much trouble, I never would have woken you. Out of the way."

"But the bracelets," he protested.

102

THE BRYNYWYN FOLK

"I'll speak to my uncle about them. See what he has to say. Move, you ol' codger!"

Tycron whipped the reins of his elk, pushing past the old guard, and waved for Anni and Kolten to follow him.

The village was almost perfectly square, with houses and shops laid out on both sides of the streets.

Every building was built from split wooden planks that had a slightly reddish tinge to them. The roofs were a combination of thatch straw and black animal skin that Anni presumed was thunder elk.

The village was quite impoverished, its roads were all dirt, and the air smelled a little like manure. But for such a poor village, it had its share of shops.

Anni couldn't read, but most of the shops had signs that hung over their doors with familiar symbols.

A hammer and anvil indicating a blacksmith shop, a barrel for a cooper, a saw for a carpenter, and a few others that Anni didn't understand.

All of the people she saw were small, and all the men had thick mustaches. Anni couldn't help but giggle as she saw one of the men with a mustache so long it reached down past his elbows, but at least he kept it neatly braided.

It seemed to have a mustache was a bit of a fashion statement in this village, and Kolten's long dwarven beard made him stand out almost as much as Anni's hair. Still, it was Anni's

103

THE BLUE HAIRED GIRL

blue hair that drew most of their attention.

"Care for an apple or a carrot?" asked a voice.

On the side of the road was a man about Tycron's age. He stood by a wooden vegetable cart hitched to a small pony. The cart was old, battered, and reminded Anni a little of Mareitsia's old wagon, but it somehow seemed friendlier. The man was selling misshapen and shriveled produce. He had apples, carrots, and a few vegetables that Anni didn't recognize. A simple wooden sign hung on one side of the wagon over the vegetables, displaying words and numbers that Anni couldn't read.

It looked like a poor harvest, but it still made Anni's mouth water, and her stomach growled furiously.

"Not today, thanks," Tycron said with a wave of his hand, and the vendor turned back to his cart with a sad look on his face as Anni's stomach growled again, voicing its disappointment.

Tycron had very little food with him, so neither Anni nor Kolten had eaten much since leaving Mareitsia a few days before, and the raven had been a meager meal at best.

"This way," said Tycron as he turned toward the largest building in the village.

Tycron hadn't told them where he was leading them to, but Anni hoped wherever it was, there would be food.

As they reached a tall building in the center of the village, Anni looked closely at it.

THE BRYNYWYN FOLK

It was the only building in the town made of stone, and even it was reinforced with wooden planks. It was a perfectly square building with a solid stone foundation. Judging by its design, it was probably the remains of a keep from many years ago, to defend the village from an attack, but someone had since converted it into a split-level shop.

It was evident by its location and position in the center of the village that this was a building of significance.

Hanging over the central doorway was a large, metal sign like the others in the village. This one showed the image of a tankard and a wine glass. On one side of the building was a pigpen with several hogs. There was talking and laughing and even loud music emanating from inside the building.

At the very top, sticking up like a lightning rod, was a long, metal spear. The spear had a blue flag hanging on it that stood quite still in the gentle mountain breeze. The flag had an emblem on it that Anni couldn't quite make out from here.

In front of the main door was a small covered area with a bench, and off to one side was a set of rickety stairs that led up to the top floor.

"Up you go," he said. "I'll see you later."

"Wait," said Kolten quickly, before Tycron disappeared into the building. "What's up there?"

"There's nothing to be afraid of," he said, responding to the dwarf's tone.

105

THE BLUE HAIRED GIRL

Anni looked at Tycron and the stairs.

"Fine, stay down here," said Tycron dismissively, nodding toward the bench. "But I'll be quite a while, and it's much more comfortable upstairs, and you can make yourselves at home."

He disappeared into the building.

Anni and Kolten looked at each other cautiously.

"What do you think?" Kolten asked her.

"Well, he did save us."

"Okay, but I'll go first," said Kolten protectively.

The dwarf climbed up the rickety stairs, with Anni following closely behind him. There was a long, black elk skin hanging over an opening at the top of the stairs as a makeshift door.

The dwarf pushed it aside, and they stepped in.

Anni and Kolten found themselves in a small but warm little wood and stone room. A crackling fire burned in the hearth, and the room had a washbasin and even a small toilet that Anni guessed hung out over the pigpen.

There were two warm-looking, human-sized beds. Never in her whole life had Anni ever known such comforts. She couldn't remember ever having slept in a bed before, and here was one sitting there waiting for her. The blankets looked warm and inviting, like the embrace of a parent that she had never had.

Anni almost cried at the sight of it, but she didn't have

106

THE BRYNYWYN FOLK

time, as her eyes fell on another object in the room.

A pair of soft-looking, skin-covered chairs sitting beside a table with a meal sitting there waiting for them.

"Food!" shouted Anni.

The table had a large plate in the center of it with bread, butter, cheese, vegetables, fruits, berries, some dried meat, and a water pitcher with two cups.

Anni couldn't even remember the last time she had seen so much food in one place. She ran toward the table, but Kolten hesitated.

"What are you waiting for?"

Kolten held up one of his arms. The darkwrist still hung there menacingly.

"I need your permission."

"Eat!" Anni laughed as she grabbed a large piece of bread.

With that, the pair tore into the meal like starving lions, all thoughts of Mareitsia and the night before forgotten.

Freedom had never tasted so good.

- CHAPTER 10 -
The Silver Spear Pub

Knock. Knock. Knock.

Anni opened her eyes and found herself staring up at the stone ceiling.

The room was warm and comfortable, and the fire burned with fresh logs. Someone had washed both Anni's and Kolten's clothes and folded them neatly at the foot of their beds.

Kolten was still sleeping silently in the bed next to Anni's.

Anni climbed out of the warm blankets and put on Mareitsia's old dress. To Anni's astonishment, the dress fit much better now. She saw a few new stitches on the chest, tightening Mareitsia's large bust-line, and it was cut shorter, tailored to Anni's size. It was much more comfortable now, and it seemed

108

THE SILVER SPEAR PUB

they had even managed to get the smell of cheap wine out of the dress, for which Anni was very grateful. The ugly, old thing looked and felt more like her dress than one she had stolen from her former mistress. They hadn't placed any more food on the table, but Anni had eaten so much that she was still full, even after sleeping all day.

There came another knock at the door.

Anni stood and pushed the elk skin aside.

It was Tycron.

"How did you sleep? I hope we weren't too loud for you."

It was only then that Anni noticed the sound of laughter and music emanating from the floor below. They had been so excited by the food and so exhausted from the night before that neither one of them had even noticed.

"It's fine. Thank you for the meal."

"Thank my uncle. He's downstairs. Is the dwarf awake yet?"

"Not yet, should I get him?"

"Yes, my uncle is very anxious to meet you both."

Anni approached Kolten's bed and lightly tapped him on his shoulder to rouse him, but the dwarf didn't move.

She lightly pressed him again.

"Kolten, wake up," she said quietly.

"Ahhhhh!" screamed the dwarf, shooting awake, flailing his arms in pain and falling out of bed completely naked.

109

THE BLUE HAIRED GIRL

"That wasn't an order! That wasn't an order!" Anni screamed in horror at the darkwrists when she realized what she had made them do.

"I'm sorry, Kolten!" she wailed. "I forgot; I didn't mean…I didn't think—"

Kolten pulled the bed sheets around his waist and gave a slight chuckle.

"Next time, just throw a bucket of water on me."

Anni gave a faint laugh. "Sorry, Tycron is here; we need to go downstairs."

Kolten nodded and got dressed as quickly as he could.

Anni and Kolten had long since gotten over any shame or embarrassment of seeing each other naked, as they both only had a single set of clothes, and when the time came to wash them, they had nothing else to wear. Still, out of respect, Anni averted her eyes, as Kolten would do for her.

When they were both dressed, they headed out the door and followed Tycron down the stairs.

It was early evening by now, and the sun hung low in the western sky and was starting to turn pink. One of the moons was visible high above their heads, but the other had not yet risen.

Tycron pushed open the small door to the main floor of the building under their room, and Anni and Kolten followed him inside.

The door was so low that both Kolten and Anni needed to stoop to get in, but thankfully, the ceiling was high enough

110

THE SILVER SPEAR PUB

that they could both stand once inside. Anni found herself in a large, perfectly square pub. The room was noisy and smelled of tobacco, beer, and pig filth from the pen outside.

If they could even detect the smell anymore, the patrons gave it no mind, as they were all laughing and joking heartily.

In the exact center of the room was a closed bar that gave the place the impression of being a box within a box. Dozens of glasses and tankards hung from the ceiling. Several wooden beer barrels were stacked in the center of the square bar, and on one side was a cast-iron cash register. High above the bar was a blue flag, displaying a bird of some kind.

On one side of the room, two small men with short, stubby, blond mustaches entertained the patrons. One played a tin whistle and the other a simple wooden drum. The music stopped abruptly as Anni and Kolten entered.

The tiny patrons fell silent at the sight of Anni's hair and all eyes were upon her. They wore expressions of utter bewilderment on their faces. As if Anni was the first person with blue hair they had ever seen, which, Anni reminded herself, she probably was.

After an awkward but brief moment, the patrons slowly began to whisper to each other and then to talk, and by the time the musicians started up again, the noisy conversations began to return to the pub.

Although Anni couldn't be sure, she had the sneaking suspicion that the other patrons kept shooting her sideways

111

THE BLUE HAIRED GIRL

glances whenever they thought she wasn't looking.

The man behind the bar had a red face and a very bushy and untidy mustache, the same color as Tycron's, and he was drinking from a large, gray tankard. He was taller than most of the other brynywyn folk, but still shorter than Anni. He wore a bright yellow tunic that clashed horribly with his blue bartender's apron, which also sported a bird of some kind.

Despite his unusual attire, the man flashed the brightest smile that Anni had ever seen.

The bartender let out a loud, welcoming laugh as his eyes fell on Tycron, Kolten, and Anni.

"Ty! There you are! Where you been, laddie?!" he shouted joyfully.

"Just upstairs, uncle," he chuckled as they approached the bar.

"These must be our new friends!" he said with a laugh, looking positively delighted to see them.

"Yes, Uncle, this is Kolten," he said, pointing to the dwarf.

To the bartender's right was a flip-up section of the counter for staff to use when going behind the bar, but the bartender ignored it entirely and climbed up and over the counter instead. As he did so, he knocked over his tankard, spilling beer everywhere, but left it abandoned on the floor.

He stumbled over to Kolten and shook the dwarf's hand violently, as if he were the first person he had ever met.

112

THE SILVER SPEAR PUB

"Jarabei, owner of the Silver Spear! Welcome! Welcome! Have a seat, my bearded friend!"

Kolten smiled broadly under his thick beard as his eyes shifted to Anni. One thing Anni was sure of immediately was that this man was extremely drunk.

He was not angry or irritable like Mareitsia had always been when drinking; it was more like he was the happiest man in all of Decareia, and he wanted everyone around him to be as well.

"And who might you be?" he asked, turning to Anni and looking her straight in the eye, as if he hadn't noticed her hair at all.

"I'm Anni," she said a little nervously.

"Lovely to make your acquaintance, my dear!" he said, smiling even more broadly. "Sit! Sit!"

Anni, Kolten, and Tycron took seats around the nearest table. The chairs were small, and Kolten's creaked dangerously under the weight of his large frame, but they were comfortable enough all the same.

"What can I get for you both?" he practically shouted at them.

"We don't have any money," said Kolten quietly.

"That's okay! Neither do I!" he bellowed, throwing his arms into the air with a deep belly laugh.

"Uncle, maybe you should have some water," said Tycron, trying to repress a smile.

"Water's for pigs!" he said, waving his hand dismissively.

113

THE BLUE HAIRED GIRL

"What can I get for you both?"

Kolten looked over at Tycron, who chuckled and nodded.

"A pint of ale?" asked the dwarf politely with an unsure shrug.

"'Course, and for you, my dear?"

"I don't know...Umm."

Anni had never had alcohol before, and from what she had seen of her time with Mareitsia, she was not sure she wanted to.

Tycron came to her rescue.

"Just get her the lightest thing you have. She's young."

"Right!" he said, slamming his hand down on their table decisively. "Two dead men from a dead man, coming right up!"

Once again, he climbed back over the bar, ignoring the flip-up section just a few feet away.

As he scrambled over it, he looked down at his own spilled tankard that rested on the floor.

"Some damned idiot spilled his drink," he muttered to himself.

Anni and Kolten giggled to each other.

Jarabei's happy and drunken demeanor made Anni laugh. But his mood was infectious, and Anni found it hard to stop herself from grinning as she watched him go to work.

Moments later, the bartender returned to their table with two drinks. This time, he seemed to decide that climbing over the

114

THE SILVER SPEAR PUB

bar while carrying something was too complicated, so he used the bar's flip-up entrance.

He placed the drinks in front of Anni and Kolten and tapped his nephew affectionately on the shoulder. Jarabei helped himself to an empty chair and joined Tycron, Kolten, and Anni at their table, without waiting for an invitation.

Kolten sipped from his tankard, and before he even lowered the drink, he sighed, looked up at the Silver Spear's low ceiling, and smiled.

"Been a long time." He grinned.

Anni took an exploratory sip of her drink and found it tasted a lot like slightly bitter apple juice.

"Thank you for everything, Jarabei," said Kolten. Given the man's generosity, this formality was long overdue.

"I don't know how to thank you," said Anni a little tearfully.

It was hard to put into words how much Anni appreciated what this bartender had done for them. Jarabei had been so kind, without any chance of reward or payment; they had nothing to offer him but their gratitude. Two days ago, they were starving and enslaved, and now here they were with food, drinks, a roof over their heads, and warm beds to sleep in, and they had been given it all for free.

"Thank you, for what?" He chuckled. "A few table scraps and a drink or two? A small price to pay for new friends."

"Well, we are very grateful." Kolten nodded. "Is there

115

THE BLUE HAIRED GIRL

anything we can do to repay you? I can fix things, if you need any help, and Anni can cook…"

"You owe us nothing," said Jarabei. "Any escaped slave will always find friends among the brynywyn folk."

"Damn the slavers," said Tycron, nodding.

"Watered it down a tad for you," said Jarabei, nodding towards Anni's cup as Anni took another sip. "So, tell me, what brings you to our village, friends?"

Anni and Kolten told Jarabei about their time with Mareitsia, their escape, and how Tycron had saved them from the fire.

Although they had told Tycron much of the story the night before, during their journey to the village, even as they recounted it again, he could only stare down at the table sadly, unable to meet their gaze.

Jarabei, however, cried like a child, tears falling from his unkempt mustache. It might have been the seriousness of their story that helped to sober him up a bit. He spoke with all the earnestness of a man who understood that they had suffered much at the hands of their former mistress.

"A t-terrible tale." He sniffed earnestly, patting Anni on the shoulder. "Horrible thing—slavery. No way for a child to grow up."

There was a brief silence at their table, and the other voices in the pub had died down slightly, as some of the other patrons might have been eavesdropping.

THE SILVER SPEAR PUB

"You don't know how to get those off, do you?" asked Anni, pointing to Kolten's darkwrists.

Jarabei and Tycron looked at each other, and down at the magical bracelets. Jarabei sighed.

"We don't have much magic out here," said Jarabei. "If I knew someone who could help…"

Kolten looked down at the darkwrists again with a look halfway between frustration and disappointment.

"Mareitsia said we should head for the Republic," said Anni.

"Probably wise; there are no slaves there," replied Jarabei. "If anyone can help you, they can."

There was a brief silence.

"Hey, things seem to be calming down," snapped Jarabei, returning to his boisterous mood from before. "Castor! Pollux! Play something a bit cheery!" he shouted at the men in the corner.

The two musicians had been taking a break, and Anni suspected they, like many of the others in the pub, were eavesdropping. They quickly picked up their instruments and began to play again.

It seemed the patrons all recognized this song, and they began to sing it proudly. Some even stood up and placed their hands on their hearts, and others held their drinks high in a toast.

117

THE BLUE HAIRED GIRL

A thousand years ago or more,
There stood a mighty drake,
A fiery beast, from dark it came,
It burned all in its wake.

The drake laid waste to armies,
They fell before its might,
None would dare to stop the beast,
It set our world alight.

But then there came a hero,
A brynywyn, you see,
Though tiny in his stature,
He wished all to be free.

He turned his gaze toward the drake,
And said with great suspense,
"Leave this land, I order you,
Or face the consequence!"

The firedrake, he didn't stall,
"You, puny one, are frail,
None can stand before me,
I am beyond the pale."

THE SILVER SPEAR PUB

"Now leave me be to rule my land,
And fear me as you must,
Or I shall use my fire breath,
And turn you all to dust."

Our hero held firm his ground,
With a determined eye,
He drew out his hunting knife,
And was prepared to die.

Letting fly a mighty throw,
With not a thought to run,
Soon the blade found its mark,
The battle, it was done.

So, remember this, our children,
Even if you're small,
When you stand for what is right,
Anyone can be tall.

The fiery drake is dead now,
And you know the epic tale,
Of the battle of the brynywyn folk,
Now, let's all sip our ale!

THE BLUE HAIRED GIRL

As they finished their song, Anni couldn't help but notice a few of the singers had tears in their eyes. The song sounded to Anni like a drinking song, but they sang it like a national anthem. She didn't think it was a perfect song, and most of them sang it out of tune, with Jarabei the loudest and most off-key of all. Still, it was clear that the song seemed to mean a great deal to them, so Anni didn't dare laugh.

Anni couldn't be sure what it was about the brynywyn folk. There was something odd about them. Not in a bad way; they had a strange pride in them. As if they all knew that they were mighty warriors, despite their small size. It was difficult to put her finger on, but there was something truly unique about these tiny people.

- CHAPTER 11 -
The Bounty

As the evening wore on, it was the most fun Anni had ever had. After a few drinks, Kolten got up in front of the bar and sang a song about a dwarf's beard that sounded like he was making it up on the spot.

"There was a dwarf who had a beard, and it was really long, and he stood up here, and I was singing my song," Kolten nearly shouted, so loudly and off-key that Anni couldn't be sure it even had a tune to begin with.

Although Kolten was drunk, he seemed happier than he had been in years.

All the other brynywyn introduced themselves to Anni one by one. She noticed, upon closer inspection, that not only did all the men have mustaches, it didn't look like any of the men

THE BLUE HAIRED GIRL

could grow beards at all. The skin where a man's stubble would be was bare and smooth, leaving mustaches as their only possible facial hair.

All the brynywyn, however, spoke with her like they were the best of friends. It seemed that if Jarabei approved of someone, that was good enough for his customers. Perhaps the job of the bartender was an occupation of high status and respect in this village.

It suddenly occurred to Anni that if Jarabei treated all strangers that came to their village this way, it might explain the town's weak defenses. Given the bartender's welcoming and friendly demeanor, and that most of the brynywyn held him in such high esteem, it was not entirely surprising that the village defenses had fallen into such disrepair. The walls might no longer be needed, as Jarabei's personality itself was protecting the village.

Anni found the apple drinks were making her feel very warm and giddy. Jarabei insisted on keeping their cups full, no matter how much they reminded him that they couldn't pay. He even brought them some more food through a pair of double doors that Anni guessed led to a kitchen.

Never in her whole life had Anni ever known a man, even a drunk one, to display such generosity.

The only thing that seemed to matter to him was that his customers were happy and having a wonderful time, whether they could pay or not.

"Oi! Anni!" hiccupped the bartender. "Lemme show you

THE BOUNTY

something."

Anni turned toward Jarabei, and she could see him reaching under the bar for something.

The bartender pulled up a strange-looking battle helmet and stumbled over to Anni's table.

The helmet was dark blue, almost black, and the face shield looked to be that of a bird. It had two wings sticking out from either side, presumably to protect the wearer's ears.

"I bought this at an antique store in the capital," he slurred. "I thought it would go with the spear."

Presumably, he meant the large spear that adorned the top of the building.

"What's the bird mean?" asked Anni.

"The bird?! It's a blue jay!" he said, shocked. "Why, it's the flag of the brynywyn folk! We are all the folk of the bird!"

"Oh," replied Anni, not wanting to be rude, although privately, she felt an elk might have been more appropriate.

"You know that ol' spear's not made of silver. S' iron," he went on. "But's magical."

"What's it do?" asked Anni.

"S' blade can't get dull. S' been up there since I was a lad. Still sharp, too."

"It's very nice."

"Bet I could kill a drake wiff this," he said, shifting the helmet in his hand, presumably referring to the song they had sung earlier.

123

THE BLUE HAIRED GIRL

"Really?" asked Anni politely, as Kolten started another verse of his made-up song.

"Oh yeah," said the bartender with the confident look of a much younger man. "I would just—UGH!" he said with a grunt and thrust an imaginary spear into an imaginary foe. "Right in the eye. See, that's the mistake people make," he said, holding up his finger thoughtfully, as if he had just made a crucial point. "You gotta go for the eye."

Anni wasn't sure what to say, so she nodded. She wasn't entirely sure what a drake was, but she guessed it was like a dragon.

"Listen ta me," Jarabei said, now pointing a serious finger at Anni. "If you ever need help, the brynywyn will come. That's a promise."

"What do you mean?" asked Anni curiously.

"I mean, if you're ever in trouble, we'll be there. All of us." He tried to snap his fingers awkwardly, but they seemed to be sticky from the spilled beer, and they wouldn't make a sound.

"Uhh, thanks," said Anni.

"You're welcome." Jarabei nodded. "We're your friends. It's what friends do."

Anni didn't dare point out that Jarabei barely knew her or Kolten, and he had already done more for them than they could have asked for.

Anni was about to answer when the pub door burst open.

THE BOUNTY

About nine or ten human men stepped into the tavern. They, like Anni, had to stoop to enter. The tops of their heads just touched the ceiling.

They wore farmers' clothing, and they all looked to be in their early twenties. Each man was carrying a sword. The tallest in their group had a stern look on his face that turned to determination as his eyes fell on to Anni.

"That's her!" he shouted, and the men started pushing tables and chairs aside as they approached the place where Anni sat. Jarabei stood next to her, the helmet still in his hands.

"Swords s'away please," slurred Jarabei. "Pud 'em away, 'nd I'll pour ya a drink."

The men approached Anni, and one of them grabbed her by the wrist and tried to pull her out of her seat.

"We're taking her," said the tall man sharply as Jarabei turned toward him.

Anni fell to the floor, but she managed to twist her thin wrist free and retreat under the table.

"Wha's goin' on?" asked Jarabei.

"We're taking her," he repeated.

"Leave me alone," shouted Anni from under the table. She had lived with Mareitsia long enough to know what these men wanted could be nothing good.

The stranger grabbed the table with his sword-less hand and started to lift it, when Jarabei stopped him. The bartender placed his hand on the stranger's wrist to cause him to lower the

125

THE BLUE HAIRED GIRL

table again, as Kolten came hurrying across the bar to help.

"Wha's she done?" asked Jarabei, who held no weapon, only the blue helmet in his hand.

The man sneered and looked down at the tiny brynywyn hand that held his wrist. It was dwarfed by his own.

"Get your hand off me, or lose it," he said as he shifted the sword in his hand.

Jarabei's look was quite stern for a man who was so jolly only moments ago, and his hand didn't move or even flinch at the man's threat.

There was a sudden commotion throughout the bar as many chairs scraped along the wooden plank floor.

All around them, the brynywyn had abandoned their drinks and gotten to their feet. Dozens of tiny faces with looks just as stern as Jarabei's stared at the strangers. All the other brynywyn in the bar wielded dining utensils, pocketknives, belts, candlesticks, and whatever else that was in arm's reach at the time and held them menacingly, looking straight at the men who dared threaten their leader.

"Easy, lads," said Jarabei, holding up his hand toward the other patrons to keep them calm.

Kolten reached the table and helped Anni out from under it. He stood between her and the men, hiding her behind his bulk.

The men looked around the pub, and though they were better armed and much larger than the brynywyn, they were

126

THE BOUNTY

heavily outnumbered.

"Leave Anni alone," barked Kolten, his fists clenched.

"What's this all about?" asked Tycron, who approached the men. Anni noticed he had loaded a sling with a large stone.

"We're here for the blue-haired girl. We heard she was here tonight."

"She's our guest," said Jarabei, finally releasing the man's wrist.

"What do you want with her?" asked Kolten as he continued to use his body as a shield to keep the men away from Anni.

The tall man turned to one of his fellows.

"Salwing, show them."

One of the other men handed Jarabei a piece of parchment for him to read. His eyes moved back and forth across the paper, then he looked over at Kolten, who read it over his shoulder.

Tycron took the parchment and turned to Anni.

"What's it say?" she said. "I can't read."

Tycron and Jarabei looked at each other for a moment, and then Tycron sighed.

"Anni, someone has put out a bounty on you," said Tycron quietly.

"What?!"

"It says right there," said the man called Salwing, pointing toward the parchment "'Ten thousand golords for the

127

THE BLUE HAIRED GIRL

capture of the blue-haired girl, approximately eleven years old, last seen in the goatlands.'"

Anni stared at the parchment she couldn't read and tried to make sense of the mysterious symbols written upon it.

"It says to deliver her to Blegor of the House of Dragmor to claim the reward," said the tall man. "She's coming with us."

"The House of Dragmor? That's Blegor the Cruel!" said Tycron. "You would sell a child to that beast?!"

"For ten thousand golords, I'd sell her to a brothel," he said lazily.

"What's the House of Dragmor?" asked Anni, peering out from under Kolten's arm.

"The people that are after you, I expect," the man said. "Now, girl, you can either come quietly, or we can kill a few of the pygmies first."

Mutterings of disapproval spread throughout the bar at the man's use of the word *pygmy,* and Jarabei tightened his grip on the helmet.

"That could be anyone," said Kolten firmly, his fists clenching more tightly. "Her hair is blue because of a concealment spell. She's staying right here with us."

"Well, let's have a close look at it, and we'll see."

Anni retreated behind Kolten again, and the man smiled. "That's what I thought."

"Let's talk about this over a pint," said Tycron.

"We're not thirsty," the man sneered.

THE BOUNTY

"Ever' one's thirsty. S'on the house," Jarabei said, nodding toward his nephew.

Tycron hurried over to the bar and started filling a few cups.

"We're not—" started the tall man, but one of his fellows was already stooping down to reach the tankard of ale that Tycron had placed on the bar for him. The brynywyn were so short that the bar was as high as the man's thigh, and the mug's handle was too small for his hand, but he sipped it and gave out a half-smirk.

"Put that down! We don't have time for that."

"But it's free!" the man protested.

"We get that reward, and you can drink yourself to death."

As the men started to argue, Anni noticed that Jarabei took a step between the men and Kolten. He was standing very close to the dwarf.

"It's really good, though!" said the man at the bar, sipping his drink again.

Behind his back, where the men couldn't see it, Anni saw Jarabei press the blue battle helmet into Kolten's hand.

"I don't care how good it is! Unless it's worth ten thousand golords, it's not worth it."

Kolten took hold of the helmet and wrapped his powerful fingers around the heavy object, and took a step closer to the gang's leader.

129

THE BLUE HAIRED GIRL

"Won't take a minute! They're small cups," said the man at the bar.

Clang!

There was a spatter of blood, and the tall man collapsed to the floor and Kolten dropped the helmet.

The brynywyn, seeing this as their signal, sprang to the attack and jumped on his fellows.

"This way!" shouted Tycron.

Anni and Kolten ran toward the back of the bar, where a set of double doors opened to the kitchen. As they pushed the doors open, Anni saw Jarabei pick up the cast-iron cash register and throw it at one of the men.

They raced through the kitchen and out the backdoor, into the streets.

In the dim light from the homes on either side of the road, Anni saw a collection of dark, human-sized figures following them and shouting.

Tycron led them down one of the side streets, away from the shouting and hollering men who gave chase.

Anni ran down the side street. Her head was still spinning a bit from the drinks.

The streets were dark, and neither of the moons was visible from their position on the road. Who it was that was after her, or how these men had found her so quickly, Anni had no idea, but it didn't matter now.

A crossbow bolt sailed over her head and stuck in the

130

THE BOUNTY

ground twenty feet ahead of them; whoever was after Anni meant business.

"Over here!" shouted Tycron as he turned a corner.

Anni and Kolten were hot on his heels.

They found themselves standing in a large corral with several thunder elk tied to hitching posts.

Two of the animals were fully saddled and ready for riders.

"Go!" shouted Tycron.

"But—" Anni started.

"Don't argue!" he shouted and practically forced Anni on to the nearest bull. Kolten mounted on an elk cow beside her.

Human shadows appeared on the wall of the nearest home.

"Listen to me; this is very important!" said Tycron, grabbing Kolten by the arm and looking the dwarf straight in the eye. "Head north to the capital, take the mountain road—it's longer but safer. She'll be safe there!"

"We don't know how to get there!" said Kolten.

"Don't worry, they know the way! Get her to the Republic of Zoltan!" he said with a nod to the elk.

"But—" Anni started again.

"He-yah!"

Tycron slapped Anni's elk on the hindquarters, and several small bursts of turbulent lightning passed from one antler point to the other as it tore down the back alley, toward the

131

THE BLUE HAIRED GIRL

village gates.

A loud snort and the clatter of hooves told her Kolten was following her.

"They're heading south! They stole our elk! After them!" Anni heard Tycron shouting as her steed made a mad dash for the gate.

A crossbow bolt embedded itself in a building to Anni's right, exactly where her head had been moments before.

She ducked low in the saddle and whipped the reins, urging the animal to go faster.

With a burst of lightning from its antlers, Anni's steed let out such an explosion of speed, she was nearly thrown off.

As the animal tore out of the village across the drawbridge, it continued to accelerate.

Anni was beginning to understand why the brynywyn folk revered these animals. It seemed their name was not only because of the magical lightning of their antlers.

Thunder elk were extremely fast.

Anni was sure that they could have easily outrun a horse at full gallop.

The elk moved across the uneven ground with the grace of a swan and the agility of a cat.

It was clear the animal knew where it was going because Anni wasn't steering, but the animal weaved left and right around rocks and trees and other obstacles, and seemed to get itself right back on course.

THE BOUNTY

After what seemed like a long time, the animal slowed down to a walk, and Kolten's steed matched its pace.

"Did you know these things could move like that?" asked Kolten, flabbergasted.

Anni shook her head. "Do you think we lost them?"

"For now," said Kolten. "But as long as that bounty is on your head, we can't risk anyone finding us."

The night was clear, and the moons were out tonight, but they could see much less of the sky than Anni was used to. The sparse trees and distant mountains hid the heavens from view, concealing many of the stars. It was a different kind of unsettling than Anni ever felt on the goatlands. It felt like being trapped, with unseen enemies hidden behind every tree.

As they trotted, Anni couldn't help but wonder why someone would offer ten thousand golords for her. That was far more than what she was worth as a slave. She had no family or distant friends who would be interested in her, and, other than Mareitsia, she had no enemies either.

Anni couldn't think of a single person who would want her for anything at all. The only thing she had ever done her whole life was work for Mareitsia, and even she wouldn't want Anni dead; at worst, she would want her back in the darkwrists and severely beaten for her escape.

Mareitsia would never have that kind of money, thought Anni. *Who in their right mind would pay ten thousand golords for me?*

- CHAPTER 12 -
The Forbidden Valley

It had been well over a week since Anni and Kolten had made their escape from the brynywyn village. They had made their way deep into the mountains, and the terrain was thick with brush and overgrowth.

The sparse trees and shrubs of the foothills had given way to an ancient pine forest and moss-covered ground. The huge trees and thick branches blocked out much of the sun, so even at midday, it felt like late evening.

The air was strangely moist, as if it had rained recently, but the ground and trees seemed quite dry. The sound of the endless goatlands winds had vanished to the chirping of distant birds and the rustling of the forest canopy. It was so different from the infinite, waving tall grass that made up so many of

THE FORBIDDEN VALLEY

Anni's memories.

Following a dirt path, the elk weaved left and right along the winding trail that took them deeper and deeper into the mountains. The trail itself was muddy in places, and roots jutted out at random intervals, but the elk were so surefooted, they didn't even stumble once.

They had long since lost any sign of the strangers that had chased them out of the village, for which Anni was very thankful. Her and Kolten had spent much of the last few days talking about why someone would put a bounty out on Anni, but their conversations went nowhere, as they still had no idea who would even know about her existence, let alone who would want to hurt her.

"Kolten," Anni had asked at one point, "do you know anything about the Republic of Zoltan?"

"Zoltan?" the dwarf had replied while looking at their map. "I know they don't allow slavery there."

"And how far is it?"

"Well, it's across the Great Sea. We'll make our way to the coast and see if we can stow away on a ship or something to get there."

The idea of crossing an ocean as a stowaway seemed like a pipe dream to Anni. Both she and Kolten stood out in a crowd. It would be nearly impossible to avoid detection on a ship, and the bounty on Anni's head wouldn't make them the most attractive of passengers, even if they could afford the fare.

135

THE BLUE HAIRED GIRL

Tycron had said the elk knew the way to the capital, and from there they should head for Zoltan. Maybe Tycron thought that news of the bounty on Anni's head wouldn't reach across the Great Sea and so she would be safe there, but he hadn't had the time to explain.

Even if it weren't for the bounty on her head, the Republic seemed to be the only place where they could find someone who could remove Kolten's darkwrists, and he could be free. If slavery was banned in Zoltan, that's where they were headed.

Anni had to hand it to the brynywyn, despite how they were forced to flee the village at a moment's notice, they had done an excellent job outfitting them for their journey.

Each of their saddlebags had two canteens of water, a large bundle of food, a warm blanket, some fishing tackle, candles, rope, a single-person tent, a map, a compass, and a large survival knife. Kolten's saddle also held a long wooden ax with a flat hammer head on the back of the blade.

The brynywyn had given them food, drinks, water, mounts, saddles, and all these tools and had asked nothing in return. Anni promised herself that if she were ever able to, she would find a way to repay them for their kindness. They were very generous, for such a small and poor village.

It was difficult for Anni to process just how much their lives had changed in such a short time frame. The cuts on Anni's back still hadn't fully healed from Mareitsia's last drunken binge,

THE FORBIDDEN VALLEY

and the cuts from her darkwrists were still fresh.

Anni could never remember not being a slave, and now she wasn't. Freedom was quite literally a dream come true. A week ago, being free had been unimaginable, and yet here it was. A part of Anni still couldn't believe it. She half expected to wake up in the morning to Mareitsia passed out in the wagon and her darkwrists inflicting pain on her for sleeping too long. Yet, each morning when she opened her eyes, her wrists were scarred and bruised but free and slowly healing. Although, Anni was sure the scars would be there forever.

It seemed strange to not suffer from constant hunger pains anymore either. The brynywyn had seen that they had plenty of food and had the means to get more if they needed it. It was like they didn't even care that Anni and Kolten couldn't repay them. The brynywyn seemed to just want to help them because they needed help.

The only thing that was missing from their supplies was a headscarf that Anni could use to hide her blue hair. She had kept the one from Mareitsia's wagon, but it was in her horse's saddlebag, and Mareitsia had taken it with her when she abandoned them.

As Anni sat, going over all the supplies, she wondered how Tycron had known they would need to make a quick escape. It would have taken time to pack all this gear for their journey, and yet they were fully loaded the moment they reached the corral. Did the brynywyn suspect they would have to make a run

137

THE BLUE HAIRED GIRL

for it? And if they had known about the reward for her capture, why didn't they try and claim it for themselves?

Still, as Anni's steed trotted along the rough path, she couldn't help but wonder. Why had the brynywyn helped them? They had given Anni and Kolten a lot, knowing they had nothing to offer in return. They even started a bar fight with much larger and better-armed foes to protect them.

Jarabei had said it was because they were escaped slaves, but did they treat all escaped slaves this way? Whatever their motivation, Anni was grateful for their help.

Anni had spent much of the last few days watching her steed display his magic powers as they went. Her elk was able to throw bolts of lightning a short distance from his antlers. The bolts, while probably not deadly to a human, looked like they would be very painful. Anni also noticed that his shots were surprisingly accurate. Her elk could snap a twig in two at a fair distance. At one point during their travel, a particularly annoying bird had been following them for more than an hour, squawking all the way as it went. When Anni's elk had finally run out of patience with it, he had jolted the bird clean off its perch, more than twenty feet away.

The bird tasted far better than Mareitsia's raven had, and the elk's lightning bolt had cooked it from the inside out before it even hit the ground.

"Why doesn't yours have any antler things?" asked Anni, looking at the antler-less head of Kolten's steed.

138

"She's female. Only male elk have antlers."

"So, does that mean she doesn't have any magic?" asked Anni, as she admired her own bull's magnificent antlers that sparked with the magical lightning.

"No idea."

The more they traveled, the more apparent it became that their elk were very familiar with the route. Whenever they reached a fork in the road, the animals turned instinctively toward one of the two paths without a moment's hesitation.

"You know," said Kolten, abruptly bringing Anni back to the present, "I think my darkwrists are getting weaker."

"What?!" said Anni, surprised.

"I haven't felt any pain in the one on my right hand for a while, and my left doesn't hurt as much when it does."

"That's good, but are you sure?" asked Anni cautiously.

Kolten sat there silently for a moment, looking down at his wrists.

"Only one way to be sure," he said with a nod toward Anni.

"Kolten," said Anni nervously, "I order you to get off the elk."

The dwarf didn't move at first.

A moment later, he flinched slightly and climbed off the saddle as ordered.

"The one on my right hand is just dead. It does nothing," he said with a half-smile.

THE BLUE HAIRED GIRL

"What about the left?"

"Still hurts."

There was no way to know why this was happening to the darkwrists. It could have been a delayed reaction to the shattering of the control crystal, or they might have been running out of magic, if that was possible. It also could have been that they sensed that Anni didn't want Kolten to be her slave but was unable to release him.

Whatever the reason, Anni felt a little better knowing her friend was in less discomfort and was slightly closer to freedom.

"Maybe it is a sign they're getting weaker," suggested Anni. "Maybe the other one will die too."

Since leaving the brynywyn village, they had tried many different approaches to remove Kolten's darkwrists, without success. Kolten had suggested having Anni try to remove the darkwrists for him, the logic being that, as she was his mistress, they could hardly punish the dwarf for what she did.

This had seemed a good idea at the time, but it proved a lot more complicated than Anni had guessed. The darkwrists were a lot harder to remove than Kolten's strong dwarven hands had made the task appear. They continued to cause Kolten pain while Anni worked on them, and soon it became too much for the dwarf to bear.

Anni had tried ordering them off, cutting them off, having her elk try to shock them off with a bolt of lightning, heating a section of the darkwrist over a small flame and pouring

THE FORBIDDEN VALLEY

water over it; nothing seemed to work.

At one point, Anni became so frustrated, she came up with a reckless idea. Using some of the rope the brynywyn had given them, she tied one of the darkwrists to each of the elk's saddles and had both thunder elk pull as hard as they could. She was hoping their combined strength could snap the darkwrist by brute force alone. They stopped instantly when Kolten screamed in pain and begged them to stop.

Later, the dwarf described the sensation as like pressing hot knives against both sides of his wrist.

They had tried nothing since then.

Despite these failures, the idea that the darkwrists could lose their powers was encouraging and might have been a sign they would soon cease to work entirely, just as Anni's had.

Thinking about this, Anni touched the bruised and reddened flesh on her right hand, and she still felt some lasting residual pain from the years of exposure to the dark magic. It felt strange to be able to touch the place where the bracelet once sat without it being there. The image of her darkwrists breaking into pieces and falling to the ground flashed through her mind again. Anni could only hope that Kolten's would come off as easily when the time came.

Soon, the elk pushed their way through a thick wall of foliage, and light flooded into their eyes.

They were standing at the crest of a huge ridge, about thirty-five feet high. Before them, stretched out like a blanket

THE BLUE HAIRED GIRL

between the mountain peaks, was a vast, flat valley. It seemed to Anni like what the goatlands would look like without the endless tall grass.

The valley was almost entirely bare, save for a few long, deep cracks scattered across the surface. As if the land under it didn't quite fit under the ground, causing it to be split open at the seams, like cloth ripping under the strain of a large belly.

The elk didn't hesitate but also didn't approach the lip of the ridge. They began to wander around the precipice, along the edge of the valley.

"Is that on the map?" asked Anni, looking down at the massive, barren wasteland.

"Yeah, I don't understand what they're doing," said Kolten, tugging the reigns of his mount, but she ignored him.

It was apparent from the elk's direction that they intended to travel around the valley and not pass through it.

"What do you mean?"

"Well, that's due north," he said, pointing into the valley. "That's the shortest route to the capital."

"Maybe they can't get down there," suggested Anni.

"They're pretty good, and it's not that high," replied Kolten, looking over the edge at the ground, which was not quite close enough to jump.

"Do you know a better way down?" Anni asked, patting her elk on the neck even though he couldn't answer.

Minutes later, they came to a steady path leading down

142

THE FORBIDDEN VALLEY

into the valley at a gentle slope. Anni tried to coax the animal down the hill, but its antlers sparked its refusal as they passed the path without setting foot off the ridge side.

It was clear that the elk did not want to enter the valley.

Suddenly, both elk stopped and turned their heads toward the forest. Their ears twitched nervously, and their nostrils sniffed the air.

"What is it, girl?" asked Kolten, trying to see what had the elk so agitated.

"I don't see anything," said Anni, straining her eyes.

With a flash of lightning, Anni's elk reared up on his hind legs and dashed down the ridge into the valley below, with Kolten's elk hot on his hooves.

"What?!" Anni shouted to her elk. "What is it?!"

Over her shoulder, Anni could hear some distant sound from up on the ridge, but she couldn't tell what it was.

As the elk reached the valley, they both slowed down and moved with extreme caution. Anni gave the reins a quick flick and kicked the saddle's stirrups. The elk barked up at her indignantly and refused to go any faster.

Anni knew well how fast these animals were capable of traveling. But no matter how she urged the elk onward, it would not move past a cautious walk. Something about this valley made the elk uneasy.

"What was that all about?" asked Kolten, looking back toward the ridge.

143

THE BLUE HAIRED GIRL

Anni shrugged and patted her elk on the neck.

Black, sandy dirt covered the valley floor. There was no sign of life anywhere. The area was so devoid of life, it made the vast emptiness of the goatlands look positively teeming.

Anni's elk kept turning his head left and right and looking down at its hooves as it walked, as if the ground was in danger of giving way.

Something was not right here, and Anni was starting to wish they had come by a different path. Whatever it was that was upsetting the animals, Anni guessed it couldn't be anything good.

Suddenly, there was a deep rumble from somewhere underneath them, and her steed nearly bucked her off.

- CHAPTER 13 -
Fire and Ash

The ground all around them began to quiver, as if shaken by the hands of an invisible giant. The nearby cracks in the surface belched with black dust and hot air that smelled strongly of burning sulfur. Several small stones clattered from the surface and disappeared into the deep cracks in the valley floor.

The elk started shifting around on the spot, nervously bleating in fear, and Anni's bull sparked with trepidation.

And then, as suddenly as it had come, the rumbling stopped, and silence returned to the valley, but the elk remained nervous.

The valley did have some small features that Anni had not noticed at first. Every few feet were small mounds of blackened earth. Jutting out of the ground at seemingly random

THE BLUE HAIRED GIRL

intervals, they looked like molehills but showed none of the typical signs of animal life. Anni could see no feces, bits of bone, nor tracks, nothing, just small mounds of dirt a few inches high.

Anni pulled on the reins of her steed to get a better look at one of the mounds. There was a loud spark, and a jolt of lightning touched Anni's hand, making her hair stand on end.

"OW!" snapped Anni. "That hurt!"

The animal ignored her and refused to get anywhere near the small mounds.

"What are those things?" asked Anni.

"The map calls the place 'the ash valley,' but it doesn't say any—"

Kolten was cut off as the land itself answered him.

The sound of the rumbling returned, and the elk got more nervous still.

Before Anni could try to calm her steed, she felt a blast of heat hit her in the face, with a blinding flash of light.

A massive jet of fire exploded from the earth and shot thirty feet into the air, nearly throwing Anni out of the saddle.

Both elk instinctively retreated from the flames, only to have another jet erupt from the earth behind them.

"What's going on?!" shouted Anni as another blast of flame to her left narrowly missed her.

Anni's elk barked, and its antlers arced with lightning.

Moments later, the first hot, flaming geyser subsided, and Anni kicked the stirrups.

146

FIRE AND ASH

The elk gave out a burst of speed across the landscape as more jets of flame exploded from the earth left and right.

The heat was so intense it made it nearly impossible for Anni to see where they were going. The smoke burned at her eyes and made her cough with every breath she took, but still, they galloped onward.

Another blast of flame forced her elk to change direction sharply, and it veered off to the left.

What kind of a valley is this? thought Anni as she smelled her hair burning.

Then is dawned on Anni—there was no sign of Kolten or his elk.

She turned around in her saddle and looked left and right, but she could see nothing but fire and dust.

He was gone.

"Kolten!" she shouted, but her yell was swallowed up by the roaring of the flames.

Her mount fought onward bravely. Dodging the flames all around them, the bull tore up the searing earth beneath his hooves with such force that they seemed to spark in his wake as much as his antlers.

Bolts of lightning passed from one antler to another and he let out another bark of fury as a jet of flame missed them by inches.

Anni could see the faintest hope through her stinging eyes. They were approaching the far ridge and could make their

147

THE BLUE HAIRED GIRL

escape from the valley.

Suddenly, Anni's mount stopped with such force that his hooves scraped across the dirt, and Anni was nearly thrown from the saddle once more.

Anni's elk had turned back toward the center of the valley.

Kolten was alive.

His steed had been cut off from Anni by several jets of fire.

Another burst of flame erupted right in front of Kolten's elk, causing her to stop suddenly in a panic.

She reared up on her hind legs and screeched defensively.

Anni's steed took a step backward at the sight of Kolten's cow rearing up on her hind legs, as if he knew something Anni didn't.

Boom!

The sound was like a clap of thunder had struck somewhere nearby. The blast was so intense that Anni had to duck down in the saddle and cover her ears to shield them from the shock wave.

It seemed the thunder elk did not get their names from the male's lightning antlers but rather from the females, who carried the power of thunder in their fore-hooves.

The scattered cracks in the valley floor began to widen with deep tearing sounds like distant echoes of Kolten's steed. The cracks started to join together like a spider, as if a cavern was

148

FIRE AND ASH

swallowing the ground itself.

A torrent of black earth flew into the air as a massive, clawed hand a hundred times bigger than Anni emerged from the ground.

The hand narrowly missed Kolten as it forced its way up, and the massive beast broke the surface.

The monster was black like the thunder elk but had none of their grace. It had six legs and was covered in large, black scales and walked like a lizard. The creature had six smaller eyes on the front of its head, surrounding a large black one in the center.

The creature took a deep breath and shut its mouth and center eye. Several huge spouts of flame erupted from its back and blasted into the air.

"Anni!" shouted Kolten. "It's an ashdrake! We're in its nest!"

Suddenly, the flat valley and the ridge all around them made sense. Anni could understand the elk's desire not to enter this valley; they had traveled this road before and had probably seen the creature from a distance.

The colossal lizard turned its massive head left and right. It turned its huge, black eye in the center of its face toward Kolten.

The creature opened its gaping maw and grabbed at him.

Kolten's elk galloped aside, and the ashdrake missed. The monster was huge and undoubtedly immensely strong, but the mounts dodged it with ease; the creature was so bulky that its

149

THE BLUE HAIRED GIRL

movements were sluggish. That and its sheer size was probably why it chose to catch prey by waiting for it to wander into its nest instead of actively hunting.

The drake let out a furious roar, and its gaze followed Kolten as he dashed alongside it.

The creature lifted its tail high into the air and dropped it down toward Kolten.

There was a massive cloud of dust, and the beast vanished from view for a moment.

When the dust settled, Anni could see that Kolten's luck had run out. The drake's legs coiled around Kolten and his elk like a black, scaly wall.

They were trapped.

The ashdrake was slowly closing its coils around Kolten, its mouth open.

Huge drops of saliva fell as it prepared to devour them.

Kolten's steed gave out a bark of defiance and looked left and right for an escape that wasn't there.

The elk reared up on its hind legs to hit the beast with another thunder blast.

This time, however, there was no loud clap of thunder, only a pathetic growl like a beaten lion. It seemed the cow was unable to generate another blast so soon after the last, paralyzed by fear. The thunder elk wielded powerful magic, but even it was not without limits.

Anni wasn't sure what made her do it, or why her elk

FIRE AND ASH

obeyed, but it didn't matter. She whipped the reins, and her elk
let out a burst of speed toward the drake. The bull lowered its
head in a full charge, challenging the beast—bolts of lightning
arcing from antler to antler.

"Hey you! Over here!" Anni shouted, waving her arms
frantically at the drake.

The monster hesitated and turned its ugly head toward
them. It paused for a moment, as if trying to figure out if this
newcomer was worth its time.

Suddenly it let out a loud, ear-piercing shriek down at
Anni's elk.

The beast's foul breath smelled like burning sulfur. As
Anni closed in on it, the creature was so close Anni could see her
blue-haired reflection in the soulless, black eye staring back at her.

Suddenly, a hazy memory of a small pub materialized in
Anni's mind and some vague advice from a drunken bartender.

"Aim for the center eye!" she shouted at her elk.

The elk barked in anger as the monster's human-sized
teeth were almost upon them.

There was a huge electrical blast from the bull's antlers.

The bolt of lightning arced through the air and struck
the drake right in the center eye in a perfect shot.

It shook its head violently, trying to dull what must have
been a painful blow to its main sensory organ.

The beast threw back its head and howled, recoiling from
pain for a moment. As it did so, an opening in its long, black

THE BLUE HAIRED GIRL

coils gave Kolten and his elk reprieve. Kolten's elk slipped out from its grasp like a snake sliding through tall grass.

The creature thrashed for a moment, flailing its six legs and head this way and that.

After a moment, the ashdrake seemed to recover from the elk's bolt. With a shake of its head, as if it were trying to shake off a fly, it turned and lumbered away.

Without her even needing to direct her mount, he ran over toward Kolten. It was nothing short of a miracle that the flailing ashdrake's massive limbs had not crushed him.

Kolten was on the ground, forcibly dismounted by the battle. His elk appeared shaken, but neither of them looked severely injured.

Anni climbed off her elk and pulled Kolten up to a sitting position.

"Are you okay?" asked Anni.

"What?!" shouted Kolten.

"Are you okay?" repeated Anni a little sharply.

"*What*?! I can't hear you!" shouted the dwarf, massaging his ears.

Anni looked at the dwarf. His blackened hands were hitting the side of his head, and he kept opening and closing his mouth, as if trying to make his ears pop.

"Kolten, can you hear me?" said Anni loudly, leaning in closer.

"What?!"

FIRE AND ASH

The thunder blast from Kolten's elk had hurt Anni's ears, and she had been some distance away from it. Kolten was right on top of it. Considering how powerful the blast was, it's a wonder he hadn't lost consciousness.

"*Kolten!*" shouted Anni. "*Can you hear me?!*"

Kolten looked at Anni for a moment, and his look softened.

"*I heard you a little that time!*" he shouted, pointing at one of his pointed ears. "*It must have been the thunder!*"

Anni breathed a slight sigh of relief. Thankfully, it seemed the dwarf was not completely deaf. She leaned in closer and spoke directly into Kolten's dwarven ear.

"Can you hear me now?" she said a little quieter.

"*Yes! I don't think the damage is permanent! It should get better in a day or two! Dwarves have really good ears!*"

Anni hoped that Kolten was right, and his deafness was only temporary.

Anni's bull elk nuzzled up to Kolten's cow affectionately. She seemed to be unhurt, and she nuzzled him back.

It then occurred to Anni they might be a mated pair. It would explain her bull's willingness to place itself in such danger. It wasn't Kolten it was worried about—it was his female.

Anni's elk nuzzled her gently on the side of her face. It nodded toward the ashdrake and snorted smugly.

She patted him gently on the side.

"Good boy."

153

THE BLUE HAIRED GIRL

The animal did not respond but held his head high. Anni couldn't help but think he was rather proud of himself, and given what he had just done, she couldn't blame him.

Kolten turned to his steed and checked on his cow. She licked his hand affectionately.

"She looks okay!" he shouted, petting her as well.

"We should get out of here," said Anni, looking back at the ashdrake. "They're may be more of them."

Kolten didn't answer.

"I said we should get out of here!" shouted Anni over her shoulder, ensuring the dwarf could hear her.

"Anni!" shouted Kolten.

Anni turned around and her stomach tightened.

"Oh, damn," she muttered.

A group of men was standing all around them.

All of the men had drawn swords.

"We saw you run down the hill," said the one Anni assumed was the leader, wagging his index finger back and forth at her.

"I—We—" she stammered.

"So," he said calmly. "You're the blue-haired girl everyone's been looking for."

154

- CHAPTER 14 -
Stonor

Anni's heart sank. These men must have been what drove the thunder elk into the valley in the first place.

The men marched them out of the valley and back up to the top of the ridge. Although the ashdrake was now some distance away, it seemed their captors were taking no chances, in case there were more of them.

"Now," said one of the men, when they had reached a secluded area atop the ridge, "both of you, sit."

Anni and Kolten sat cross-legged in front of one of the men. He was middle-aged, and his dark hair was streaked with gray. His face was an arrogant, disgusted scowl, like a man looking down at a drowned rat on a riverbank.

THE BLUE HAIRED GIRL

"That was quite a sight," he said to Anni.

"Who are you? What do you want from us?" asked Anni.

"That depends," he replied. "If you are who I think you are."

"What do you want?!" shouted Kolten.

The man looked very irritated at the volume of Kolten's voice.

"He's gone deaf," said Anni.

The man's eyes moved to Kolten's dwarven ears and then darted down to Kolten's darkwrists. His face filled with understanding, and he turned to Anni. "I take it the dwarf belongs to you?"

Anni decided against explaining what had happened to her and Kolten and nodded. Instead, she placed a gentle hand on Kolten's shoulder and put her index finger over her mouth to tell him to be quiet.

Kolten nodded, unable to communicate with the men anyway.

"My name is Geldman Stonor," said the man to Anni. "A lot of people have been looking for you."

Anni nodded, not knowing what else to do.

"What's your name?" he asked.

"I'm Anni."

"Are you the blue-haired girl from the wanted posters?"

This was a difficult question to answer. Anni couldn't be

156

entirely sure if she was the one from the posters; however, the men in the brynywyn village had undoubtedly thought so.

Anni hesitated for just a moment before answering. The sides of Stonor's mouth raised, as if her silence told him more than her actual answer ever could.

"Some people think that," said Anni, trying to recover from her moment's hesitation, but from the look on Stonor's face, it was too late.

"You're a witch," he said. It wasn't a question; it was a statement.

"What?" asked Anni, quite sure she had misheard him.

"You're a witch," he repeated.

"Uhh, no."

The man's face twisted into a scowl.

"Are we really going to play this game?" he asked in an exasperated tone.

Kolten, unable to hear what was said, massaged his knuckles aggressively at the sight of Stonor's scowl.

"I'm not a witch," said Anni firmly.

"Don't lie to me," he snapped. "We just saw you nearly kill an ashdrake with some kind of a lightning spell."

Although Anni had nothing to do with what had happened to the ashdrake, she couldn't blame Stonor for thinking she had. Sorcerers and other magic users were rare, but they did exist. And it must have been quite a sight from the men's

THE BLUE HAIRED GIRL

perspective seeing a blue-haired girl, riding an elk and stun an ashdrake by appearing to throw a bolt of lightning at it.

Anni had been living in the goatlands for as long as she could remember, but she had never heard of thunder elk before. If Stonor hadn't heard of them either, there wouldn't be any other explanation besides her having some powerful magic.

"It wasn't me; it was the thunder elk," explained Anni.

"Thunder elk are a bedtime story," he replied, his voice getting increasingly annoyed.

"Let me show you," said Anni.

Not bothering to wait for permission, and in spite of the armed men all around them, Anni got to her feet.

She approached her elk, who stood a few feet away and patted him on the neck.

"Go on," she said to the animal, "show them your powers."

Anni's bull barked at her. He shifted his antlers slightly, and with what looked like a great effort, a small spark appeared on one of his antlers but was probably too small for Stonor to see.

Anni then tried to coax Kolten's cow to use her thunder hooves, but she wouldn't even lift them. It seemed the battle with the ashdrake had weakened their powers.

"I don't like to be lied to," said Stonor.

"They're thunder elk, I'm telling you," pleaded Anni. "Look at their antlers and their coats."

158

STONOR

The elk's unique silver antlers looked oddly dull and opaque, as though they too had been weakened by the battle. Even their signature black coats looked dark brown in the patchy light of the forest clearing.

They looked inconveniently like ordinary elk.

"You can drop the act. You and I both know what you are," said Stonor, his face getting angrier.

"But—" Anni started.

Kolten looked over at Anni for some indication of what they were saying, but Anni didn't have time to explain before Stonor spoke.

"Everyone from here to Golairia knows that Blegor is after the blue-haired girl," said Stonor. "And now I know why."

Anni had absolutely no idea who these men were, who this "Blegor" was, or why he would be interested in her, but she was pretty sure he was the one that had put a bounty on her head.

"I don't know who Blegor is," she said.

Stonor rolled his eyes and nodded to one of the men, who quickly grabbed Kolten by the beard and placed one of their swords to his throat.

"No! Please! Don't!"

"Then don't lie to me."

"I'm not lying. We really don't know who that is!"

Stonor hesitated for a moment and studied Anni's face carefully for any sign of a lie. He then nodded to his man who

159

THE BLUE HAIRED GIRL

held the sword to Kolten's throat, and the man lowered his blade.

"Fine, but it's lucky for you that I'm a very clever man. I think Blegor wants your magic."

"But I don't—"

The man's blade returned to Kolten's throat.

Telling the truth wasn't helping right now. Anni knew, from having been Mareitsia's slave for so many years, that sometimes, it's best to tell people what they want to hear.

"Okay! Okay!" she replied. "You caught me. I'm a witch."

"I knew it. Tell me, what kind of powers do you have?" Stonor asked Anni in an inquiring tone as his man lowered the blade again.

"I—You—You wouldn't understand."

"Try me."

"I don't know, they just sort of come out when I need them to," Anni invented.

"You were never trained?" he asked.

Anni shook her head.

"What does Blegor want with your powers?"

"I don't know," said Anni.

The man with the sword twitched.

"I really don't! I have no idea what Blegor wants with me, and I'd rather not find out."

Stonor paused again. "Well, lucky for you, it doesn't

160

STONOR

matter that much anyway. I'm not interested in Blegor or the reward."

"You're not?" asked Anni, confused.

"I'm a very wealthy man," he said in a casual tone. "Ten thousand golords won't make much of a difference to me."

It was then that Anni noticed this man was not like the others. His skin was smooth and showed none of the signs of hard work, and his hands were free of blisters and callouses. He was a man of means.

"Then what do you want from us?"

"I want my questions answered. Who exactly are you?" Stonor asked.

"I told you, I'm Anni."

"No, I mean, who are you really? What's your last name? Where do you come from?"

"I'm from a long ways from here, where we don't have last names."

This was technically true; Anni had chosen to phrase it in a way that made it sound like she was from a community where no one had last names. Mareitsia had never bothered to give Anni a surname, and she couldn't remember her former owners at all.

"Let's try this, then. Where are your parents?"

"I don't know. We're out here looking for them," said Anni.

161

THE BLUE HAIRED GIRL

"Did they do something to Blegor?"

Anni shrugged.

"Do they have powers too?" he asked.

"No," said Anni quickly. "It's just me."

The man paused for a long time, as if choosing his words very carefully.

"Could you do that again?" asked Stonor, nodding toward the valley.

"Do what?"

"What you did to that monster. Could you do it again?"

"Probably," said Anni, hoping it would help get them away from Stonor and his men.

There was a brief pause.

"I need your help," he said quietly, in a business-like tone.

"My help?" asked Anni, quite sure she had misunderstood him.

"Yes, I have a...sort of a...problem, and I need a witch."

"What sort of problem?"

"The magical kind," he said vaguely.

"And why should I help you?"

"Maybe you don't understand," he scoffed. "You have no choice; you're my prisoners."

"No, you don't understand," said Anni, unable to think of anything else. "You either let us go, or I'll destroy you."

162

STONOR

The man's face hardened.

"And how exactly are you going to do that?"

"Ask him," said Anni, pointing in the direction of the enormous ashdrake that was reburying itself in the valley below. This man was quite convinced that Anni had magic, and so it seemed only logical that if Anni did have powers, she could use them to escape.

There was a brief silence as the man studied her.

"I'm a very powerful man; you wouldn't dare," he replied. His voice sounded a little tighter.

"You don't know what power is," Anni spat back with her best impression of condescension; it would have put Mareitsia to shame. "I'll do whatever I have to do to find my parents."

The man stared at her; the look on his face was one of anger and fear. It seemed this man was not used to being challenged, and was even less accustomed to threats.

Anni opened both her hands and placed her palms one against the other in a steeple in front of her chest, in a passable impression of Mareitsia's magic act.

While he stood his ground, the man gave out an involuntary flinch and a slight intake of breath.

Anni knew she had him.

She smiled and slowly lowered her hands.

"Let us go," she said.

"Calm down, Anni," he said in the tone of a man hiding

163

THE BLUE HAIRED GIRL

his fear and raised one hand soothingly. "I think maybe we got off on the wrong foot. I can reward you—"

"I said, let us go."

"I can even help you find your parents…"

"We're leaving, *now*."

"Let them go," said Stonor, with just a hint of fear in his voice.

"Sir?" asked one of the men.

"You heard her. We're letting them go."

"But, sir…"

"We're letting them go or I'll sell you to the slavers myself," he snapped.

"But—"

"That's an order!" he roared.

Kolten climbed to his feet as soon as the man sheathed his sword.

"Dwarf! Check on the elk!" shouted Anni, pointing to the elk in her best impression of Mareitsia.

Kolten, who got the hint, lowered his head submissively and retrieved the elk.

Anni climbed on to her mount.

As the pair were about to leave the clearing, Stonor raised his arm to stop her.

"You can leave now if you want, but I have a great deal of influence in this country, and I still have a job that needs

STONOR

doing. I *will* see you again."

"Good-bye forever, Stonor," said Anni as she kicked the elk's stirrups.

- CHAPTER 15 -
The Old Man and the Apple

It had been more than a day since they had escaped from Stonor and his gang of thugs, and thankfully, they had not encountered anyone since then. By now, Kolten's hearing had returned, but Anni did notice he massaged them once in a while, and he complained about an occasional ringing in one of his ears.

Anni knew it was only a matter of time before they found people again. They would have to find a way to conceal her hair somehow. Maybe they could smear it in mud to darken it, or find her a hat. Anni hoped they wouldn't have to cut it.

They had continued pressing north, and the forest had thinned out slightly, leaving many open clearings along the rough path they now traveled. The elk had gotten them back on course

THE OLD MAN AND THE APPLE

with ease since their encounter with the ashdrake and Stonor. In addition to their magical storm powers and impressive speed, it seemed that they could add an excellent sense of direction to their many useful traits. The animals knew where they were going, and despite how hopelessly turned around Anni had gotten since their escape, the elk still moved with confidence, continuing to make their way north. Anni had no idea how far they had gone, but it was a long way.

As they trotted along, Anni couldn't help but wonder about what Stonor had said. He needed a magic user to help him with some job, but he hadn't said what it was. It didn't much matter what he wanted, as Anni could never help him with it, but it was hard not to be curious all the same.

What kind of job requires magic? Anni thought.

Magic was rare, but if Stonor were as powerful as he had said, surely he would be able to find someone else who could help him with whatever it was he needed.

Anni's former mistress being a fraud, she hadn't seen much in the way of real magic. Until they first saw the thunder elk, the only real magic Anni had ever seen was the darkwrists themselves. Even if Anni had any magical powers, she would rather die than help Stonor with something like that.

In any case, it was Anni's blue hair that had tipped Stonor off. The wanted posters had mentioned her hair specifically. So Blegor probably thought it was necessary. Then

167

THE BLUE HAIRED GIRL

again, it was the only identifying mark that she had. So maybe it was just to help the bounty hunters find her.

And, for that matter, why did Anni have blue hair in the first place? This was a question Anni had asked herself many times in the past, but she had never gotten an answer. Blue wasn't exactly a typical hair color, and hers was especially unique.

It was a deep, watery blue like the midday sky on a clear day, or the surface of a lake in summer. Completely exotic, which might have been why Mareitsia had bought her in the first place all those years ago. As a potential sideshow to add ambiance to her show, though she had always ordered Anni to keep her head covered when customers were around.

Still, there had to be a reason for its color. Anni had used her parents as a ruse to fool Stonor, but as far as she knew, she was an orphan and had never known her parents. But she must have had them at one time. Someone must have given birth to her. Did her mother also have blue hair? Were her parents even human?

Anni had always assumed she was a human, but she didn't know. Mareitsia had never cared enough to discuss it. Anni was far too short for an elf and much too tall for a brynywyn, and she certainly wasn't a dwarf like Kolten.

Mostly, her entire existence was a mystery. Was she from Yuspiereia? Or was she from Golairia or the Republic, or somewhere else entirely?

168

THE OLD MAN AND THE APPLE

"Kolten?" Anni asked when the questions finally came to a head. "Do you remember when Mareitsia bought me?"

Kolten stroked his beard thoughtfully.

"Anni, I've told you this story."

"Yeah, but I still want to know what you remember."

The dwarf took a deep breath and began to recount the tale again, though he had told it to her many times before.

"All right," he sighed. "It was at that big slave market in Golairia. I'm not sure where, exactly. Hell, it might not even exist anymore. You were just a little wisp of a thing, couldn't have been more than three years old. Standing there in line, chained to the other slaves, bright blue hair, just absolutely terrified. The old hag needed someone to cook and clean for her. She thought you looked good, so she bought you."

"How much did she pay for me?" asked Anni curiously.

"I can't remember, if I ever knew. Not enough, as it turns out," he said with a half-smile.

"Was there anyone else there with hair like mine? Maybe my parents were there too."

Kolten looked down at the ground beside them awkwardly.

"It was eight years ago, Anni. But I really don't remember seeing anyone like that."

Anni looked down at the reins of her thunder elk.

"It would be nice to know where I came from."

169

THE BLUE HAIRED GIRL

Kolten rubbed his bald head uncomfortably.

"I don't know, Anni. I really wish I did."

"Do you think the people in the Republic of Zoltan will be able to help?"

Kolten stopped his elk and looked straight at Anni.

"Anni, you're the toughest girl I've ever known, so I'll be honest with you," he said in a serious tone. "They don't keep records of where slaves come from. It just isn't done. I doubt even the Republic will have any answers."

Anni rubbed one of her eyes with her knuckle to dry it. She would probably never know where she came from, and if her parents were out there somewhere, it was entirely possible that she would never find them.

Kolten leaned over to her and patted her on the arm; his kind eyes had their usual fatherly look.

"It's going to be okay, you're f-free now," he said, staggering slightly on the word "free." He was still wearing the darkwrists, even if they weren't working properly.

"But, Kolten, what am I going to do when we get to the Republic? I don't have any family or anything," asked Anni, her eyes watering again.

"Anni, we can do anything we want," said the dwarf kindly.

"W-We?" she said weakly.

"You're not getting rid of me that easy! You didn't really

170

THE OLD MAN AND THE APPLE

think I was just sticking around because of these damned things, did you?" he said with gritted teeth, holding up the darkwrists.

"R-Really?"

"Anni, I don't have a home to go to, either. I know where I'm from, and I'm no better for it. I was born in Golairia, and my family was killed in a raid ages ago, and I've been a slave ever since. It's not very interesting."

He continued, "I don't even remember how long ago it was. Hell, even if I had a home, you think I want to go back there and risk getting enslaved all over again? The whole damned continent can be swallowed up by the sea, for all I care. I'm staying with you."

Anni hesitated and gave a watery smile.

"Thanks, Kolten."

He smiled from under his thick, bushy beard.

As the thunder elk trotted around a bend in the path, they stepped onto a cobblestone road. It was a bit worn and had moss in a few places, but it looked like someone had been maintaining it recently.

"Thank the gods," said Kolten in relief. "We must be getting close."

It had been so long since they had seen any sign of habitation that just walking along a road was refreshing.

"How much further do you think it is?" asked Anni as she looked down at the paved road.

171

THE BLUE HAIRED GIRL

"I'm not sure, but they wouldn't be maintaining the road if it didn't go anywhere. The capital has to be in this direction somewhere."

The sun broke in through the thinning forest canopy, and patches of sunlight decorated the cobbles of the road, creating a lovely and welcoming pattern on the mossy stonework.

As they continued down the road, more thoughts raced through Anni's mind.

What would life be like in the Republic? she wondered. Would she have to get a job? She didn't have much in the way of skills, other than what Mareitsia had ordered her to do. She only knew how to build fires, cook, and clean. Would that be enough to support herself? Maybe Kolten could get a job, and Anni could do the cooking and housekeeping.

As they rounded the bend, they spied an old man with a long, wooden cane.

There was no time to head into the brush to hide. The man must have seen them already, and Anni's hair was like a lighthouse beacon. If this man had heard about the reward for her, they were in trouble.

"Hello there," said the old man. "Come have a chat with old Gill."

"Uhh, we really do need to be going," said Kolten nervously as he beckoned his elk to move onward.

"In a rush, eh? Well, best be careful, they say there's

THE OLD MAN AND THE APPLE

strange folk abroad, making trouble around these parts."

"Strange folk?" said Kolten, his elk trying to move around the man, but he extended his wooden cane out in front of Kolten's steed.

Anni leaned back in her saddle, trying to hide behind her elk's antlers as best she could, but it was utterly pointless.

"Aye, nothing to worry about though; local rumors, I expect."

"We will keep an eye out," said Kolten, very anxious to get away from this man.

"Well, can either of you two spare a copper for an old, blind man?" he asked softly.

Anni felt a rush of relief wash over her as she noticed the man's cloudy eyes, knowing that he could not possibly recognize her.

"What makes you think there are two of us?" asked Kolten, as if trying to keep attention on himself.

"I may be blind, but I'm not deaf," he chuckled. "Two sets of hooves."

"We don't have any money," said Anni honestly, deciding it was safe to speak up.

Kolten looked over at her disapprovingly.

"Not even a single coin?" he pressed.

"No, we don't have any money. We really have to be going," repeated Kolten.

173

THE BLUE HAIRED GIRL

"What about a bite of food? I haven't eaten since yesterday morning."

"No, we—" Kolten started.

"I have some food," said Anni, kindly. She heard the man's stomach growl, even from up in her saddle.

Kolten shook his head at her furiously, but Anni ignored him.

Anni knew all too well how horrible hunger could be, and she was not going to stand by while this helpless old man starved to death if she could help it. He was blind, so there was no chance of him recognizing her. Judging by his advanced age, they could probably outrun him if they needed to, even on foot, to say nothing of the speed of the thunder elk.

Anni reached into her saddlebag and pulled out an apple that the brynywyn had given to her as part of their rations.

The old man's eyes stared straightforward into nothingness.

"Hold out your hand," said Anni.

The old man extended his hand in front of him.

Anni reached out and placed the apple on his open palm.

"Wait!" said the man sharply, grabbing Anni by the wrist.

"*Let me go!*" shouted Anni.

"I sense something…" he said.

"Let go of me!"

174

THE OLD MAN AND THE APPLE

"I may be blind, but some things I still see. There is something strange about you."

"No, I'm not anything!" shouted Anni, still trying to free her arm as Kolten scrambled down off his saddle to help her.

"It's true; I sense great darkness. Something's wrong."

Anni finally freed her wrist but didn't run.

"What do you mean?"

"Anni, let's go," said Kolten quickly, pulling her away from the old man.

"There is something different about you…"

"We're going now," said Anni sternly.

The man stood there, looking sightlessly in Anni's general direction and breathing heavily, a look of pure horror etched across his face.

"You are one who suffers from misfortunes," he said, his sightless eyes staring straight ahead. "I've not felt anything like this before." Suddenly, the man started screaming, *"Go away! Leave me alone! And take your darkness with you!"*

He threw the apple in Anni's direction, and it sailed over her head and disappeared into the forest.

He took his cane and stumbled away into the woods in the opposite direction.

"Wait!" said Anni, but the old man was already gone.

"Let's go," said Kolten. "Someone might have heard the old coot shouting."

THE BLUE HAIRED GIRL

When they had mounted their elk and reached what Anni felt was a safe distance from where they had met the old man, Anni turned to Kolten.

"What do you suppose he meant by that?"

"By what?"

"All that stuff about darkness."

"Anni, it's the same garbage we used to hear Mareitsia say to her customers," he explained. "He's just an old soothsayer, looking for a few coins."

"But Mareitsia used to say good things about people, not all that darkness stuff."

"Anni…" said Kolten in an exasperated tone.

"Okay…why didn't he eat my apple?"

"Must have been mad. He didn't strike me as the normal sort."

Before she could answer Kolten, another sound joined the clattering of the elk's hooves on the cobblestone road. The sound of crashing waves nearby filled her ears, and the smell of salt entered Anni's nostrils.

There was a loud squawk of a seagull, as it passed overhead.

They had finally reached the coast.

- CHAPTER 16 -
The Yuspiereian Guard

The vast sea stretched to the horizon until it touched the sky itself.

The blue waves broke on the rocky coast, turning to snakelike lines of white, and some of the breakers were even taller than Kolten.

The sea was unimaginably vast. Anni had scarcely imagined there could be an expanse of water so vast that it seemed to go on forever.

"I've never seen the sea before," said Anni earnestly.

"I don't think I have either."

The air smelled like salt, and the wind swept Anni's hair. But it wasn't like the wind from the goatlands—it was different.

THE BLUE HAIRED GIRL

It felt clean and fresh. Anni could almost feel the spray of the sea on her skin.

The road snaked along the coastline, giving travelers a beautiful view of the sea. Anni could see many ships in the distance; some had dozens of sails and looked massive, like they could carry a hundred men across the ocean, and they probably could.

Up ahead was a fork in the road, and several people were going about their daily business. They probably hadn't noticed Anni and Kolten yet from this distance. So they couldn't risk getting any closer.

They steered the elk off the road and back into the forest, soon hidden by the trees.

It seemed they were forced to face a problem they had been avoiding for their entire journey because they had no idea how to solve it. How could they find a ship that would take them to the Republic, if they couldn't risk talking to anyone? The closer they got to civilization, the more people they would encounter. If news of the bounty on Anni's head had reached this far north, it would be even harder because she was very easy to spot.

"Anni," said Kolten sternly, when they had reached a secluded clearing well away from the road, where the thick foliage hid them. The sounds of the sea were still nearby. "We may need to cut your hair."

THE YUSPIEREIAN GUARD

"My hair…" Anni had known this was coming, but it didn't make the prospect any easier. She instinctively touched her blue hair defensively.

"We'll never get on a ship otherwise."

Kolten and Anni climbed off their elk, and Kolten reached into his saddlebag and pulled out a knife.

Anni had always hated her deep blue hair. Still, something about being forced to sheer it off did not sound all that appealing to her. But like Kolten, she couldn't see any alternative.

Kolten took hold of a tuft of Anni's hair and held it before the blade of the knife.

"Sorry," he said apologetically as the blade touched her hair.

Then, he tried to pull the blade across.

"OW!" said Kolten, swearing loudly at his darkwrists.

"It's okay!" said Anni hotly to the wretched bracelets. "Kolten can cut my hair!"

A moment later, Kolten tried again to cut it, but his one functioning darkwrist refused to let him.

"Anni, they won't let me."

"But I said you could," she replied defensively.

The defective darkwrists seemed to be behaving even more erratically as time went on.

"*Damn it!* I want these things off!" shouted Kolten, a

THE BLUE HAIRED GIRL

little louder than was wise.

The dwarf fumbled with the magical manacles with gritted teeth, grunting in pain as he tried to pry them off with the flat of the blade.

The one on the right still hung there uselessly, as it had before. It still appeared to have lost its magic. It did not resist his attempts to remove it.

The other on his left, however, sensing his defiance, shifted and cut into his wrist, fighting against him with every ounce of magic its weakened form could muster.

"Err!" he grunted.

"Kolten! It will cut your hand off!" said Anni loudly, trying to pull his hands apart as he fought with the manacle.

Soon, the dead darkwrist on Kolten's right hand snapped off, fell to the ground in pieces, and disappeared.

"Ha, ha!" the dwarf laughed excitedly.

The one on his left hand, however, refused to cooperate. Despite being defective, he could not remove it. It continued to fight fiercely against him.

"Damn it! Off!" Kolten roared as his wrist turned blue.

"Kolten calm down," said Anni, trying to help him.

"Get off!" he shouted.

There was a rustling in the trees, but Kolten didn't seem to notice.

"Arrrrg!"

180

THE YUSPIEREIAN GUARD

Anni could hear something, and the elk started to twitch nervously.

"Kolten…"

"*Oooooooffffff!*" he screamed as some blood dripped onto the ground.

The foliage to the side of the clearing opened up.

Several heavily armed men stepped into the clearing and looked straight at Anni.

"*Holy shit*! We found her!" one of them shouted.

Both Anni and Kolten climbed up on their mounts, as they had many times before.

The elk seemed more nervous than usual. Escaping danger was something the thunder elk were good at, yet something was amiss this time. Their ears twitched, and they looked every which way. The only time the elk had ever acted this way before was days ago, when they entered the ashdrake's valley.

Something was wrong.

The forest gave way to an open, grassy area. They were at the base of a hill, and a ridge towered over them, cutting off their escape.

The ridge was low but steep, and shaped like a horseshoe; it would be difficult for Anni and Kolten to climb and impossible for the elk.

The elk must have sensed that they were heading into a trap.

181

THE BLUE HAIRED GIRL

"Halt!" shouted a voice.

Within moments, a gang of official-looking men had them surrounded. Anni didn't bother to count them, but there must have been at least thirty. Far more than she and Kolten could fight, even with the thunder elk's help. The men were standing in a perfectly square formation.

Each man wore a colored tunic and chain mail armor. They carried perfectly round shields painted in two colors, with yellow on the left and orange on the right. Separating the two colors was a black anchor in the middle.

The men wore wide-brimmed kettle helmets to protect their heads and presumably to keep the rain off. The helmets were held together with rivets painted with yellow and orange.

Anni's bull lowered his head, and his antlers began to spark threateningly at the approaching gang. Kolten's cow leaned low on her front legs, preparing a thunderclap.

Although they were outnumbered, at least the elk's magic had had time to recharge.

"Anni, take the knife," muttered Kolten.

Anni reached over to Kolten, and he handed her the small knife that he'd been planning to use to cut her hair only moments before. She held it tightly in one hand and grasped the reins in the other.

Kolten held the wood ax the brynywyn had given him and brandished it threateningly.

182

THE YUSPIEREIAN GUARD

As if to taunt them, just over the trees Anni could make out the top of a towering brown spire. It could only be a keep of the Yuspiereian capital. They were so close to the city, it was infuriating. Freedom was just out of reach.

"You will stand down," said one of the men.

"What do you want from us?" shouted Anni.

"I am Sargent Kayell of The Yuspiereian Guard," said the same soldier. "I am here on the authority of the High Council. You will lower your weapons."

"The Yuspiereian Guard?" said Kolten. "Are you from the capital?"

Sergeant Kayell nodded as several spears pointed at them.

"Turn yourselves over to us, and no one will be harmed. This is your first and only warning."

"Like hell, we will," sneered Kolten.

"Are you refusing to comply?" asked Kayell sternly.

Neither Anni nor Kolten answered.

"Corporal," he said.

"Yes, sir!" shouted one of his men. *"Advance!"*

The entire contingent took a few steps forward, their spears pointed straight at Anni and Kolten, their shields in a tight wall formation.

Kolten looked over at Anni as their elk started to get nervous. Anni gestured for him to lower his ax, and she placed her knife back in the saddlebag. Kolten threw her a disapproving

THE BLUE HAIRED GIRL

look, but the darkwrist forced him to comply.

"Wise choice," muttered Kayell.

The men took hold of the reins of Anni and Kolten's elk and led them away. The thunder elk did not resist when Anni and Kolten ordered them not to.

"You will stay on your mounts," said Kayell sharply, and Anni nodded.

Soon, they returned to the road. The guards formed a square formation around Anni and Kolten, keeping them from escaping, and they marched in perfect unison.

The many travelers they had seen up ahead gave the soldiers a wide berth. It was clear they didn't want any trouble.

"Where are you taking us?" asked Anni.

"Yuspiereia city," said Kayell without looking at her.

"Why?"

"We have standing orders from the High Council to bring the blue-haired girl to the city for questioning. That's all we know."

Anni was getting tired of everyone referring to her as "the blue-haired girl" and of everyone chasing after her, and she still had no idea why. What Kayell meant by "questioning," she didn't know, but it didn't sound good.

"What's the High Council?" asked Kolten.

"They run things around here," said Kayell vaguely.

"So, are we prisoners?" asked Kolten.

184

THE YUSPIEREIAN GUARD

"Don't try to escape, if that's what you're thinking," said Kayell.

Anni and Kolten both tried several more times to engage Kayell in conversation, but he continued to give nondescript answers, and it was possible he didn't know any more about their current situation than they did. His men, on the other hand, said nothing at all when Anni addressed them.

One thing that did give Anni a little cause for hope was that the Yuspiereian guards didn't seem to be interested in the reward for her capture. At least, they made no mention of it.

It wasn't long before the forest disappeared entirely, and only a grassy field stood between them and their destination on the coast.

Jutting abruptly out of the coastline and into the sea was the biggest city Anni had ever seen. It looked like it housed many thousands of people. Surrounding the city was a massive wall, flanked by brown, rounded towers that rose out from the water itself. Each wall had battlements all around it and guards wearing the same-colored tunics as Kayell and his men on patrol.

There were dozens of ships sailing around the city. Undoubtedly full of goods from all around Decareia. It seemed this was quite a trade hub for The Southern Continent.

There were people from every walk of life bustling outside the city walls. Farmers, merchants, elves, dwarves, children, all hurried about their daily business. A few of them

185

THE BLUE HAIRED GIRL

stared and pointed at Anni, possibly discussing what they would do with the reward. Some might have been merely ridiculing her hair.

The gates of the city were a pair of massive oak doors that were twice as tall as a man and broad enough for two large carriages to pass through with ease.

As they passed through the gates, the scents of horses, vegetables, and bread filled Anni's nostrils. The buildings were stone and timber, and most of the roofs were straw or wooden shakes.

Shopkeepers of every kind lined each side of the city's narrow streets, far more than the brynywyn village, and most of them Anni didn't understand. Stretched overhead from one side of the road to the other were long ropes displaying laundry from the various inhabitants of the city for all to see.

There were more people in the streets than Anni could even count. Some selling goods, some gambling, and some were drinking. As they passed a darker back alley, Anni made out what she could only assume was a prostitute servicing a customer behind some crates.

The elk were clearly uncomfortable with all this activity; they had the same nervousness they displayed whenever danger was near. Still, neither of them attempted to run or use their powers. It was probably all the activity of the city that made them nervous. The brynywyn village was what they were used to, and it

186

THE YUSPIEREIAN GUARD

was nowhere near this size.

The soldiers led them down several streets, until finally, they rounded a corner and Anni gasped.

- CHAPTER 17 -
The Yuspiereian Marketplace

The city streets opened into a large courtyard. Before
Anni was a huge outdoor market that stretched for miles. There
must have been hundreds of stalls all arranged in rows upon rows,
creating a street-like layout. She had no idea how many
individual shops there were, but there could have easily been
more than a thousand. It would have been easy to get lost or
turned around in the chaos.

Anni had seen a few village markets in her time with
Mareitsia, but nothing like this. The crowded marketplace looked
almost like an anthill abuzz with activity.

The noise was deafening; the sound of haggling,
bartering, the crying of wears, and arguing assaulted her ears from
every direction. Anni could even hear the distant sound of music

THE YUSPIEREIAN MARKETPLACE

wafting on the air from somewhere in the maze of shops.

It looked like you could buy almost anything at this place. Anni spied beautiful rugs, jewelry, food, bath oils, pets, horses, clothing, magical objects, and things she didn't even recognize.

One of the Yuspiereian guards approached Kayell from the direction of the marketplace; they talked in hushed tones, and he handed Kayell something. Anni couldn't hear what they were saying, but a moment later, he turned to her.

"The High Council has been informed of your arrival, and you will be meeting with them at five o'clock."

"What time is it now?" asked Kolten.

"Almost three," replied Kayell.

"So, what do we do now?" asked Anni, even though she couldn't tell time.

"Well...First of all, put this on," he said, turning to Anni.

Kayell handed Anni a green piece of cloth with a familiar triangular shape.

It was a new headscarf, just like the one Mareitsia had had.

"I don't—"

"Put it on, *now*," said Kayell in a very threatening tone.

Anni looked over at Kolten, and his face was serious.

She reached out and took the headscarf from Kayell and started to wrap it around her head like she had done many times

THE BLUE HAIRED GIRL

in the past before Mareitsia's shows.

The guards very carefully examined her head to make sure every last strand of hair was hidden by the green cloth.

Kayell sighed with relief.

"Keep that on at *all costs*," he said, heavily emphasizing the last two words. Anni noticed that Kayell wasn't talking to her, he was talking to the other guards, who nodded and glanced down at Anni's green headscarf.

"Now that that's out of the way, we should see if we can get you cleaned up a bit. You can't go visit the High Council looking like that."

Anni looked down at the tattered remains of Mareitsia's old dress, with its stitched-down bust-line. It was never in the best condition, but it had taken some very severe punishment in the last few days. Everything from getting caught on branches as they walked, to the blackened scorch marks from their battle with the ashdrake. The ruined dress looked almost as bad as the one Blade had vomited on back at Mareitsia's wagon.

"This is Malo," said Kayell, indicating one of his men. "I have some other matters to attend to, so Malo will take you around the shops to get the things you need for your appointment."

"We don't have any money," said Anni.

"The council will cover the costs," replied Kayell. "In the meantime, I'll see that your…uh…horses…and your gear will be taken to the stables," said Kayell, indicating Anni and Kolten's

190

THE YUSPIEREIAN MARKETPLACE

thunder elk.

"They're elk," said Kolten, climbing off his.

"Whatever," he said dismissively. "They don't seem to like it here very much."

He was entirely right; all the activity in the marketplace seemed to overstimulate the elk. The elk displayed the same nervousness they had when they had entered the ashdrake's nest, even though they weren't in any real danger here—at least not at the moment.

The elk did not take kindly to Kayell's men trying to lead them away, and Anni's began to spark and pull against his reins.

Anni didn't want to leave her precious steed, given how many times he had saved her life, but they were both clearly very uncomfortable here, and she could see no alternative for now. Anni patted her elk on the neck and reassured him as best she could.

"You'll be fine," she said calmly. "We'll see you later."

The elk nuzzled her affectionately and allowed one of the guards to lead him and Kolten's away from the busy marketplace.

"Now, remember," said Kayell in his stern tone. "As long as you wear that"—he indicated the scarf—"and stay close to us, you'll be fine. This means it's in your best interest to not try and escape. If you don't make your appointment this evening, the council may issue a warrant for your arrest."

Anni understood why he felt the need to tell them this. If Anni or Kolten were inclined to try and escape, it would have

THE BLUE HAIRED GIRL

been easy to get lost in the crowded marketplace. The idea of being chased through the busy city streets by Kayell's men did not sound fun, and Anni had experienced enough of that lately. Besides, Anni very much wanted to explore this vast marketplace, even if it meant being under guard.

"We won't cause any trouble," said Kolten gently.

Kayell nodded and left them.

The guard named Malo had two other unnamed guards with him, and he turned to Anni and Kolten.

"I guess we should start by trying to find you both some clothes," said Malo.

Anni and Kolten looked at each other, and Kolten smiled. "I guess we have some shopping to do."

The group walked along the long, wide rows of stalls. Soon, it became clear that this market was even more diverse than Anni had initially thought. There were barbershops, doctors, map sellers, blacksmiths, brewers, pawnshops, and hundreds more.

As they passed an open-air brothel, a busty, full-bodied madam threw her arms around one of Malo's men, causing him to beat her back and mutter, "Not now, I'm on duty."

As Malo chuckled, Anni was pretty sure she heard the guard say something about "tonight."

Suddenly, the smell of cooking meat filled Anni's nostrils, and she recognized it instantly as pork. There was a fat, shirtless, and very sweaty man in one of the stalls, standing over a metal grill and tending to huge, sizzling chunks of meat. Every

THE YUSPIEREIAN MARKETPLACE

once in a while, he pulled them off the rack and rolled them in what looked like salt and spices and drizzled them with some kind of sauce. A young man was with him, who looked to be around twenty years old, watching the fat man cook the meat with all the pride a son could have for his father.

The fat man turned toward Anni and smiled.

"Fancy o' taste?" he asked in a thick foreign accent.

"I—I—" Anni started.

The man had already pulled out a small wooden stick, about the size of Anni's finger, with a small piece of the juicy meat on the tip.

"Go on," he said, handing her the sample.

Anni looked at the guards and Kolten, and she took a bite.

The taste was sublime. It was hot, but not too hot, just right. The spices, salts, and the sweet sauce had permeated the meat, making it delicious.

"Thank you," said Anni, nodding furiously, almost laughing from the meat's juicy flavor.

The enormous man smiled broadly, clearly very proud of his dish. "Be 'ere till closing, four silvers a plate."

Next to the meat vendor was a large, open area with several people playing musical instruments. There was a guitar, two flute-like instruments, and in the center was an instrument Anni didn't recognize. It was held by an older woman, who sat on the ground cross-legged, holding it in her lap. It looked like

193

two cooking bowls sandwiched together, and the woman was tapping on dents in the bowls' surface to make metallic tones. She was singing something in a language that Anni didn't know, but she sang so beautifully that it would have put the brynywyn to shame.

Anni soon found herself swaying to the beat alongside the crowd who had stopped to enjoy the music. The guards, however, would not let her pause long, and soon, they left the musicians behind.

"This is us," said one of the guards, pulling Anni toward one of the stalls.

Across the line of stalls was a sizable open-air vendor with stacks upon stacks of cloth, and clothes hanging from ropes strung across the shop.

A bearded man with a mouth full of sewing pins bent down before a tall woman in the dress that he was working on. She stood on a plinth-like table and wore a midnight-blue dress that the man was fussing over.

"I'll be right with you," he muttered with a look over at Anni and Kolten. The collection of sewing pins in his mouth muffled his speech.

"Tima!" he called. "The seams need to be adjusted."

A young human girl a few years older than Anni came over to help the woman on the table. The man with the pins in his mouth spat them out and turned toward Anni.

"And what can I do for you two?" he said in a slightly

THE YUSPIEREIAN MARKETPLACE

effeminate tone.

"She needs a new dress, and we need something for the dwarf too," said Malo. "The High Council has summoned them."

"Well, you certainly can't go dressed like that!" he said, waving his finger. "And sweetheart...Sorry, but the headscarf...doesn't work."

The tailor reached up for it, presumably to pull it off her, but he stopped short.

Malo's hand was on his wrist, and the other two guards had their spears pointing at him.

"You touch that headscarf, we'll kill you where you stand," Malo muttered into the tailor's ear. "She needs a dress, that's it. *Got it?!*"

The tailor slowly nodded and lowered his hand away from Anni's head, his eyes wide with fear. He indicated for Anni to climb on to a stand like the one the woman in the dress had been using a moment ago. He took a long piece of measuring tape and ran it up and down Anni's body, checking her every measurement. It wasn't entirely clear what he was thinking, but at the very least, he seemed to know what he was doing.

"Right," he said, putting down the tape measure and jotting down something on a piece of parchment. "I'm thinking a dark green; it will go with the scarf."

Anni nodded, only half listening as she climbed off the plinth because it was Kolten's turn. She already knew the dwarf

195

THE BLUE HAIRED GIRL

wouldn't be so patient with the tailor's hands, not to mention his sharp demeanor.

Not surprisingly, within moments, the tailor found himself flat on his back the moment he started to take Kolten's measurements. The guards only laughed, with disapproving looks on their faces as the tailor stumbled to his feet, looking stern.

"Fine then," he snapped. "I'll just guess."

"Works for me," muttered Kolten, not caring in the slightest.

"Come back in a few hours. I should have something ready for you," he said sharply as Kolten stepped off the stand.

As they walked along the line of shops, Anni suddenly noticed that something was missing from the market. The one thing no one seemed to be selling, or indeed shopping for, was slaves. There were no shackled workers, or signs of beating, anywhere to be seen. Perhaps, this part of Yuspiereia didn't practice the trade; this was something that they had in common with the brynywyn. Anni couldn't help but feel a little more affection toward the people of the capital at the thought of their having abolished slavery.

A few stalls down, Anni couldn't help but stop again, as they came to one of the most massive tents in this part of the marketplace. The guards stayed very close to Anni and Kolten, but they did not attempt to stop her when she approached it.

This tent was full of animals; some Anni had seen before, but others were entirely alien to her.

196

THE YUSPIEREIAN MARKETPLACE

She couldn't resist entering the tent to take a closer look. Cages lined one of the walls full of birds of many colors and sizes. Not black and menacing, like Mareitsia's pet raven, but much more pleasant to behold.

The largest was an enormous, deep-brown owl that was bigger than Anni was tall. The magnificent bird stood on its tree-stump-sized perch, sleeping with its beak tucked under its wing, probably waiting for nightfall. There were other birds so tiny they could have sat on Anni's fingernail, and they beat their wings so fast they were a blur.

There were also common dogs, and dire wolf pups play-fighting in a pen on the other side of the tent. Anni smiled with glee as they climbed on top of one another in mock battles of dominance, barking in high-pitched yelps.

At the rear of the tent, all alone, was a huge, wooden pole driven deep into the ground. A large, gray mass about the size of a wagon slept chained to the pole. Anni assumed it could only be a Golairian battle boar, but she couldn't see it too clearly, and she didn't want to get any closer to the hulking beast.

A pure white unicorn was eating out of a dish next to a desk where a young, attractive elf woman sat scribbling with a long feather quill. She placed the quill on the counter at the sight of Anni.

"Hello," she said brightly. "Is there anything I can help you with?"

"No, no, we're just looking," said one of the guards.

THE BLUE HAIRED GIRL

"No problem, feel free," said the elf woman, bending down with a smile to look Anni straight in the eye. "You know, there's someone I would like you to meet."

She gestured for Anni to follow her over to her desk.

The elf woman reached out from behind her desk and pulled out a small bundle of cloth.

"Now, be careful. He's really young," said the elf woman to Anni softly.

She handed Anni the bundle of rags, and Anni coddled it like a baby. In her arms, wrapped in the bundle, was a tiny baby tiger. It was ice-blue, and its stripes were white. The cub opened its eyes and looked up at Anni, and it nuzzled in its wrappings deeper to get more comfortable.

The cub had large eyes and a bulbous, over-sized head, and it cooed like a well-behaved human baby.

He was adorable.

Suddenly, the little creature let out a hiccup, and there was a burst of hot air, and a few sparks came from its mouth.

"It's called an icecat. They live in the mountains of northern Sydonea. Their blue coats help them survive in the high altitudes, and they use their fire breath to keep their caves and their young warm."

Anni couldn't help herself; she was overcome with emotion at the sight of the tiny bundle. A tear fell down her cheek as the icecat cub batted at her headscarf playfully, and it almost seemed to smile up at her as it snuggled more deeply into

198

THE YUSPIEREIAN MARKETPLACE

its blankets. It was the sweetest thing Anni had ever seen. She didn't want to put it down ever again.

"It's okay," said the shopkeeper as she saw that Anni was crying.

"He's s-so cute," sniffed Anni.

Kolten patted her on the back kindly.

"He's just like you, Anni."

"What do you mean?"

"Blue on the outside and fiery on the inside," smiled the dwarf.

Anni let out a tearful laugh.

This was not what she had expected for their time in the capital.

- CHAPTER 18 -
The Yuspiereian High Council

Finally, five o'clock came, and Anni and Kolten found themselves at the High Council building in the center of the city.

Anni had to admit, the tailor knew his craft well. She was wearing a new, dark-green dress that was cut just below the knee; the headscarf was still bound tightly around her head. Anni had even been able to take a bath inside the tailor's private tent while the soldiers stood guard outside.

Making clothes for Kolten had probably been more difficult, as his dwarf frame was quite broad even by dwarven standards, and of course, he had refused to let the tailor measure him. Still, they managed to make him a dark blue tunic and a pair of brown trousers. Kolten had refused to let them cut his

THE YUSPIEREIAN HIGH COUNCIL

beard and nearly injured the tailor in the process. Instead, the dwarf had compromised and allowed his beard to be washed, combed, and done up into a long, tidy, triangular braid.

Anni had giggled when she saw him. His pointed beard and long, birdlike nose made Kolten look a bit like an oversized woodpecker.

The council building was in the heart of the city, and it towered over the shops and houses around it. It was a large, cylinder-shaped building that must have been ten stories high.

Arch-shaped windows with a colored glass surrounded the building, and between each window were various flags. The only one Anni could recognize was a large yellow and orange one with a black anchor in the center. It looked just like the shields that Kayell and his men carried.

Two large doors, like the ones at the city gate, stood at the top of a small flight of stone stairs leading into the council building. A pair of guards wearing the same garb as Kayell and his men stood before them.

Kayell was at the entrance, waiting for them.

"Search them first," ordered Kayell. "Not the scarf," he added, pointing to Anni's head.

The guards obeyed and poked and prodded Anni and Kolten, searching presumably for weapons, being careful to avoid Anni's scarf.

"Come on," said Kayell when they had finished, and he

THE BLUE HAIRED GIRL

led them through the front doors.

They walked in the entryway, and there was a hallway lined with many arch-shaped doors that snaked around the circumference of the round building. At the end of the corridor was a set of spiral stairs.

"Kolten, you'll have to wait," said Kayell. "The council wants to speak to Anni alone."

Anni and Kolten turned at each other with almost identical looks of horror on their faces. It had not occurred to them the council would want to separate them.

"I'm not leaving Anni!" said Kolten firmly, taking hold of Anni's arm.

"This is not a discussion," said Kayell. "Corporal!"

Several other guards took hold of Kolten and wrenched Anni's arm out of his hand. The dwarf put up quite a fight but soon was dragged away from her down the hallway, fighting the guards every step of the way.

"Where are you taking him?!" shouted Anni.

"Just to a holding area," he explained, taking hold of Anni's arm himself. "The High Council may want to question him as well."

"I'm not going without him!" said Anni sharply.

Kayell sighed and reached down.

Before Anni could protest, Kayell had lifted her off the ground and hoisted her over his shoulder. Anni tried to put up a

202

THE YUSPIEREIAN HIGH COUNCIL

fight, but it was useless. Kayell was much older and stronger than she was, and he was determined to get her to the council.

They began to climb the stairs at the end of the hall.

As they reached the top of the stairway, they reached another corridor lined with doors, and several important and busy-looking people ran around the halls.

"Is that really necessary?" asked an official-looking young man at the sight of Kayell and a struggling Anni held over his shoulder.

"The High Council summoned her, and she doesn't want to go," he said, shrugging his free shoulder.

Soon, they reached another pair of huge doors, similar to those in the streets, guarded by another couple of soldiers.

Kayell lowered Anni to the floor so, like the guards at the main gate, these two could search her as well before letting them pass.

"It's fine, I'll walk," said Anni in an exasperated tone when Kayell bent down to pick her up again. Although she wanted to know where they had taken Kolten, there didn't seem to be much she could do about it right now.

They reached a flight of stairs just like the last, followed by another hallway and a pair of guards who searched her again. This cycle repeated itself several times until, after going up several flights, they came to what Anni could only assume was the top story. A set of double doors loomed before them. The one on the

THE BLUE HAIRED GIRL

left was painted yellow, and the right was orange. Each of the door handles was black and shaped like half an anchor.

They must really like that symbol, thought Anni.

In front of the doors were four guards dressed more elaborately than the others. They wore masked helmets that concealed their faces, but in the same yellow and orange colors. Each guard searched her one by one, checking for anything the other had missed.

Kayell turned to Anni.

"I can't go in with you," said Kayell. "Speak only when spoken to, answer all questions asked of you, and for gods' sake, don't lie."

Anni noticed that he had just a hint of fear in his voice.

He knocked on the door.

"Enter!" said a voice.

Two of the guards grabbed each of the half-anchor door handles and pulled them open.

Anni found herself in a round chamber that probably took up an entire building floor all by itself.

The room, like the building, was completely circular and was lined with white stone marble. It was mostly empty, but several sets of raised stone benches with tables in front of them surrounded the room's walls in perfect circles. As many as forty important-looking people dressed in yellow and orange robes were sitting on the benches, and most of them had parchment,

THE YUSPIEREIAN HIGH COUNCIL

books, or quills on the stone tables before them. Anni noticed that most of the seats were empty.

The entire room seemed like a coliseum and gave Anni the uneasy feeling of marching into a fighting pit. The only gaps in the seating ring were the main door that Anni had just come through and one on the exact opposite of the entrance, where a woman was sitting.

The woman sat on a bench that was built much higher than all the other seats, to make it visible from everywhere in the room. Like the doors to the chamber, and indeed, just about everything of consequence in this building, it too was colored yellow and orange.

There were only two sources of light. In the center of the ceiling was a dome-shaped glass skylight that cast a perfectly round sunbeam on the floor in the center of the room, and the light bounced off the white stone floor, illuminating the rest of the chamber.

The other light source was a pair of stained-glass windows above the woman on the raised seat, bathing her in a yellow and orange hue. Anni noticed there were many windows in the ceiling above the benches surrounding the dome-shaped skylight, but all the other windows had their shutters closed.

The woman held a long stick with a diamond-shaped crystal on the top in her right hand.

"Step into the light," said the woman on the raised

THE BLUE HAIRED GIRL

platform.

Many faces stared at her, whispering to those next to them in hushed voices.

Anni stepped into the disk of light; as she did so, she felt the eyes around her stare at her even deeper.

"Remove your headscarf," said the raised woman.

"That guard said I shouldn't," said Anni.

"You will remove your headscarf," she said, a bit more forcefully.

Anni reached up and unwrapped the cloth from her head and placed it beside her on the floor.

Suddenly, the room burst out with arguing and shouting like a back-alley bar as her blue tresses were exposed. Some were shouting questions, others making accusations, and others were barely coherent. Oddly enough, many of the loudest voices seemed to be the ones demanding quiet.

Thud!

A blinding purple light flashed from the crystal on the woman's stick, and the room fell silent. It reminded Anni of the hooves of a female thunder elk. It was much louder than would be possible without magic, and Anni guessed it was to keep the room silent.

"The chamber does not recognize the Honorable Councilor Kollin at this time," snapped the raised woman with the stick, looking at one of the councilors that had been loudest.

206

THE YUSPIEREIAN HIGH COUNCIL

"The chair would like to remind the chamber that if a member wishes to speak, they should first raise their hand."

Several of the councilors nodded their approval.

"I call this emergency meeting of the Yuspiereian High Council to order," said the woman with the stick. "The chair would like to take this moment to express its gratitude to the councilors who found the time to attend this meeting on such short notice."

How a chair could be made to want or say anything was a mystery to Anni, but given the situation, she thought it best not to ask.

"What is your name?" asked the woman.

"A-Anni," she stammered nervously.

"Anni what?"

"It's just Anni."

"We need your full name for our records, please."

"I don't have any other name," said Anni uncomfortably. "I've never had one."

The woman turned to the man sitting on the lower seats next to her, who appeared to be taking notes. He shrugged, and the woman turned back toward Anni.

"Very well. As you may have guessed, we have some questions for you."

Anni didn't answer, still unsure what to say.

"Now, before we begin. All rise."

207

THE BLUE HAIRED GIRL

All the men and women in the room, including the woman on the raised platform, stood up.

"We are the High Council of Yuspiereia," they chanted in unison. "Only the words of truth and liberty shall be uttered in this chamber. For we are the throne of kings, the sword of justice, and the book of wisdom. We serve only the people of this nation. For we are the voice of Yuspiereia."

They all returned to their seats.

"Anni," said the raised woman. "Do you solemnly swear to all who bear witness to abide by this chamber?"

Anni started to sweat, and she had no idea what the woman was asking. Anni was beginning to wish she had tried harder to get more details from Kayell and his men about the High Council, but she had allowed herself to get distracted by all the activity in the marketplace.

"I-I don't understand." She shifted her feet uncomfortably and wished Kolten was here with her.

"This is absurd!" snapped one of the councilors. "We're don't have much time!"

"You're out of order," said the woman sharply. "Anni, it means, do you promise to tell the truth?"

"I—I, yes," Anni stammered.

"Let the record show that the witness has agreed to abide by this chamber. Your hair, Anni. Did you color it somehow? Maybe using a dye or some form of magical concealment?"

208

THE YUSPIEREIAN HIGH COUNCIL

Anni shook her head.

"I will remind you that you are under oath not to lie."

"It's always looked this way."

Once again, arguing and shouting broke out throughout the room.

Thud!

With another blinding, purple flash of light from the crystal on the woman's stick, the shouting stopped.

The woman turned and looked down at one of the few councilors who had bothered to raise her arm.

"The chamber recognizes the Honorable Councilor Valama at this time."

She tapped the bottom of her stick on her raised seat as the woman councilor stood up.

Suddenly, the window above the woman with the stick snapped shut, and another one opened directly above the Councilor Valama. She was now bathed in yellow and orange light, and all eyes fell upon her.

"Thank you, Chairwoman. Now, Anni, why are you here?" she asked.

"I, well—that guard told me you wanted to see me."

A few members laughed in serious tones.

"Not in this room, I mean in this city, Anni."

"We're trying to reach Zoltan."

"The Republic?" she asked. "Why?"

THE BLUE HAIRED GIRL

"Because of Kolten's darkwrists," Anni explained.

"Kolten—you mean the dwarf?"

"Yeah, they punish him whenever he doesn't listen to me," Anni said without thinking.

"The dwarf is your slave?" asked a male councilor, getting to his feet.

"You're out of order," snapped the woman with the stick.

"Oh, sorry," muttered the man earnestly, and he returned to his seat.

The raised woman with the stick nodded back to Valama to continue.

"Are you aware that slavery is illegal in this country?" asked Valama sternly.

"Kolten isn't my slave," Anni said quickly. "Well, he is, sort of...It's complicated."

Anni took a few moments and told them about her and Kolten's time with Mareitsia, including their escape and how they had tried several times to remove Kolten's darkwrists, but instead of coming off, they had malfunctioned. Anni noticed that when she reached the part of the story involving the bounty on her, several councilors shifted in their seats uncomfortably and a few whispered to one another, but the chairwoman ignored them.

As Anni finished her story, another councilor was lit up and rose to his feet. This man dressed differently from all the

210

THE YUSPIEREIAN HIGH COUNCIL

others. He wore robes of purple and gold, but they were just as formal and elegant as the others, despite their unique colors.

"Chairwoman?" asked the man in unique colors. "Could you remove a pair of defective darkwrists?"

"Possibly," she said.

Anni's head turned toward the chairwoman so fast that her neck cracked.

"It's highly complex magic, so I'll need to do some research first," she replied.

"You could help Kolten?" asked Anni.

The chairwoman gave a half-smile with a noncommittal shrug.

"How?" asked Anni.

"Witchcraft," muttered another voice.

"Shut up!" snapped another.

The chairwoman raised her staff threateningly to head off the speakers before the room could break out in chaos again.

"You know what?" said another councilor loudly when it was his turn to speak. "Everyone is thinking it, so let's just take the goat by the horns here. Anni, why is Blegor the Cruel after you?"

Several of his fellow councilors nodded their approval at this question.

"I don't know who that is," replied Anni.

"How can you not know?" he asked with raised

THE BLUE HAIRED GIRL

eyebrows. "He's offered a king's ransom for your capture."

"I don't know anything about him." Anni shrugged.

"She's lying!" shouted another voice.

Once again, the chamber erupted in shouting, and a few councilors stood up from their seats, screaming at their fellows across the room.

Thud!

Once again, the room fell silent as the chairwoman's purple-lit staff flashed and then went dark.

"Thank you, Chairwoman," said the councilor standing in the light. "If you don't know Blegor the Cruel, why would he be after you?"

"No idea," replied Anni.

The man that spoke shrugged and sat down, looking confused, and the window above his head snapped shut with another tap of the chairwoman's stick.

A moment later, another window opened above a stern-looking councilor, and he stood.

"You made an oath to abide by this chamber. You will tell us what we want to know."

"I don't know anything," said Anni, a little louder.

The councilor hesitated for a moment to compose himself. "So, do you think that this Mareitsia woman has had anything to do with Blegor or the reward?"

"I don't think so," replied Anni. "It was only when we

212

THE YUSPIEREIAN HIGH COUNCIL

reached the brynywyn village that we first heard about it."

A stunned silence fell over the room.

"Anni, when exactly did you escape from the gypsy?" asked the chairwoman. She had now taken the questioning away from the councilors, who all wore looks of utter shock on their faces.

"Well over a week, closer to two; we've been running ever since."

"And that was the first time you ever heard about the reward for your capture?"

Anni nodded.

There were several odd looks from members of the High Council.

"Then you really don't know?"

"Don't know what?"

"Anni, Blegor the Cruel put out the reward for your capture ages ago. The entire continent has been looking for you for nearly ten years."

- CHAPTER 19 -
A Council in Chaos

"That can't be," said Anni, as the council continued to ask her questions.

"Anni, we've all read the wanted posters. It has to be you."

The idea that there had been a bounty on Anni's head for so many years and she was only just hearing about it now seemed ludicrous.

Surely, she would have heard something about it before now.

Anni had spent her entire life out on the goatlands, though, and almost no one lived out there. The few people they had met only interacted with Mareitsia, and Anni had always

A COUNCIL IN CHAOS

been forced to keep her head covered whenever there were people around.

As much as Anni and the council found it hard to believe, it was entirely possible that Anni was the girl from the wanted posters and news of the reward had just never reached that deep into the goatlands.

It still didn't explain both the council's and Anni's main question: what did Blegor want with her in the first place? If it had been close to a decade, it might have been something from Anni's past, before Mareitsia had bought her, that Blegor was interested in, but there was no way to know for sure.

The only thing Anni could be sure of was that Mareitsia certainly couldn't have known anything about the reward for Anni's capture. If she had had any idea how much Anni was worth, she would have turned her in years ago. Instead of running a traveling fortune-teller's scam, she could have bought an entire circus, maybe more than one.

"What does he want with me? Why me?"

"That's why we're here, to figure this out," said the chairwoman.

"But, I'm nobody!" said Anni exasperatedly. "I've been a slave my whole life. I have never done anything to anyone, besides cooking and cleaning for Mareitsia, and she's probably dead by now."

"A side motion for the chamber, Chairwoman," said a

THE BLUE HAIRED GIRL

female councilor when it was her turn to speak. "I motion for this chamber to issue a special warrant for the arrest for this gypsy woman Mareitsia for suspected violation of the anti-slavery act."

"We don't have time for this," muttered a man from somewhere behind Anni.

"Any second voices?" asked the chairwoman, ignoring the interruption.

The man who stood next to the woman raised his hand, and the chairwoman called on him to speak.

"Yes, Chairwoman, I second that motion under the premise that the gypsy woman be brought before this chamber for questioning with regard to the current issue, as she may have more information for us."

"Motion will be tabled for now," said the chairwoman. "But point of order, please hold all motions until after the witness has testified."

Anni had absolutely no idea what had just happened or what any of these people were talking about, but it sounded like they wanted to talk to Mareitsia.

Anni thought back to the grass fire that had been tearing across the goatlands the last time she had seen her former mistress. Fire moved so fast on the dry goatlands grasses, it was hard to imagine that Mareitsia had escaped the flames on her exhausted horse. If the High Council were trying to find Anni's former mistress, they would find it a lot easier said than done.

216

A COUNCIL IN CHAOS

The goatlands were enormous, and Mareitsia was quite good at avoiding detection when she wanted to—if she was even still alive and had somehow managed to avoid the raiders in the area.

"Anni," asked yet another councilor, "do you know where you were from before you ended up with Mareitsia?"

Anni thought back to what Kolten had said to her on their journey to the capital.

"Well, Kolten said she bought me in a big slave market in Golairia," explained Anni. "I've been with her ever since."

"Well, we'll probably ask the dwarf after we're done with you," he replied. "So, it's possible that Blegor was your former master?"

"Could be; I don't remember." Anni shrugged. "Why don't you just ask that Blegor guy what he wants with me? If it's been ten years…"

Several members of the council shifted in their seats nervously as Anni spoke the name.

"Eight years by my count, actually, but anyway, Blegor the Cruel has the rather bad habit of killing or enslaving our diplomats when they meet with him," said the councilor. "And as far as the High Council can tell, he has kept his reasons for hunting you a carefully guarded secret."

"Why would he do that?"

"We don't know," he said. "Blegor the Cruel has spent years burning villages, destroying whole cities, slaughtering

217

THE BLUE HAIRED GIRL

thousands of innocent people in his search for the blue-haired girl. He's been tearing the Southern Continent to pieces for nearly a decade looking for you. Then, one day, out of nowhere, you just show up at our front door…"

It seemed that Anni didn't know much more than the council did about what Blegor wanted with her. She was starting to get frustrated with their constant questions about things she knew absolutely nothing about.

A few more questions were asked of Anni, wherein she answered, *"I don't know,"* until finally, the chairwoman's window opened.

"Anni, Blegor the Cruel has, on many occasions, threatened this country and this chamber," the chairwoman continued. "Our scouts report that his raiders have been moving deeper into the goatlands, and you're the one he wants. It won't take him long to figure out that you're here. So, if you know anything at all…"

Several of the other councilors nodded in agreement.

Anni looked up at the chairwoman. She was a tall and formidable-looking woman, even when seated. Her hair was pulled back into a tight bun, and her face had all the look of a wise, childless woman who had devoted her entire life to the service of a nation. The staff in her hand glowed slightly with the recent use of her powers and was ready in case she needed to summon them again.

218

A COUNCIL IN CHAOS

"I don't know anything."

Another councilor stood up.

"Chairwoman, given that this girl doesn't seem to know anything we would expect her to, I'm inclined to think this whole thing could turn out to be a goat race. We don't even know for sure if this girl is the one Blegor is looking for. Has anyone actually bothered to examine her hair—"

"Oh, come on! Look at her! We're not idiots!" shouted a new voice across the chamber as it erupted in shouts and threats more loudly than ever before. In seconds, fists were slammed on tables and obscenities were hurled across the room like spears.

"I demand that this chamber order an investigation!"

"By the time we start investigating, Blegor will be at the gates."

This time, the shouting got so bad that one of the councilors jumped down from his seat. He wasn't running toward Anni—he was looking at one of the other councilors across the chamber.

The man he was shouting at jumped down from his bench as well, screaming at him, his chest puffed out and his hands clenched into fists.

Two beams of light emanated from the chairwoman's crystal, and the men found themselves magically lifted off the floor of the chamber and forced back into their seats.

"If Blegor wants her so badly, I say we give her to him!"

THE BLUE HAIRED GIRL

shouted one of the men.

"She's a child!" shouted the other.

Thud! Thud! Thud!

"The longer we wait, the closer Blegor gets!" said a third.

"There's nothing but grassland between him and the capital!"

Thud! Thud! Thud! Thud! Thud! Thud!

"The High Council should be immediately evacuated to Zoltan!"

"You would have us rule in exile?!"

"We can't just run!"

"He's the most dangerous man alive!"

"We should order conscriptions!"

Thud! Thud! Thud! Thud!

"If Blegor finds out she's here, he's coming!"

"He's probably already on his way."

"I say we seal the gates!"

"We should call the Senate and demand Zoltan send help!"

"That will take weeks!"

Thud! Thud! Thud! Thud! Thud! Thud! Thud! Thud!

The room only got louder as the chairwoman's thundering continued. She was rapidly losing control of the chamber.

Suddenly, the chairwoman stood up, her staff held high over her head as a beam of light exploded from the crystal.

220

A COUNCIL IN CHAOS

"Silence!" she bellowed.

There was a massive crack, and the dome-shaped glass ceiling over Anni's head shattered, and chunks of glass rained down on their heads from above.

Anni was in the center of the room and had no time to find cover, so she threw her arms over her head, trying to protect herself.

The glass shards never hit the floor.

Anni looked out from under her arms, and she could see all the councilors were ducking in cover as well. The chairwoman was suspending the glass shards in midair with a magical beam from her staff. The look on her face was furious.

Slowly, the glass shards raised back up to the top of the chamber on their own and returned to their places. As they did so, the cracks in the glass vanished as the roof repaired itself, piece by piece.

As the councilors fell silent and slowly returned to their seats, the chairwoman was breathing hard, as if she had just run a mile. The chairwoman adjusted her graying hair, which had come down from its bun, and she sat down as the window over her head opened.

"The chair would like to remind the council that if they continue to disobey the rules of this chamber, the meeting *will* be adjourned," she said sternly. "I know the council is frightened of Blegor, we all are, but we need to focus here."

221

THE BLUE HAIRED GIRL

The councilors, taken aback by the chairwoman's show of magical strength, did not dare speak out of turn again. Anni couldn't blame them; this woman was obviously a very powerful sorceress, and she could have destroyed the entire chamber if she had wanted to. The councilors would have to be idiots to cross her again.

A moment later, the one councilor who was wearing purple-and-gold-colored robes stood up.

"Honorable members, we will discuss our options for dealing with Blegor after the witness has been dismissed," said the oddly dressed man. "I would, however, like to remind the chamber that we are not speaking to Blegor, or one of his henchmen, we are speaking to a child. And a child who has suffered greatly, at that. It would do this chamber great honor for us to keep our heads. Anni's had a hard life, keep that in mind."

He spoke in a soft and gentle tone. Several councilors nodded, and the chairwoman smiled at him.

Slowly but surely, calm returned to the chamber and the councilors resumed asking Anni questions, but each time her answer was, *"I don't know."*

Eventually, the chairwoman stood up.

"Are there any further questions from the council for this witness?"

No hands went into the air.

"Very well, does the witness have anything she wishes to

A COUNCIL IN CHAOS

add?"

Suddenly, the door that Anni had entered through opened, and a familiar figure entered the chamber.

The man had graying hair and a disgusted scowl on his face.

It was Stonor.

"You!" Anni shouted. "What are you doing here?"

All eyes fell on Stonor, who looked bored and completely apathetic to his late and unannounced arrival.

Stonor glanced down at Anni for a very brief moment, but then he faced forward as he walked slowly along the edge of the room toward an empty seat.

Stonor had changed into the same formal-looking robes that most of the councilors wore, but he still had the disgusted scowl on his face.

"Councilor Stonor," said the chairwoman in a sharp tone. "You have been warned about this in the past repeatedly. If you wish to be a member of this body, you'll need to make sure you arrive on time. The meeting is nearly over."

Stonor didn't respond but dropped down in his seat and crossed his arms defensively, with a look of pure loathing on his face directed not at Anni but at the chairwoman.

Anni gazed up at Stonor, who looked even more disgusted than the last time she had seen him. As if the council was lucky just to have him in the room with them. Stonor refused

223

THE BLUE HAIRED GIRL

to look at Anni; his eyes were set squarely on the chairwoman and his scowling face was transfixed upon her.

The chairwoman turned back to Anni after throwing Stonor a cold look.

"Does the witness have anything she wishes to add?"

"Huh?" said Anni, puzzled, looking back up to the raised platform.

The woman offered a hint of a smile.

"Anni, is there anything else you want to say to the council?"

"I want to see Kolten and get his darkwrists off," she said quickly.

"All right, I am issuing an order of remand," said the chairwoman. "The witness will be placed in the holding cells while the council deliberates, and a final decision is made."

"*What*?! But I didn't do anything!" said Anni, as she was pretty sure that was a bad thing.

"Are there any objections?" the chairwoman said, ignoring her.

Only a few hands went in the air, including that of the soft-spoken councilor in the odd-colored robes.

"Noted. The motion passes. Guard!"

- CHAPTER 20 -
Prison

Anni was forced by a pair of guards into a tiny stone cell. It had three bare stone walls and a wall of iron bars with a door in the center.

She heard the rattling of metal in metal as the door was locked behind her.

"Hey! Let me out of here!"

The guard gave the door a hard shake to ensure it was locked, then left her there without another word.

The cell block was windowless and dark. The hall was lit only by flickering glass lamps hanging from the ceiling, well out of arm's reach.

Anni's cell itself was small and had nothing in it but a cot

THE BLUE HAIRED GIRL

with a blanket and a bucket that smelled like feces. All she could see through the bars was a long hallway with several other prison cells along both walls.

Anni tried in vain to squeeze through the bars of her cell. Despite how thin and malnourished she was, even her small frame was too big to fit through them.

After several tries to open the door or fit through the bars, she decided it was impossible to escape and sat down on the cot, defeated.

Kayell had said they were taking Kolten to the "holding area." Anni had assumed that it would be a cell like the one she was in now. But she was completely alone in this cell block. All the others were empty.

Where was Kolten? The city was huge—they could have taken him anywhere. For that matter, Anni wondered where they had taken their thunder elk.

She wished with all her heart she and Kolten had never come here. They should have just shaved off her hair and stayed in the brynywyn village. Kolten could have gotten a job fixing things there. Anni could have worked in the pub, cleaning dishes or washing floors. Maybe Kolten's darkwrists would have eventually stopped working on their own.

It only made Anni feel worse when it dawned on her that Kolten was still wearing one of his darkwrists. Wherever he was, there was a good chance he was in pain because the darkwrists

226

PRISON

would probably know she didn't want him there.

It wasn't her fault that she didn't know why Blegor was after her. She didn't know why *any* of these things had been happening to her.

There was a loud clang, followed by some footsteps down the hall. Anni peered through the bars and leaned over to see who it was.

The man reached her cell and stared down at her. Standing before her was the soft-spoken councilor wearing the purple and gold robes from the meeting.

"Hello, Anni, my name is Ackleman."

The councilor was tall and appeared to be human. He had dark hair with streaks of gray and tired gray eyes to match. He had a softness about him that Anni had rarely seen in anyone before.

"You were in that meeting," said Anni.

"Yes, I was. I'm not an official member of the High Council but, yes, I was there."

"Where's Kolten?" she demanded.

"Your dwarf friend is fine; I just came from there."

"Why are you keeping us here?"

"The chairwoman feels it's in everyone's best interest if you stay here," he explained. "Temporarily," he added at Anni's look of horror.

"How long will that be?"

227

THE BLUE HAIRED GIRL

"Soon," he said vaguely.

"Why do these things keep happening to me?!" said Anni, finally losing her temper.

"Anni, we've been over this. We don't know why Blegor is after you either, that's why the council summoned you in the first place," he said calmly.

"Who is Blegor?!" shouted Anni. "Everyone just assumes I should know who he is! I've never even heard of him, until those men came after me in the brynywyn village!"

Ackleman paused, as if considering if Anni was old enough to hear this.

"He's a gloknore warlord, and he's…not very nice."

Anni didn't know a lot about gloknore, but she remembered the stories she had heard from Mareitsia's show about them, and what she did know was terrible. They were humanoid creatures who lived in the mountains of Golairia. They had big tusks, bad tempers, and were merciless warriors.

"Anni, they call him Blegor the Cruel, and it's a name that he's earned," Ackleman continued coldly. "He has a huge army at his command just across the goatlands. As you may have noticed, the High Council is utterly terrified of him, and for good reason. He's absolutely ruthless. There have been stories of him eating prisoners alive, and forcing children to murder their own parents."

Although Anni had no memory of her family, she was

228

PRISON

close to Kolten in that regard and she couldn't imagine being forced to do something like that. Anni knew all too well what cruelty could be like from her time as a slave, but it was hard to picture even Mareitsia doing the type of things that Ackleman described. Anni hated her former mistress, but Mareitsia was mostly just a mean-spirited, selfish, old drunk. If what Ackleman was saying about Blegor was true, and Anni had no reason to doubt him, Mareitsia seemed downright tame by comparison.

"For years now, every time Blegor destroys a village or sacks a city, he leaves just a handful of survivors with the message, 'Bring me the blue-haired girl'; we just don't know why. He has thousands of warriors at his command, and just a few days ago, the guards caught some of his scouts right here in the capital, so it's a good bet he already knows you're here. It's got both the High Council and even the Republic of Zoltan very worried. It's probably best that you stay here for the time being because we think he's heading this way."

"What?!" said Anni, a little more loudly than she meant to.

Ackleman nodded.

"His troops have been spotted in the goatlands to the south."

"But, why me?!"

"We don't know, Anni, but here you're safe until we can figure this out."

229

THE BLUE HAIRED GIRL

"I don't want to stay here."

Ackleman paused again.

"I just wanted to see if you needed anything," he said kindly.

"Like what?"

"I don't know—food, water, or something to read?"

"I can't read."

Ackleman looked at Anni awkwardly.

"So, there's nothing you need? There's nothing I can do for you?"

"You can tell me where Kolten is and open the door."

Ackleman gave a half-smile.

"You know, Anni, I have a daughter about your age. She's back home in Zoltan."

"Zoltan?" said Anni, surprised to hear that her tone had softened at the sound of the word. "The Republic of Zoltan?"

He nodded.

"You're from the Republic?"

Ackleman rolled up his sleeve. He had an unusual tattoo on his arm. It was comprised of a series of numbers written in fiery purple ink.

"That's my Republic ID."

Anni's eyes fell on the numbers written on his forearm; there were close to ten digits printed on it, but Anni didn't bother to count them. Anni looked up at the councilor's gentle

230

PRISON

eyes and back down at the tattoo.

"I never met anyone from there before."

The Republic of Zoltan had been their ultimate destination since they had first escaped from Mareitsia, but it had always seemed like a fantasy place to Anni.

"Is it true there are no slaves there?"

"There have never been any slaves in Zoltan, nor will there ever be," said Ackleman, sounding a little indignant. "The Republic prefers to rely on free men with good ideas who build great things."

It was hard to believe that there could be a whole country without slavery. Yet, here, standing before her, was living proof that the place really existed.

"Well, you can see it for yourself, soon enough."

"What do you mean?" asked Anni.

"Once the council is finished deliberating, I think there's an excellent chance that the High Council will vote to have you extradited."

"What does *extradited* mean?"

He smiled. "It means, they'll let me take you and Kolten back to Zoltan with me, where Blegor can't get to you. The council would probably have voted to do that already, but you weren't able to tell us very much."

"But the bounty…"

"Yes, ten thousand golords for your capture, I believe it

THE BLUE HAIRED GIRL

was," he said with a smirk. "Anni, golords are not a recognized currency anywhere in the north. Zoltan, Torus Island, Sydonea, even here in Yuspiereia, golords have been declared worthless in their borders. No one in any of those countries will have any reason to come after you because the reward is worth nothing outside of Golairia."

"But those men in the brynywyn village…"

"Anni, you need to understand," he said in an imploring tone, "Yuspiereia is a weak nation. The southern borders haven't even been drawn yet. The High Council is relatively new, and they haven't worked out all the problems yet. Building a democracy takes time. That's why I'm here; the Senate has sent me to oversee it."

Anni didn't understand all of what Ackleman was saying, but the word *democracy* sounded vaguely familiar to her. Still, Anni was pretty sure she thought she got the gist of what he was talking about.

Now that Anni thought about it, it made a lot of sense, what Ackleman was telling her. The lawless goatlands, the chaos of the council, the fact that slavery was still practiced in the borderlands but nowhere else. All this added up to a weak nation.

"What's the Senate?" she asked.

Ackleman gave his kind half-smile again.

"We'll get to that in good time, Anni. In the meantime, the High Council will come to a decision on this soon."

232

PRISON

Anni highly doubted this; the council looked more like a flock of squabbling, screeching birds than a group of statesmen. If it weren't for that woman with her magic staff, Anni would probably still be in there, watching them screaming at each other.

"Who was that woman?" asked Anni.

"You mean the chairwoman? Her name is Valentia; she was appointed chairwoman at the urging of the Senate. She has been a strong advocate for these reforms. She helped build the High Council."

"She didn't do a very good job," muttered Anni.

Ackleman smiled.

"Anni, the council is young. Once they vote on what to do about all this, I'm confident that I'll be taking you and Kolten back with me."

There was a brief silence.

"When can I see Kolten?"

"I don't know, he did injure a guard when they were taking him to his cell…"

"They shouldn't have made him mad," said Anni, grinning slightly at the thought of Kolten throwing one of the guards across the room.

Ackleman stood there awkwardly.

"I'll speak to the guards," he said with a nod. "Are you sure there's nothing I can get for you?"

"I just want to see Kolten."

233

THE BLUE HAIRED GIRL

Ackleman nodded. "I'll be right back."

Ackleman turned and walked down the hall. Anni watched him until the door shut behind him. Anni wasn't entirely sure she trusted Ackleman, but she remembered that he had voted on her behalf in the council meeting. If Ackleman was up to something, he had chosen not to reveal it yet.

The door to the hallway opened up, and Anni looked back through the bars.

That was quick, thought Anni.

It was not Ackleman.

Standing before her was a shorter and nastier-looking man, wearing a deep scowl on his face.

It was Stonor.

Anni retreated deeper into her cell, staying well out of arm's reach from the man, using the bars as a shield, but she kept her look fierce.

Stonor wore the same yellow- and orange-trimmed robes that he had worn in the council chamber. The robes were quite elaborate and well cared for. They were decorated with gold buttons and a black anchor on the breast pocket, with a pair of animals on either side that Anni didn't recognize. She guessed it was Stonor's family crest. They would have looked nice were it not for the distasteful man that wore them, or the scowling look on his face.

"What are you doing here?"

234

PRISON

"Look, that old cow might have swallowed your 'helpless little girl' act, but I haven't. I *know* what you are!"

"Oh, go away!" said Anni hotly as she scowled right back up at the man. It felt good to be able to talk back to someone like Stonor, and Anni inadvertently touched the place where her darkwrists had been. Stonor took no notice.

"Listen, girl, you have no idea what you've wandered into. What's about to happen. If you don't start treating me with some respect, you'll live to regret it."

"I'm not afraid of you!" spat Anni, her temper rising.

"You should be. The council won't be able to protect you forever."

Anni said nothing and just scowled up at the foul man.

"Fine then, I have a job for you to do," he said, taking a step closer toward the bars.

"Not interested," said Anni.

"You *are* going to help me," he said, reaching into his pocket.

Anni pressed her back up against the rear wall of the cell to maximize the distance between her and Stonor. She had been beaten enough times in her life to know that distance was the key to avoiding pain.

"Ah, councilor," said a soft voice. "It's nice of you to come visit our guest."

Ackleman had returned and placed his hand down on

235

THE BLUE HAIRED GIRL

Stonor's shoulder very hard in a mockingly friendly manner to announce his presence.

Stonor removed his hand from his pocket with nothing in it.

"I...I..."

"No need to bother, councilor," Ackleman said in a bright tone. "I've already spoken to Anni. She doesn't need anything."

Anni guessed that Ackleman knew that was not what Stonor was doing there; Ackleman was cleverly offering him a face-saving way out of the situation.

Stonor took the opportunity.

"Oh well, good to hear, Ackleman. Well, if you need anything else, Anni, just have the guard call on me. I'll see you in the council meeting later, Ackleman."

"Yes, you will."

Stonor turned to leave.

"Oh, and Stonor..."

Stonor turned back toward Ackleman.

"Try not to be late this time."

Stonor threw him a cold look, gave a slight nod of recognition, and left without another word.

As Stonor's robes disappeared from view, a figure was revealed behind him.

"*Kolten!*" Anni shouted as he came into view.

236

PRISON

The dwarf looked a little worse for the wear. His eye was a little puffy where someone had hit him. A trickle of blood dripped from his birdlike nose and down onto his beard, but other than that, he looked okay.

Both his hands were bound behind his back by thick, iron chains, and his left hand was still wearing the defective darkwrist.

"Are you okay?" she asked.

"I've had worse, you know that," he said simply.

"What happened?"

"Oh, they brought me into that big stone room at the top of the stairs, and they yelled at each other a lot."

"I mean, what happened to your face?" asked Anni.

"One of the guards thought it would be a laugh to try and pull my beard. Didn't work out so well for him."

"What did you tell them?" asked Anni.

"Nothing, didn't say a damned thing. Darkwrist wouldn't let me. Not that I minded."

"I've convinced the guards to let you both be kept in the same cell block," Ackleman explained.

The guard standing behind Ackleman opened the cell door straight across from Anni. He led Kolten into it and locked the door behind him.

"Arms," said the guard.

Kolten reached one of his bound arms through the bars,

237

THE BLUE HAIRED GIRL

and the guard removed the iron shackles, then repeated the process for the other.

Anni noticed that the guard did this while touching Kolten as little as possible, and he stayed as far back from the dwarf as he could. He might have witnessed Kolten's fight with one of the other guards and thought it best to keep his distance.

"Is there anything else?" asked Ackleman gently.

"Yeah, let us out of here," snapped Kolten.

Ackleman smiled gently. "Anni already tried that. I'll have some food and water sent down here."

Ackleman and the guard turned and left.

As the door closed behind them, Anni could hear only one set of footsteps going up the stone stairs. Clearly, the guard remained stationed outside the door at the foot of the stairs.

"Well, this is a fine situation we've landed ourselves in," said Kolten.

- CHAPTER 21 -
Stonor's Bargain

"Are you sure you can't bend those bars?" asked Anni.

"No chance, I've tried," he said, looking at the thick iron bars. "Maybe if they were cut first, but I'd never fit through."

The dwarf's dense, powerful frame gave him a great strength, meaning he could potentially force his way out. But the cost of his strength was his body was slow, bulky, and cumbersome, making an escape from the cell by forcing his way between the bars impractical.

It had been a few hours since Kolten had been moved to Anni's cell block. The only contact they had had with anyone since then was every half hour or so, one of the guards walked down their dark corridor and made sure they weren't trying to

THE BLUE HAIRED GIRL

escape. They would not answer Kolten's or Anni's attempts to engage them in conversation, and even if they had, it was unlikely the guards would have any better idea of how long they would be kept here than Ackleman did.

Anni had since told Kolten everything that Ackleman had said to her about Blegor and that the council might vote to have them taken to the Republic, but Kolten didn't trust Ackleman. After all, they had been chased, captured, separated, interrogated, and thrown into prison without any idea how long they would be forced to stay, and their only possibility of escape depended on a vote of the squabbling council.

Ackleman had said that Yuspiereia was in reform, as if things were getting better. But as far as Anni was concerned, if the High Council was considered progress, she couldn't imagine things being much worse. They could barely shut up long enough to let each other ask questions. If it hadn't been for that Valentia woman, real fights would have broken out in the council chamber.

Even with Anni's near ignorance of Yuspiereian politics, the problems with the council were clear, even to her. It wasn't hard to see why there would be so many problems in the goatlands and the surrounding area, or why the possibility of Blegor the Cruel attacking them would terrify the council as it had. If they were attacked, it would be hard to imagine the council being able to launch a successful defense, given their

STONOR'S BARGAIN

constant bickering.

"Did that woman say anything about getting your darkwrists off?" Anni asked Kolten across the hall.

Kolten shook his head. "Not really; she said she was going to read up on them."

"What do you think she meant by that?"

"It means she's not going to help."

There was a brief silence.

"We need to find a way out of here," she said to Kolten finally.

Kolten looked over at her, looking slightly defeated, but he nodded. Anni couldn't be sure if it was the defective darkwrist that made him speak or if he just wanted to get out of there as much as she did, but she didn't ask.

"Is there anything long and thin in your cell?" asked Kolten, sounding a little hopeless. "Something I can use to pick the lock?"

Anni dropped to the floor and crawled around on her hands and knees.

She had already looked over the cell pretty thoroughly, but there was little harm in being sure. If there was any chance of escape, she needed to make sure they had exhausted all their options. As her fingers caressed the smooth floor, they poked and prodded around but found nothing, even little in the way of dirt. It seemed the floor had been swept clean before they were

THE BLUE HAIRED GIRL

imprisoned.

The cot in Anni's cell was bolted to the floor, and there was nothing underneath it. The cot's fabric was double-stitched around its secure metal frame. Anni knew from her time mending Mareitsia's clothes over the years that the quality of the stitching was excellent, so there would be little hope of taking the cot apart without the proper tools.

They needed something long and thin. Finally, Anni gave up her fruitless search when she was quite sure she had checked the entire cell.

She turned back to her remarkably well-assembled cot and sat down on it, chewing her bottom lip, defeated.

"There's nothing in here," said Anni.

Kolten had returned to his own cot with the same glum look on his face.

"Well, unless you have another idea, there's not much we can do but wait and see what happens," said Kolten.

Anni shook her head. "They said the council was going to vote and decide what they were going to do with us."

Kolten stroked his beard.

"In that case, we'll be here for a while," said Kolten, his hand full of beard. "From what I saw, they would be lucky if they could decide what color their flag is."

Anni laughed mirthlessly.

Several hours passed, and Anni and Kolten said little to

242

STONOR'S BARGAIN

each other. Anni had checked her cell several more times to see if she could find something to help them escape, but it was hopeless.

This was not exactly a surprise; the guards probably cleaned the cells before and after each use for just that reason.

Eventually, the door down the hall opened again, followed by a set of footsteps.

As the scowling face of Stonor looked down at her from outside her cell, Anni refused to look him in the eye. Instead, she gazed up at the ceiling, as if Stonor wasn't even there.

"What do *you* want?" snapped Kolten, with particular emphasis on the word "you."

"I brought you your dinner," he said.

Anni turned her head instantly, and her eyes fell on something in Stonor's hands.

He was holding two trays of food, and Anni's stomach growled longingly.

"Why would you bring us food?" asked Anni distrustfully.

"I would like to talk to you," he said simply.

"Tell someone who cares," spat Kolten, rolling over in his cot, turning his back to the councilor and facing the far wall of his cell.

Stonor ignored Kolten's rudeness and pushed the trays of food through a small slot in the bars at the floor of each of their

243

THE BLUE HAIRED GIRL

cells.

Anni didn't much like Stonor, and she was pretty sure he didn't like her either, but there was no doubt what he was giving her was food, so she took the tray. She had learned from years of living with Mareitsia never to hesitate when she had the chance to eat, as meals could be hard to come by.

Anni completely ignored the wooden fork and started eating the plate of lemon bread and fish with her bare hands.

"You forgot to say '*thank you*,'" he said coldly.

Anni thanked Stonor by spitting a fish bone through the cell bars at him.

Stonor's jaw was tight, and his fist was clenched as he wiped the fish bone off his face, but he did not respond. The look on his face was that same look of loathing that he had given the chairwoman in the council meeting when she had reprimanded him for being late.

"How would you like to get out of here?" he asked simply.

Anni looked up at him but did not stop eating.

Stonor looked back at the door he had come through and then down at Anni, who still sat on the floor eating.

"I can get you both out of here," he said in a slightly hushed tone.

"How?" asked Kolten, turning his head toward Stonor slightly but still facing the rear of his cell.

244

STONOR'S BARGAIN

Stonor reached into his pocket like he had during his last visit, and this time he pulled out a small, brass key.

"I can open these doors right now," he said simply.

"And why would you do that?" asked Kolten.

"I've told you: you're going to do a job for me."

"What job?" asked Anni, taking a sip of water.

He looked at the door to the cell block again.

"You're going to kill Valentia for me," he said simply.

Anni snorted into her water cup, and Kolten sat up in his cot.

"The chairwoman from the meeting," he said. "I want you to get rid of her for me."

"Ackleman said he could get us out of here." said Kolten. "Why would we want to mess that up?"

"Because the council is deeply divided," he explained. "As you probably saw, it doesn't function very well. I, however, can have you on a ship heading for Zoltan, before sunup tomorrow morning. Along with food, money, identity cards, clothing—everything you need to start a new life in the Republic. You can leave this place forever."

There was a brief silence, broken only by the sound of Anni's chewing.

"Ackleman said he can get us out of here," Anni retorted, echoing Kolten. "He can probably get us all those things, anyway."

245

THE BLUE HAIRED GIRL

"Only if the council votes to have you released," he said with his nasty smirk. "Anni, Blegor the Cruel is after you, and he'll do whatever he has to, to get his claws on you. I don't care what that fool Ackleman says, some of the council will want to hand you over to him, and none of them are just going to let their best leverage over Blegor leave the country. If you want to leave this cell ever again, you have no choice but to help me."

"Why do you need us?" asked Anni, diving into the bread.

"Do not ask stupid questions!" he snapped.

The distant sound of footsteps echoed from somewhere beyond the cell block. All three of them sat there quietly, waiting to hear if anyone came in, but the footsteps slowly faded away.

"I want to rule Yuspiereia, and the High Council is in my way," he said in a hushed tone. "Valentia is a powerful sorceress; magic-users are not easy to kill, but it can be done," he went on. "I need another magic-user to destroy her, and I saw what you did to that beast in the ash valley. With Valentia gone the council will collapse,"

Anni looked over at Kolten, who shrugged.

"Then what? You're planning to take over?" asked Anni.

"Won't matter; you'll be halfway to the Republic by then."

"So basically, you're planning a coup," said Kolten.

The councilman looked back toward the door at the end

246

STONOR'S BARGAIN

of the hall, and then back at Anni and Kolten.

Anni knew Stonor must have been right about one thing: Valentia was the only thing keeping the High Council together, and without her intervention, it was hard to imagine it surviving for even one meeting. Stonor, it seemed, had reached the same conclusion.

Anni looked up into Stonor's cold, dark eyes. Anni hated the idea of being used like this; it felt like being back with Mareitsia again. But, unlike her former mistress, who was just a stupid drunk, Stonor seemed to be quite clever.

Despite her poor upbringing with Mareitsia, Anni knew perfectly well that killing was wrong. Many times, Anni had seen Mareitsia's past slaves worked to death and their bodies left to rot in the grass, and even that had always seemed wrong to her. But what Stonor was asking her to do was far worse. This was cold-blooded murder, plain and simple.

If Stonor were to enact his plan, people would get hurt; Valentia would just be the beginning. Even if Anni had been a witch or a sorceress, she would want no part of this. Although Anni didn't much like the High Council, she would never want to hurt them—or anyone, for that matter.

"I'm not going to kill anyone," said Anni simply.

"Everything is all set," said Stonor, ignoring her response completely.

"If you're so sure that Anni has powers, why would we

247

THE BLUE HAIRED GIRL

still be here?" scoffed Kolten. "Wouldn't we have escaped by now?"

"You've already told me why," replied Stonor observantly. "You think the council is going to let you go, so you have no reason to escape, and besides"—he rapped on the iron bars with his knuckle—"magic-resistant iron."

Anni looked at the metal bar in front of her. She hadn't noticed earlier, but they seemed to emit a very faint light that was almost too weak to see, but it was there.

"Here's the plan: my men will escort you to Valentia's home. Once you've taken care of her, there'll be a ship waiting for you in the harbor, bound for Zoltan and loaded with all your supplies. Then, once you're gone, the High Council will collapse, and I'll seize control of the city."

"Hang on a minute," said Kolten. "What about that Blegor guy, who's been after Anni all this time? Isn't he going to be mad about you sending her to the Republic?"

Stonor gazed down at Kolten with an eyebrow cocked.

"Dwarf, you're a lot smarter than you look," said Stonor.

Kolten said nothing.

"What Blegor doesn't know, won't hurt him," he replied shrewdly. "Anyway, if she's in the Republic of Zoltan, then Blegor will have no reason to attack us. Instead, he'll be forced to focus his efforts up there, and he'll be Zoltan's problem, for a change. Blegor's not stupid; he's not going to invade a country

248

STONOR'S BARGAIN

that doesn't have the thing he's after, just out of spite. Besides, if it comes down to it, once I'm in control of Yuspiereia, I'll be able to organize a defense. I'm not worried."

Anni had to admit, it was a well-conceived plan. Stonor had cleverly found a way to use the High Council against itself. He had probably been waiting for an opportunity like this for quite a while, and it just happened to be that Anni and Kolten had ended up in the right place at the right time.

There was, however, one fatal problem with the plan.

"I can't destroy her," said Anni, finally deciding it was time to give up on the ruse. "I don't have any magic."

"I know what I saw in that forest," he sneered.

Anni didn't know how to convince Stonor that fighting off the ashdrake hadn't had anything to do with her. It had all been the thunder elk. It was hard to see how she could convince Stonor of this. If she had seen what he had in that valley, she probably would have thought the same thing.

"That being said, Valentia's magic is probably a lot more powerful than yours is," said Stonor. "So I have a plan."

Stonor reached into his robe pocket and pulled out a small, glass vial of clear liquid.

"All I need your magic to do is find a way to get this poison into Valentia's wine glass and I'll take care of the rest."

"And how am I supposed to do that?" asked Anni.

"I don't know, an invisibility spell, or levitate it up above

249

THE BLUE HAIRED GIRL

her glass—you're the sorceress. I'm sure you'll think of something."

"You know, Ackleman will be coming back to check on us eventually," said Kolten, as if trying to draw Stonor's attention away from Anni. "We could just tip him off to what you're planning."

Stonor's scowl morphed into a look of cocky satisfaction, as if he had heard exactly what he was expecting to and was already well prepared for it.

"Oh, I'm quite confident that you won't be doing that," he said with a triumphant smirk. "You have no choice but to help me."

"I'm not going to kill or hurt anyone," said Anni firmly as she finished the last of her meal.

"Oh yes, you will," he said with a scowl. "You have no choice," he repeated.

Anni looked up at him blankly.

Then Stonor bared a merciless smile. He reached into the pocket of his robes and pulled out a second glass vial, just like the first one—but this one was empty.

"Tell me, Anni, how was the meal?"

Anni looked down at the empty plate in front of her and her jaw dropped as her stomach let out an uncomfortable growl, and she felt a sharp pain.

250

- CHAPTER 22 -
The Chairwoman

"You son of a bitch!" shouted Kolten. *"I'll kill you!"*

He shook the bars of his cell violently, but they would not budge. The dwarf's teeth were bared, and his face was so red with rage that his birdlike nose looked like some kind of overripe vegetable.

Stonor stepped back from Kolten's cell.

Anni sat there in shock. Stonor smiled, satisfied with himself. The look on his face reminded Anni of Mareitsia when she had just conned someone out of their life's savings. He knew she had no choice but to try and help him.

"The poison acts slowly, but steadily," he explained coldly. "I have given the antidote to a man at the harbor. Once you've done this little job for me, he has been instructed to give it

THE BLUE HAIRED GIRL

to you. If you *don't* help me, you'll be dead by midnight."

Anni didn't feel any different, but she knew he must have been telling the truth. It would have been so easy for him to slip something in her food while he was bringing it to her, and she hadn't thought to examine it first.

"I'll take care of it for you," said Kolten, looking straight up at the scowling man. His huge dwarven hands were clenched so tightly around the bars of his cell that they were blood-red. He had a violent look in his eyes. "Just open the door, Stonor."

"No, no, I don't think so," said Stonor simply. "I think Anni can handle this perfectly well on her own."

"But," Anni said, looking over at Kolten, "you said the antidote—" Anni stammered.

"The dwarf's food was clean," he said simply.

Kolten's food looked much the same as Anni's, but the dwarf had left it sitting on the floor of his cell, untouched.

"I wasn't hungry," muttered Kolten, his jaw clenched tightly.

"Once the job is done, I'll have control of the city. I'll order the dwarf to be released and you both can leave."

"But I can't!" protested Anni. "I don't have any magic!"

Stonor rolled his eyes, unconvinced.

"If you think I'm just going to sit here, while Anni risks her life—" snapped Kolten.

"You, also, have no choice," said Stonor, as if this were

252

THE CHAIRWOMAN

his new favorite expression.

"When I get out of here…" snarled Kolten.

"You keep talking like that and you won't," said Stonor dismissively.

Kolten sneered at Stonor and turned to Anni. "Are you okay?"

Anni wasn't feeling any effects of the poison yet, but if Stonor's timeline was accurate, she only had a few hours.

"Now listen to me very carefully," said Stonor, looking down at Anni. "Valentia's home is on the north side of the city. One of my men will take you there. You sneak in, destroy her, and then they'll take you to the harbor and you'll be given the antidote."

"What about our elk?" asked Anni.

Stonor rolled his eyes exasperatedly.

"Once the job is done and I have control of the city, no one will stop you. I'll see that the damned things are brought to you at the harbor."

"If you're so sure that Anni has magic, what makes you think she won't use it to cure herself or force you to hand it over as soon as you open the cell?" asked Kolten sternly.

"It's a calculated risk, to be sure," he said in his shrewd tone. "But the poison I chose is very potent, and I don't have the antidote on me, so I'm betting she won't try anything. The only way you're getting the antidote," he said, turning to Anni, "is

253

THE BLUE HAIRED GIRL

when my men get confirmation that the job is done."

Anni opened her mouth and closed it again.

"And put on your headscarf," he ordered. "I don't want any complications."

Anni reached over to her cot and picked up the headscarf that Kayell had given her and wrapped it around her head, hiding her hair.

Stonor took a deep breath and opened Anni's cell door, allowing her to enter the hallway. When Anni didn't use her non-existent powers, Stonor exhaled, satisfied that his plan had worked.

"What about the guards?" asked Anni.

Stonor grinned menacingly and cupped his hands around his mouth.

"Did you check the gate?" he shouted down the hall.

There was a sudden commotion from somewhere up above them. The sound of men struggling and fighting echoed down the stairs.

"Clear," came a voice from up the stairs.

"That's it," he said, nodding to Anni.

Anni turned toward Kolten, lost for words.

"Be careful, Anni," said Kolten gently.

"Off you go," said Stonor impatiently.

Anni walked down the hall and pushed open the door to the cell block, finding it unlocked. Then she climbed the stairs.

THE CHAIRWOMAN

It might have been brought on by nerves rather than the poison, but her stomach gave another uncomfortable gurgle.

As Anni reached the guard room on the ground floor, she saw several men with swords standing around the room. A few wore guard uniforms, but most were dressed as civilians.

None of them made any effort to stop her leaving.

A few men wearing Yuspiereian yellow and orange guard uniforms were in the center. They were all on their knees; they had been beaten and bound with ropes and chains.

Apparently, that thing Stonor shouted up the hall was a code phrase for his men to make their move.

Among the beaten and bound men on the floor was Kayell. His hands were bound behind his back, his face was bloody, and a gag had been forced into his mouth. A man was standing over him with a sword tip to his throat.

The solider stared up at Anni, his eyes wide, full of fear and pleading.

Anni forced herself not to look at him and made her way out of the guardhouse.

The sun was setting, and the streets looked oddly quiet. Many of the locals had closed shop for the evening, and the streets were starting to empty. Anni guessed that many of the shopkeepers from the marketplace were returning home for their evening meals.

These people have no idea what's happening, thought Anni.

THE BLUE HAIRED GIRL

If Stonor's move in the prison was any indication, Yuspiereia City was probably in for a very rough night.

A man in plain clothes from down the street looked at Anni and gestured for her to follow him.

"Not too closely," he muttered.

Anni nodded and followed the man down the quiet streets at a distance.

She was still not feeling many ill effects from the poison, but her stomach was cramping.

Her guide turned down an alleyway, and Anni followed him.

The sound of the ocean returned to Anni's ears, and the man stopped near the end of the alleyway, hidden in the shadows.

"The big house at the end, with the white bench out front," he muttered.

"Okay, how do I—"

But her guide had already left her, heading back down the alleyway and disappearing around the corner.

Anni walked down the street toward the house the man had indicated.

The house was painted a pinkish hue and was the largest on the street. There was, indeed, a large white bench in the front yard, just as the man had indicated.

It was a pleasant-looking house, although in Anni's

THE CHAIRWOMAN

opinion the pink paint job was a bit tacky. The home had a wrought-iron fence surrounding it, and in the center was a large, metal gate. A stone walkway led to a lovely wooden porch; lights were on in the house.

Anni headed toward the fence and saw a few men moving around inside the home; she assumed that they were servants. By the time her hands found the metal of the fence, the sun had gone down completely and the street was in near darkness.

Stonor had made killing the chairwoman sound so easy, and in a way, it was. Anni could be very stealthy when she wanted to be. Years of stealing from Mareitsia's customers had taught Anni how to avoid detection. Anni knew how to move silently when she wanted to. As long as she could find a way into Valentia's house, it was at least conceivable that she could enact Stonor's plan.

The problem wasn't so much practical, it was ethical. Could Anni really kill someone? She was about to murder an innocent person to save her own life. It was one of the most despicable things she could think of doing.

Anni knew it was wrong. She wouldn't even let Kolten kill their mistress back when they had first gained their freedom, and arguably Mareitsia deserved it. Valentia's only crime was that she was in Stonor's way, and that made what Anni was about to do even more contemptible.

257

THE BLUE HAIRED GIRL

The thought of killing someone absolutely disgusted Anni, and she hated herself for even considering it. But she needed to do something, and it didn't matter how Anni looked at it; she couldn't think of any other way out of this. As horrible as the thought of murdering someone was, it didn't change anything.

The fact remained, Anni didn't want to die, and Stonor was the only one with the antidote. What choice did she have?

A sudden pain shot through Anni's stomach and forced her to not think about it and just focus on the task at hand.

She looked to see if anyone was watching. She could see no one on this part of the property.

Once Anni was satisfied that there was no one watching her, she climbed up over the fence near one of the corners and crept around the side of the house.

It seemed odd that such a powerful woman as Valentia would not be surrounded by whole teams of security, but then Anni reminded herself that the chairwoman was a powerful sorceress, so she could probably take care of herself.

Anni's eyes fell on a single iron kettle helmet that lay abandoned on the ground by the side of the home. It seemed that Stonor had taken care of any guards that had been protecting Valentia, just like he had with the guards in the holding cells.

This coup really must have been something Stonor had been planning for quite some time.

258

THE CHAIRWOMAN

There was a single open window nearby that was just outside of Anni's reach. She could hear voices inside.

"…a glass of wine. Thank you, Massie," said a voice that Anni recognized as the chairwoman.

The chairwoman went on, "You know, Massie, Ackleman really did bring some good ideas for how to help stamp out the slave trade in border regions."

"Yes, Ma'am," said the servant.

Anni couldn't hear what the chairwoman said next, as it was muffled by the distinct sound of liquid being poured, but it was followed by the same servant's voice saying, "Yes, Ma'am, he is in town."

"Why don't you take tomorrow off and visit with him? I'll be in the council chamber all day tomorrow."

"Thank you, Ma'am."

Anni looked up at the open window above her, but there was no way she could possibly reach it without something to stand on.

Maddeningly, an old yet delicate hand placed a silver wine goblet on the windowsill and disappeared, but it was hopelessly out of reach.

Anni winced as her stomach cramps worsened.

Seeing no way of doing anything with the cup from here, Anni abandoned the out-of-reach window and crept around the rear of the house.

THE BLUE HAIRED GIRL

The back door was wide open.

Stonor, you're good, Anni thought.

Anni climbed the back steps and slipped into the house.

The whole place smelled like fresh-cut flowers and had the same sort of tacky pink color scheme as the outside.

The rear of the house opened into the kitchen, where a servant hummed to herself as she prepared something to eat with her back to Anni. Apparently, Valentia liked to take some food with her evening drink.

On the table in the center of the kitchen was a silver wine pitcher that matched the chairwoman's goblet perfectly.

The servant in the kitchen seemed to be in a complete trance and hadn't noticed Anni yet. She then stopped and headed over to the pantry on the other side of the kitchen, with her back still to Anni.

In a desperate move, Anni darted over to the table and pulled the stopper out of the vial of poison.

Anni was starting to feel lightheaded and dizzy. It was a similar sensation to what she had felt when she drank the apple drink at The Silver Spear pub in the brynywyn village. But this feeling was far less pleasant, as it came with an increasing pain in her stomach, and it might have been made worse because of what she was about to do.

Anni lifted the open vial of poison toward the wine pitcher.

260

THE CHAIRWOMAN

The pain in her stomach was getting worse now, and she had trouble focusing.

Then, she hesitated.

Anni had been so worried about getting the antidote that she hadn't stopped to really think about the implications of what she was about to do. If she somehow managed to kill Valentia, she and Kolten could make it to the Republic and no one would ever know.

Anni had never cared about Yuspiereia at all because she had never had any reason to, but leaving all Yuspiereia to suffer under Stonor and his cronies to save her own skin was something that Anni simply couldn't bring herself to do. Poison or no poison, murder was wrong.

Stonor had made it perfectly clear that he didn't seem to care about anyone.

Images flashed through Anni's mind. The tailor, the musicians, the elf woman with the menagerie—even that crazy, old, blind man she and Kolten had passed on the road. What would happen to all the people of the city if Stonor took control?

In her mind's eye, Anni saw Ackleman having his head cut off, the brynywyn village burned to the ground. The thunder elk forced to fight one another for entertainment, or simply killed for sport.

Then she saw the imagined sight of a scowling Stonor, placing a fresh pair of darkwrists on Kolten's beaten, bloody

261

THE BLUE HAIRED GIRL

hands.

Anni retracted the still full vial of poison and pulled it away from the wine pitcher.

"Guards!" shouted the servant.

"They won't come," said Anni, lowering the vial and pouring its content harmlessly to the floor. "Stonor has seen to that."

"What's going on in there?" asked a voice that Anni recognized as the chairwoman's.

"There's a child in here, Ma'am," said the servant. "She is tampering with your wine."

Valentia came around the corner and stepped into the kitchen. She wore a pink robe and carried her crystal staff in her hand. She looked at Anni, the servant, the vial of poison on the ground, and back at Anni again.

Suddenly, a beam of purple magic burst from the crystal at the top of Valentia's staff.

A moment later Anni was magically pinned flat on her back against the kitchen ceiling. She found her arms and legs frozen in place, and she was forced to stare straight down at the kitchen floor below. Everything around her was tinted by the purple light from Valentia's staff.

"Massie, are you all right?"

"Yes, Ma'am, I'm fine. I saw her trying to pour something in your wine."

THE CHAIRWOMAN

"What are you doing here, Anni?" asked the chairwoman sternly, as the magical beam tightened.

Anni didn't know what to say, and she didn't know if the chairwoman's magic would allow her to speak.

"How did you get out of your cell?"

Anni found her voice as the magic spell loosened slightly.

"I'm sorry! I had no choice! He forced me to!"

"Forced you to what?"

"I'm supposed to kill you!" said Anni as her eyes teared.

The chairwoman looked up at Anni, her expression hard.

"Is that why you came to Yuspiereia City? To kill me?"

"No! Stonor, he poisoned me!"

The magical beam released her and lowered her to the floor.

"Stonor put you up to this?" she asked sternly.

Anni nodded. "He said if I killed you, he would give me the antidote and let me and Kolten go."

Anni had a hard time focusing her eyes. Valentia and her servant were starting to get blurry.

"Is he after any other members of the council?" the chairwoman asked quickly.

The pain in Anni's stomach went away as her limbs went numb.

"Anni!"

The room began to spin.

263

THE BLUE HAIRED GIRL

"What did he give you?!"
Then everything went dark.

- CHAPTER 23 -
The Coup

Slowly, feeling returned to Anni's limbs, and she became aware of the darkness all around her. As consciousness returned to her, Anni's eyes snapped open, and she found herself staring at wooden planks.

A series of organized wood beams floated above her, spaced in regular intervals, supporting a dark, stone ceiling.

The pain in her stomach had vanished and had been replaced with a splitting headache, and her vision was still blurry.

But there could be no doubt, she was definitely alive.

Anni tried to sit up, but her arms wouldn't cooperate, and she heard the clattering of chains as she tried to move them.

"She's awake," said a voice.

THE BLUE HAIRED GIRL

"W-Where am I?"

No one answered her.

Anni heard a series of footsteps, followed by the creaking of a door.

Then she remembered Stonor, Valentia, the poison, and that something had happened to her.

Anni tried to sit again. She found she was able to reach a sitting position. She was lying on a cot; it was like the one from her prison cell, but this one was a bit more comfortable. Both Anni's arms were bound to it, not by darkwrists but simple yet very heavy iron shackles. They had no magic about them as far as she could tell, but they were nonetheless very effective.

Anni was lying in a windowless stone room with a ceiling reinforced by wooden beams. It was lit by gas lamps that were so bright, Anni couldn't look directly at them.

She wasn't alone in the room.

Two men stood in the room, wearing the typical yellow and orange Yuspiereian uniforms.

Standing over Anni was Valentia. Her eyes were sharp and narrow in the light of the gas lamps.

Valentia was no longer wearing her robes. She had changed into more practical attire and was wearing a metal breastplate over her clothes. Her staff was in her hand, and the crystal glowed red with worry.

"What happened?"

THE COUP

"You passed out, probably a side effect of the poison," said Valentia.

"Poison?! I need the antidote, now!"

"You'll be fine," she explained. "If it was going to kill you, it would have done it already."

"But Stonor said—"

"Anni, you've been unconscious for more than a day. Stonor may not have given you enough of it to do the job, or the batch may have been tainted. Either way, if you survived this long, I think you're out of the woods."

"Where am I?" asked Anni again.

"You're in a safe house," said one of the guards.

"A what?"

"A secret, underground bunker," she explained. "Zoltan had several of these safe areas built and magically concealed all around Yuspiereia while the High Council was being created. They serve as a fail-safe in case of a power struggle."

"We're underground?"

"Yes, Stonor and his followers have taken control of most of the city. He's declared himself First Emperor of all Stonorland."

"What?!"

"I know, it's a horrible name," she said with a cold smile.

"But what about Kolten? And Ackleman?" asked Anni. "Are they okay?!"

THE BLUE HAIRED GIRL

"Kolten should be fine. He's no threat to Stonor locked up in the cells, so he has no reason to hurt him. The rest of the council have either been arrested or gone into hiding. If they're lucky, they escaped the city."

It seemed that Anni's change of heart in the chairwoman's kitchen was all for naught. Stonor had taken the city without her help, and if he had control of the capital…It wouldn't be long before he would have control of the entire country.

"What about the guards? And everyone else, the shopkeepers?"

"Anni, the city is in chaos. Stonor has legalized slavery, and the men were pillaging the city. Taking whatever and whomever they want."

"It's all my fault," said Anni sadly. "If I hadn't been stupid enough to eat that food, none of this would have happened."

"Anni, Stonor has been planning this for a while," said Valentia in a consoling voice. "He would have done this either way."

"But he needed me to kill you."

"And you didn't. You poured it out on the floor," she replied. "What I don't understand is why Stonor chose you."

Anni went on to explain Stonor's ridiculous theory about Anni having magical powers.

268

THE COUP

The chairwoman said nothing as she pondered this.

"So, what are we going to do?" asked Anni.

"Well, there's no way Zoltan's Senate is going to take this lying down," replied Valentia. "The Republic has spent years pushing for the creation of an elected council in Yuspiereia, so they're not going to let Stonor just take it away."

"So, is the Republic of Zoltan sending help?"

Valentia looked down at the floor awkwardly. "Anni, Zoltan doesn't even know anything has happened yet. The Republic is across the Great Sea. It will take weeks for them to hear about this. Even if we send a ship right now, it will be well over a month for help to arrive, at the earliest."

"A month?! But Stonor could have enslaved half the country by then!"

"Yes, and that's assuming Stonor hasn't shut down the harbor to stop a message getting out, and he probably has," she replied. "So just waiting him out is probably not our best option."

"So, what are we going to do?"

"Did Stonor tell you anything that could be useful to us?"

"Like what?"

"How many men does he have? Are they all in the city? What towns and villages nearby support him?"

Anni racked her brain for some small scrap of

269

THE BLUE HAIRED GIRL

information that Stonor had let slip, but she could think of nothing. She had been so distracted by the poison and her desire for the antidote that she hadn't paid much attention to anything else.

"I don't know."

Valentia sighed.

"What are we going to do?" asked Anni.

"There's not a lot we can do. I only have four men."

"Four?!" shouted Anni, pulling on her chains.

"And two of them aren't here right now," said Valentia. "Nowhere near enough to take the city back by force. Even with my magic."

"So, what do we do?"

The chairwoman sat there awkwardly and glanced up at her men and back to Anni.

"Right now, I've sent two of my men to check the other safe houses. See if any of the council survived," she said simply.

"Then what?" asked Anni.

"Then, we'll see."

This was not good enough. Even though it wasn't really her fault, Anni still felt responsible for all this. A few days ago, the only thing Anni had wanted was to reach Zoltan and be free. But the people of Yuspiereia didn't deserve what Stonor was doing to them.

Anni knew all too well what life as a slave was like.

270

THE COUP

"What if we kill Stonor? Would that stop this?"

"Maybe," said Valentia. "But that's easier said than done. He'll have his best and most loyal men guarding him."

Anni pulled on her chains.

"Will you take these things off!" snapped Anni, pulling on her chains.

Valentia's guards looked down disapprovingly at the chairwoman as she nodded for them to remove Anni's bonds.

A moment later, Anni's chains clattered to the floor.

"Are you hungry?" asked the chairwoman softly.

Anni had never had less of an appetite her entire life. The chairwoman seemed to have almost given up. Anni doubted very much that Stonor would honor his bargain, seeing as how Anni had failed to kill her. Now that Anni had time to think about it, she wasn't sure he was ever going to give her the antidote at all. For that matter, he might not have even had one in the first place.

The possibility of ever reaching the Republic was starting to look like a dream. If Valentia was right, with the harbor shut down, there would be no way of reaching Zoltan, and she still needed to find some way to get Kolten out of his prison cell.

There was no escaping it. Like it or not, Yuspiereia was in a state of civil war, and Anni had found herself on the losing side of it. The city around them was falling apart, and for all she knew, Kolten could be headed right back to a life of slavery. She

THE BLUE HAIRED GIRL

had no intention of just sitting around and hoping it would all get better.

"I'm going out there."

"No, you're not," said one of Valentia's men firmly.

"There has to be something we can do!" Anni protested.

"Anni, we need help," said the chairwoman. "Stonor caught us off guard here. We don't even know how much of the army is on his side. We need someone who can help us stand up to his gang of thugs."

At these words, something came to Anni's mind. A distant memory from way back at the start of her journey.

A race of tiny, child-sized, and kindhearted people. A people who hated slavery and had come to Anni's aid before, and had promised to do so again. Their village was much closer than the Republic, and most importantly, they possessed the means to travel great distances at high speed. One thing Anni was sure of, they would never side with Stonor.

"The brynywyn!" Anni shouted, standing up.

"Who?" asked one of the guards.

"The brynywyn folk! The little people! They have a village on the other side of the mountains! They can help us!"

Anni went on to tell them about her and Kolten's time with the brynywyn, and how Jarabei had promised to help her if they ever needed it.

"You're talking about that pygmy village to the south?"

272

THE COUP

asked one of the guards skeptically.

"They're not pygmies!" she said sharply. "They said if I ever needed help, they would come. Well, we need help."

"Anni, it sounds like Jarabei was drunk when he said that," said one of the men. "I don't know if—"

"They'll help; I know they will!" Anni cut in. "And they can be here soon! Thunder elk are really fast!"

Valentia looked at one of her men; he shrugged.

"We'll take all the help we can get," said Valentia.

"They'll help; I know they will," repeated Anni.

There was something about the brynywyn that Anni couldn't help but admire. They had a strange pride about them that one wouldn't expect of a race of such tiny folk.

"How many men can they bring?" asked Valentia.

"I'm not sure, probably not a lot. How many do we need?"

"It's hard to know how many men Stonor has," explained Valentia. "Some of the Yuspiereian guard may only be supporting him because they feel they have no choice, and some will have gone into hiding. If we can show them that the tide is turning, they may side with us."

"So, it's possible?" asked Anni.

"It's risky, but I don't see that we have any choice," she said. "We can't wait around for Zoltan."

"Do you know how to *get* to the brynywyn village?"

273

THE BLUE HAIRED GIRL

asked one of the guards.

Anni already knew exactly what to do.

"I won't have to," she replied, remembering the thunder elk's uncanny sense of direction. "I just need to get to the stables. The place where the guards would have taken our elk while we were seeing the council."

"That's on the other side of the city, Anni," replied Valentia.

"We just need to send them a message. Can you write one for me?"

The chairwoman raised her eyebrows and nodded.

She stood up and fetched a piece of parchment and a quill, and placed it down on a wooden supply crate and jotted down a quick message in an elegant, slanting hand.

"That should do it," she said and handed the note to Anni.

Anni stared at her for a moment.

"Anni, I can't leave the safe house."

"But you have magic," said Anni in a pleading tone. "I could really use your help out there."

Valentia smiled awkwardly.

"Anni, you don't understand. It's not that I want you to go out there on your own—believe me, I don't. But I physically can't leave this place. The safe houses were designed to protect the High Council, and I'm the chairwoman. The same magic that

274

THE COUP

keeps Stonor and his thugs out of this place also won't let me leave. I can't cross the magical barrier that guards this place, at least not until the city starts to stabilize—it's a security measure. For the time being, I'm stuck here."

"And we're her bodyguards, we can't leave her," said one of the guards.

"You'll need to go and get help."

"But my hair…"

In all the confusion, Anni had lost her precious headscarf. It was probably still in Valentia's kitchen, where this had all started.

"Use this." One of the guards took off his iron kettle helmet and handed it to Anni.

The helmet was too big and didn't cover her whole head, but its broad rim would at least make her hair less noticeable if she kept her head down.

"Which way to the stables?"

Anni listened intently to every word the chairwoman said as she described the directions in perfect detail. She could almost see the streets of the capital in front of her as the chairwoman described them. They were burned into Anni's memory like the mark of a branding iron.

"Remember, look for a sign that looks like a horse," said one of the guards helpfully.

Anni nodded. She rolled up the message and tucked it

THE BLUE HAIRED GIRL

into the folds of her dress for safekeeping.

The guards and Valentia walked Anni down a short
hallway outside the room that Anni had awoken in. At the end of
the hall was a wooden step ladder and a wooden trapdoor.

Anni climbed the stairs and looked back at the
chairwoman.

"Take this," said one of the guards.

He handed her a small, sheathed dagger and belt.

"Just in case…"

Anni took the weapon and strapped it around her waist,
under her dress to keep it hidden.

"Good luck, Anni," said Valentia with a hopeful smile.

Anni turned back toward her, and the chairwoman's
guards gave her a worried nod. Then she pushed open the
trapdoor.

- CHAPTER 24 -
Anarchy

The trapdoor clicked open, and the darkness of the capital city streets reached Anni's eyes. She poked her head out of the safe house and into the streets above.

As she climbed out of the hidden trap door, a warm rush of air flowed over her. She had passed out of the magical concealment spell that hid the trapdoor from view.

The ground where she knew the opening was now appeared ordinary. As long as the door was kept closed to keep anyone from falling in, the safe house would remain hidden.

Anni took a mental picture of where the entrance was, in case she ever needed to return to it.

It was well after sunset, and the streets were noisy, but

THE BLUE HAIRED GIRL

she didn't see anyone. The sounds of a city in chaos assaulted her ears. Several fires burned out of control in the distance, a few streets away, and the sound of yelling and screaming emanated from all around her.

Besides the light of flickering fires in the distance, the city was in complete darkness, and it took a moment for Anni's eyes to adjust. Ironically, the entrance to the safe house was right next to one of the city's wooden lampposts. Anni could just barely make out the image of a white wax candle housed in a glass lantern. They had probably been built by order of the High Council, but with the city in chaos, no one had lit them.

Although a little light would have been helpful for Anni to make her way through the noisy streets, it was probably good the lamps had been left out, as it would make it much harder for anyone to recognize her hair in the darkness.

The cobblestone streets were uneven and bumpy, and Anni had to tread carefully to keep herself from stumbling on the dark roads. She reached the first turn toward the city stables and quickly ducked behind a pile of wooden crates.

A group of citizens were bound together by thick ropes, and several of Stonor's men stood over them with swords. A pile of valuables on the other side of the street was being loaded onto a horse-drawn cart by their former owners.

Anni could only imagine what was going on in the city's marketplace, but that was on the other side of town, and this was

278

ANARCHY

no time to go sightseeing.

It could not have been clearer that Stonor's men were pillaging the city. That was probably how he had been able to amass such a sizable force without anyone finding out what he was up to. He was allowing his men to take whatever they wanted.

Most of the male prisoners showed signs of beatings, and at least one dead body was splayed out on the ground. Even in the dim light, Anni saw it was lying in a pool of dark, red liquid.

Crouched beside the corpse were two young, attractive women in their late teens or early twenties. Both had been stripped naked and tied up. They were both crying.

Anni gritted her teeth, and the image of that arrogant, scowling man in Yuspiereian robes flashed through Anni's mind.

Stonor, you'll pay for this, thought Anni.

Anni forced herself not to look at the women. She crept behind the crates and the assorted pile of pilfered goods. The looters were so distracted by their prizes that they didn't seem to notice Anni.

She ducked down a side street and passed several other deserted lanes. With every turn that Anni made, she went over the directions in her mind, always keeping on track toward where Valentia had told her the stables were located. The last thing she wanted right now was to get lost.

The road ahead of her opened up into one of the city's

THE BLUE HAIRED GIRL

main streets. Anni found herself in the center of a massive urban brawl. Several of the buildings on this street were on fire, but no one seemed to be trying to control the blazes. A few hundred people were engaged in a massive melee that filled the street. Using clubs, swords, kitchen knives, and bare hands, the battle raged on.

Anni could only guess that some members of the High Council, or possibly just ordinary citizens, had decided not to roll over and let Stonor have control of the city, at least not without a fight.

Yells, grunts, and taunts echoed up and down the street, and there were many motionless figures on the ground; a few might have been unconscious, but no doubt many of them were dead.

Some of the combatants were civilians, some were Yuspiereian guards. But there didn't seem to be any logic to the fighting—guards were fighting guards, civilians fought civilians; everyone was fighting everyone.

Yuspiereia was entering a true state of civil war.

In all the chaos, it was impossible to tell whose side she was on, so Anni kept out of the whole affair.

Ahead of her was the next side street she needed to take. Keeping close to the side of the street that was not on fire, Anni thought it best just to make a run for it.

She let out a burst of speed, dodging left and right,

ANARCHY

weaving in and out of battles. Guards, men, women, and even children were all beating, stabbing, and biting all around her.

Suddenly, Anni felt something grab her, and she fell to the ground, skinning her hands and legs as she landed.

One of the fighters dressed in civilian clothes had grabbed her dress, and it tore as she hit the ground.

Her over-sized kettle helmet clattered to the ground.

In the light of the fire blazing across the street, her hair stood out like a beacon. The man's jaw fell open as his eyes landed on Anni's hair.

"Hey, you're—"

"NO!" Anni shouted as she pulled away from the man, determined not to let anyone get in her way.

A huge boom, like a clap of thunder, was lost in the chaos of battle, and her attacker sailed backward through the air and disappeared into fray.

Anni paused for a moment and looked around for any sign of a thunder elk, or any other source of the commotion, but she could see nothing.

I need to get to the stables, Anni thought.

Anni let out another burst of speed and ducked down one alleyway after another.

Finally, after what seemed like hours, Anni saw a wooden building with a sign hanging on it. The sign displayed the image of a horse standing up on its hind legs.

THE BLUE HAIRED GIRL

She had made it to the stables.

Anni tried the door but found it to be locked.

She pounded on the door furiously, screaming at the top of her lungs.

"Open the door!"

She stood there pounding on it for several minutes. Finally, there was a commotion inside.

The door opened a crack and she could see a single blue eye looking out at her.

"Go away!" a voice ordered sharply. "This is my hiding place!"

"I don't have time for this!" shouted Anni.

She took several steps back and prepared to throw herself at the door, to try to force it open.

Before she could start running, the door burst open like it had been hit by an invisible battering ram.

Anni entered the building, readying her dagger in case the occupant was armed.

The man who had blocked her at the door lay on the floor, unconscious, as if someone had hit him over the head.

Anni quickly scanned the room, but she could see no one else anywhere. Only the unconscious man, who Anni noticed was armed with a farmer's scythe.

The stable was much larger than any Anni had ever seen, and it was extremely dark. Before her was a long hallway, with a

282

ANARCHY

series of open compartments lining the inside of the building on both sides.

She passed a few compartments. Some stalls were empty, some contained horses, and one even had a few civilians hiding from the battle in the streets. Anni ignored them and they did the same.

"Where are you?!" shouted Anni as she wandered up the aisle.

The was no sign of the elk.

Suddenly, it dawned on her, all the days that she and Kolten had been traveling with their mighty steeds. How her elk had saved her life many times, and yet she had never once thought to give him a name. One would have been very useful just now.

"Thunder elk! It's me, Anni! Where are you?" she shouted again as she ran along the hallway of compartments, doing her best to look into all the compartments as she passed.

Suddenly, a bright flash of light exploded from one of the compartments, somewhere up ahead.

"Good boy!" she shouted as the elk's flashes of light guided her toward it.

Other, smaller bursts of light came from several stalls ahead on her left.

As Anni reached the compartment, her eyes fell on a pair of large, antlers that she knew well.

THE BLUE HAIRED GIRL

But something was very wrong.

Anni's bull was standing over Kolten's female. She was lying on her side, and her breathing sounded shallow.

She was ill.

Not a good time! thought Anni as she looked down at the sick animal. It occurred to Anni that the stable boy must not have known how to care for thunder elk and might have fed her something he shouldn't have.

Anni reached over to the bull and tried to pull him toward the exit, but he wouldn't leave her.

"Come on!" she pleaded. "We don't have time for this! If we don't stop Stonor, we're all dead!"

Still, the elk refused to move.

"Look, we need to get to the brynywyn village!"

He stared at her.

"Please! It's really important! We need to stop this!"

The elk looked down at the sick cow and nuzzled her affectionately. She returned his caress but seemed too ill to move.

The bull then turned toward Anni and leaned down, allowing her to mount him.

Suddenly, the door to the stable opened, and several men with swords entered.

Anni ducked into the stall and reached into the folds of her dress to extract the letter from the chairwoman.

It was gone.

284

ANARCHY

The note must have fallen out of the folds of her dress when the man grabbed her. It could be anywhere right now.

Unfortunately, the elk wasn't saddled, and Anni couldn't see one nearby.

The men near the entrance to the stables grabbed a few cowering citizens and dragged them screaming into the street.

"Hey, some idiot threw a deer in here," said one of the men.

Anni noticed that, standing up, her elk's antlers were visible over the wall of the compartment.

Without a saddle, Anni would have to ride bareback to the brynywyn village. She clambered up on his back.

Before she could even begin to settle herself, a pair of huge, meaty hands grabbed her from behind and hoisted her off the elk.

"Got one!" her attacker shouted.

There was a bright flash of light from Anni's bull, and the man recoiled, but his grip held her firmly.

Anni struggled with all her might, and there was another flash, but this man was strong, and he refused to let her go.

"*Will you hold still!*" grunted the man who held her.

In an act of sheer desperation, Anni drew the dagger from her belt and jammed it into the muscular arm that held her.

"*Ahhhhh!*" The grip loosened, but the man's other hand reached for the blade.

285

THE BLUE HAIRED GIRL

I need to do this! she thought, her arms almost exhausted from struggling against the attacker.

"S'matter?" said a voice. "Can't handle a little girl?"

The elk let out another blast of lightning as the attacker finally managed to turn Anni around and pinned her to the floor.

"That was not smart!" hissed the man as a trickle of blood poured down his massive forearm.

With a look of fury, the man reached up and grabbed a tuft of her blue hair. He painfully cut it off with her own dagger and let the hair fall to the floor.

"Don't do that again!" the man snapped, covering the gash in his arm as one of the other men pulled Anni off the floor and threw her over his shoulder.

As they dragged Anni away from her precious thunder elk, the animal let out a spark of rage. He lowered his head and charged straight at the men, his antlers sparking violently.

The men, including the one who held Anni, dove out of the way. The animal reached the open door to the stables and entered the chaos of the city. Without a letter, there was no way the brynywyn would get the message, even if the elk got there.

Anni listened intently to the sound of the elk's galloping hoofs until it was drowned out by the noise in the streets.

There was no point in pretending.

Anni had failed; help wasn't coming.

- CHAPTER 25 -
The Empty Cell

Anni's hands were bound by what felt like thick ropes, and a large cloth sack was pulled down over her. She could see nothing but darkness.

"I suppose you were hoping that beast would trample us to death," said one of her captors.

"How's the arm?" said another.

"I'll live," replied the voice of the man that had grabbed her.

"Stupid girl."

Something hard struck Anni in the face, and she tasted blood.

"Where are you taking me?" said Anni, her voice muffled

THE BLUE HAIRED GIRL

by the sack.

"Shut up," snapped the man, shaking her a bit as he walked.

The only thing Anni could think of doing to help her stay alive and unharmed was to follow orders and pray that the sack would stay on her head. She hoped that, with all the chaos going on around them, the men hadn't noticed her hair in the shadows of the dark stable.

Without the letter, the brynywyn would have no way of knowing what was happening in the capital, let alone that she was asking for their help. The animal might not even make it out of the city.

"How many horses are there?" asked a voice.

"I counted forty-seven," said the man carrying Anni. "There's a sick deer in there too."

"A deer?!"

"See for yourself."

"Nah, I believe you. Stonor wants a count of everything we find."

Anni was dropped down hard on a cobblestone street and bumped into someone else, who was lying next to her.

"Easy," said a familiar, soft voice, "it's going to be okay."

"Ackleman?" whispered Anni.

"Yes, who are you?"

"It's me, Anni!"

288

THE EMPTY CELL

"Shh!" he hissed. "Listen, we're going to get out of this. The Senate—"

"No talking!" shouted one of their captors.

"You know, Zoltan will never let you get away with this," said Ackleman, who had apparently reached the same conclusion as Valentia.

"Shut up!"

As Ackleman began to verbally harass their captors, Anni started shifting her hands in front of her against the thick ropes. Despite her thin hands, the ropes were bound tight. Anni couldn't gather enough purchase to let even one of her hands slip out.

"The Republic will consider this to be an act of war," Ackleman continued. "I don't know what Stonor offered you for this, but he can't protect you from an armada of Zoltanian ships."

"I said, shut up!"

"If you don't stop all this now, you're going to be sorry."

"Zoltan is weeks away!"

"They're not as far as you may think. They have ways of monitoring the situation down here. The gallows are—"

There was a sudden crunching sound of a fist hitting flesh, and Ackleman said nothing more.

"Zoltan will not come!" spat the voice. "Stonor told us they wouldn't interfere!"

THE BLUE HAIRED GIRL

"He lied," said Anni, unable to help herself. "He doesn't care about you."

"One more word out of either of you, and you won't live to see dawn."

Anni thought it best not to push her luck any further, and she gave up her futile battle against her bonds. All that needed to happen was for one of them to remove the sack over her head and recognize her, and she was as good as dead.

"I have orders from Stonor," said another voice, paired with approaching footsteps.

"What's he say?"

"He doesn't want the prisoners standing in the streets, in case more fighting breaks out. Have this lot taken back to the cells."

Anni felt a blast of relief wash over her. They weren't going to execute her just yet, and she might even be able to check on Kolten.

Anni was forced to her feet by a pair of muscular hands.

She felt some tension placed on the ropes binding her hands. Someone pulled a second rope in between her wrists, and she was pulled along with it like a dog on a leash.

As they walked, it had occurred to Anni it would have been a good idea to try counting their steps and remembering which way they turned. That might have helped her get her bearings, but they had already been walking for several minutes

290

THE EMPTY CELL

by the time she got the idea, so there was no point.

It wouldn't have helped much anyway, as Anni had been carried from the stables. Still, the fact that Stonor wanted them to be moved to the cells suggested they couldn't have been that far.

Anni could hear about a dozen footsteps all around her. They could have been prisoners or more of Stonor's thugs, probably both, but they all seemed to be heading in the same direction.

Anni could still hear the distant screams and shouts and the occasional sound of wood, stone, or glass breaking. The battle, while not as heavy in this part of the city, still raged in parts nearby.

It might have been citizens standing up to Stonor, or it might have been some guards and remains of the council organizing a counterattack. Either way, Anni didn't care, as long as there was someone trying to thwart Stonor's plans.

After walking blindly through the city streets, her sack still on her head, Anni heard a door open. She almost tripped as she was forced to step upward on to a set of stairs.

"Where is everyone?" asked the voice that had threatened Ackleman not long ago.

"No idea. Stonor ordered guards here at all times."

Anni heard a door shut behind them, and they were soon walking down several flights of stairs.

As a final door opened, the man shouted, *"Where the hell*

THE BLUE HAIRED GIRL

are they?!"

"I'll check the other cell blocks."

Anni couldn't help herself; she leaned forward to give some slack on her rope-leash and lifted her sack just enough to peer out from under it, then dropped it again after scanning the scene.

They were standing in the same hallway that her and Kolten had been locked in hours before. She knew it was the same one because the empty food tray that Stonor had used to poison her the day before was still visible on the floor of her cell.

Kolten was gone, and all the cells were empty, doors open.

It actually made Anni smile slightly to see all the cell doors wide open—and an ordinary wooden fork jammed into a lock in one of cell doors.

It was the same type of fork that had been with the plate of food Stonor had given Kolten. One thing was clear: Stonor had definitely underestimated just how resourceful the dwarf could be.

Kolten had been Mareitsia's slave for longer than Anni had even been alive. One of his main duties had been to fix things around the camp. The darkwrists didn't work mechanically, so Mareitsia had had no reason to worry about Kolten working with locks, latches, and other mechanical things over the years.

292

THE EMPTY CELL

Interestingly, Anni and Kolten had been the only ones in the cell block when she was here last, and yet now all the cell doors were open, the cells empty. Kolten would never have bothered opening an empty cell.

In her mind's eye, Anni could see a cell block, packed full of Stonor's political enemies, hours after launching his coup. Kolten, seeing his chance, took the fork off his plate and snapped off a prong or two. In the dwarf's skilled hands, it would have made a passable lock pick. Then, after opening his own cell, he went on to release all of Stonor's prisoners just for good measure.

Kolten could have opted to help them out of necessity, or because his one malfunctioning darkwrist had forced him to. But Anni knew the dwarf well enough to know that a major factor in doing it was that Kolten probably just wanted to give Stonor a headache.

"They're all gone!" shouted a voice from down the hall.

"Stonor is going to be furious," said the other. "There were a couple of members of the High Council in there."

Good to know, thought Anni.

"I told you," said Ackleman simply. "You were never going to get away with this."

"So, what do we do with them?" asked the other, ignoring Ackleman's words. "Do we still lock them up?"

"We can't. The keys are gone, too."

Very clever, Kolten! thought Anni, as she wished with all

THE BLUE HAIRED GIRL

her heart that she had not been so stupid as to eat Stonor's poisoned food or she would probably be with him right now.

This was some much-needed good news. It seemed that Stonor's insurrection was probably not going as well as he had hoped. As far as Anni knew, his main target, Valentia, was still alive. There was clearly still some resistance going on in the streets, and now some of Stonor's key political prisoners had escaped.

"We should take them to Stonor and see what he wants to do with them."

"*You* can tell him about the prison break."

"Hell no! You tell him!"

"It wasn't our fault, anyway. We just found it like this."

Anni felt herself get turned around, and she marched back in the direction they had come from.

As they reached the streets, Anni wondered where Stonor was. He must have set up his main base of operations somewhere nearby. They walked blindly for a long while, until Anni turned a corner. There was a commotion not far from them.

A familiar voice was yelling at the top of his lungs.

"What do you mean, they've escaped?!" shouted Stonor.

"Sire, we arrived at the guardhouse and the place was deserted. All the cell doors were open, and the keys were gone."

Stonor let out a stream of swear words, and Anni heard the distinct sound of one of Stonor's own men being beaten.

THE EMPTY CELL

After a long bout of grunts and struggling, the beating suddenly stopped, suggesting the man had lost consciousness.

"Take their hoods off."

Before Anni could resist, she felt the sack on her head get whipped off, exposing her to the darkness.

"I..." Anni started.

But Stonor wasn't looking at her. His attention was drawn to Ackleman.

"I should kill you right now."

"And tell Zoltan what?" said Ackleman in a surprisingly business-like tone. "They're not stupid, Stonor. They're never going to let you get away with this."

Anni couldn't help but admire Ackleman's calm head under pressure. The entire city was tearing itself apart, and here he was, face-to-face with the man who had caused it, yet he was able to keep his voice remarkably even.

Stonor slapped Ackleman across the face with the back of his hand.

"You are to refer to me as 'sire' or 'your excellency,'" snapped Stonor.

Ackleman didn't flinch at Stonor's assault, nor did he agree to refer to him by his new titles, but he also didn't argue. Ackleman stayed perfectly silent and stared Stonor straight in the eyes.

"It's a good thing I have a few hostages. I'll trade your

295

THE BLUE HAIRED GIRL

life for Zoltan staying out of this."

"Zoltan will never do a deal with you," said Ackleman with a passable attempt at a chuckle.

"Then you're worthless to me, and I should kill you right now."

Ackleman finally broke gaze with Stonor, and his eyes focused to the ground, but again, he didn't answer.

Stonor's eyes fell on Anni.

"You?!" shouted Stonor.

"I…" Anni said again.

Stonor reached out and grabbed Anni by the front of her dress.

"Is she dead?" he asked sharply.

Anni knew exactly who he must have been talking about. But she wasn't sure whether she should tell him the truth.

Stonor himself looked a little worse for the wear. He had a black eye and was missing a tooth. He had abandoned his formal High Council robes for plate mail armor. A long sword hung at his side, and the blade was stained with blood.

All of Stonor's men were injured to some degree. They had taken so many prisoners, Stonor's men were far outnumbered by them. It would be difficult to control so many if they decided to fight back. It seemed that the resistance to Stonor's regime change was much more enthusiastic than he had anticipated.

There was murdering, raping, and pillaging going on all

THE EMPTY CELL

around the city. So, it shouldn't have come as a big surprise that the High Council wouldn't have trouble finding support among the citizens.

"Well, is she dead?!" he asked again, shaking Anni.

"Yes!" said Anni, not knowing what else to say.

"You killed her? She's dead?!" he asked excitedly.

Anni slowly nodded, in the most convincing way possible.

Out of the corner of her eye, Anni saw Ackleman hang his head sadly. But there was no way to tell him it was a lie.

Stonor smiled slightly, but then cocked an eyebrow curiously.

"Why are you still alive?" asked Stonor. "There was no antidote."

Anni shrugged.

Stonor was no fool. He had never had any intention of saving Anni's life after she had done his dirty work. He was just going to use her to get rid of Valentia and then let her die.

He was a disgusting man.

"She is dead," said Anni firmly.

"How can I be sure you're not lying?"

"If she was alive, she would be fighting."

Stonor seemed reassured by this and he released Anni and turned back to Ackleman.

"You see that!?" he shouted at Ackleman. "It's over!!

297

THE BLUE HAIRED GIRL

With that old cow gone, it won't be worth Zoltan's time!!"

"What about me?!" shouted Anni. "You said if I helped you, you would let me and Kolten go!"

"When this is all over, the dwarf will fetch a fine price."

"What about me?!"

"You?" he scoffed. "If Valentia is dead, then I have no more use for you. If Blegor still wants you, he can have you. I'm not going to say no to an extra ten thousand golords."

- CHAPTER 26 -
Reunited

As the sun rose and peeked over the tops of the buildings in Yuspiereia, the civil war only showed signs of intensifying.

The High Council's escape from the jail seemed to have provided a much-needed boost to their cause. Stonor and his men had fallen back toward the harbor to regroup. Anni had no way of knowing how much of the city was under Stonor's control.

Although the battle did seem to be turning against him, it was still far from over. Stonor still had a sizable force at his disposal. Most of the citizens in this section of the city had been killed, captured, or had fled.

It had been three days since Anni's capture at the stables, and most of the prisoners had been moved to a warehouse by the

THE BLUE HAIRED GIRL

docks, where they could be guarded by relativity few men. The warehouse was hot and crowded, though thankfully there were a few water barrels and crates of dried fruit that they all made good use of.

It was probably a good thing that Kolten wasn't there, as it suggested he was free, but it didn't make Anni any less worried about him. She hadn't seen him since Stonor had poisoned her.

Even if Stonor lost the battle, he could still choose to hold them all hostage. Anni held out little hope that Valentia and the High Council would pay much in the way of ransom for her; they certainly wouldn't outbid Blegor's standing bounty on her head. Assuming, of course, Stonor didn't kill her outright for lying about the chairwoman's death once he found out she was still alive.

Ackleman sat with his back up against the wall of the warehouse next to Anni. His face was red and puffy. He had endured an obvious beating during one of Stonor's interrogations. When he had finally joined Anni in the holding area, he had told Anni, somewhat proudly, that he had told Stonor nothing.

"Hey," said Anni gently. "How's your head?"

"I used to be in the Republican National Guard," replied Ackleman with a slight smile. "I had worse than this in basic training."

"Oh," said Anni, not sure how to respond to this. "So

REUNITED

how are we going to get out of here?"

"Well, I don't suppose you actually *have* any magical powers, do you?" asked Ackleman.

Anni shook her head.

"But, if you don't have any magic powers, then Valentia, she's..."

"Alive," Anni mouthed silently, nodding her head in case anyone was listening.

Ackleman's gentle face softened.

"Then we need to escape. This war is just getting started."

Suddenly, Anni heard voices on the other side of the warehouse wall. Anni pressed the side of her sweaty face up against it and listened.

"...taken the city center," said a voice. "We've no choice but to hold here and wait for reinforcements."

"Stonor sent out a call for allies just before the fighting broke out."

"Is anyone coming?"

"Rumor is—"

There was a sudden commotion in the far side of the warehouse as a few of the prisoners started pounding on the doors.

"Let us out! We can't breathe in here!"

They were kicking and beating on the doors, screaming

THE BLUE HAIRED GIRL

at the guards to free them.

"Shut up!" said a voice from outside.

There was a huge, booming thud, and the doors shifted slightly as one of the guards outside it slammed something against it to silence the prisoners.

Far from quieting them down, the other prisoners only got more restless and the shouting continued.

The shouting continued for several minutes, until finally, the door opened. About half a dozen heavily armed men stepped inside, carrying swords and brandishing them aggressively.

The crowd fell back, retreating from the entrance.

"Kill a few of them," said one of the guards. "That'll shut up the rest."

There were several screams of fear and the prisoners fell back toward the rear of the warehouse.

Anni was slow to react. Ackleman tried to pull her behind him, but the guard grabbed hold of her, and Anni slipped out of Ackleman's grasp.

The next thing Anni knew, she was being dragged from the wall of the warehouse, toward the men with swords.

"You'll do, sweetheart," snapped one of the men.

Anni was yanked to her feet and her hair was pulled back, exposing her neck.

"Give me the knife," said the man holding her.

There were several shouts in protest from the crowd, and

302

REUNITED

Anni started fighting fiercely against the man holding her.

He brought a small dagger toward her throat.

Anni shut her eyes.

There was a loud boom, like a clap of thunder, and the man released her.

Anni fell to the floor and the entire warehouse fell silent.

As she pushed herself up from the floor, Anni saw that everyone was looking at her. The men with swords had lowered their blades, their eyes wide with shock.

"W-Wait! N-Now, hold on," said one of the guards, his hands held out in front of him defensively, his eyes wide and his sword sheathed. "There's no reason to get all upset! No one is going to hurt you."

Anni didn't know what had happened, but everyone around her had retreated from her, as if she were a rabid animal.

She looked down at her hands. They were smoking like a doused campfire, but they didn't feel hot or painful.

Anni turned toward the man who had been ready to kill her moments before. He was slumped up against the far wall. His face and clothing were badly burned, as if he had been held too close to a flame, but there was no sign of fire anywhere. His skin was charred black, and he wasn't moving.

He wasn't just unconscious, he was dead.

"L-Look," stammered the guard. "There's no reason to get all excited. W-We can talk about this."

303

THE BLUE HAIRED GIRL

"She's a witch!" said a voice in the crowd.

"I've heard rumors about the blue-haired girl."

Anni stood there dumbfounded for a moment. It must have been some form of magic that had killed the man; there was no other explanation. But there were no thunder elk or other magical creatures in the warehouse with them, and Valentia was nowhere to be seen. There only explanation Anni could think of was someone nearby had used a magical spell to save her life and had chosen not to reveal themselves. At this point, it didn't matter; all Anni wanted was to escape. If whoever had cast the spell didn't want to show themselves, Anni would be happy to take the credit, if it would help them escape.

She held her hands out in front of her with a determined look on her face.

The guards all fell backward.

"Let us go!" ordered Anni.

"Look, we—"

"Get! Out! Of! The! Way!" said Anni through gritted teeth.

The guards stepped aside and left the door to the warehouse open.

"Well," said Anni, turning toward the crowd, "what are you waiting for?! Go!"

Most of the prisoners made a run for it to find their own escape, but a few didn't move.

REUNITED

"Go on! Go!" said Anni, coaxing them out of the warehouse. "You're free to go."

"I'm staying with you," said one of the prisoners, nodding toward Anni.

Several others nodded in agreement.

This was not something Anni was prepared for. Most of these people were adults, much older than she was. She had no idea where to go or what to do next. Whatever had happened to kill her attacker had clearly convinced the others that she was their best bet for survival.

Ackleman came to her rescue.

"Anni, I don't know why you didn't tell me about this, but don't you think we should get out of here?"

"Uhh, right. We should go."

There were several shouts from somewhere outside the warehouse.

"Anni, their swords," said Ackleman.

The men who were guarding them had lowered or dropped their swords, and a few had simply fled.

"Drop them," said Anni to the few guards that still stood in their way.

Their weapons clattered to the ground, and Ackleman gathered them up and distributed them to a few of the prisoners. He kept one for himself.

"Where are we going?" asked one of the prisoners.

305

THE BLUE HAIRED GIRL

"Are you Valentia?" asked another voice.

Anni rolled her eyes. She really didn't have time for this. She looked over at Ackleman, who took the lead toward the warehouse exit. He peered out of the warehouse door and gestured for them to follow.

Anni had been blindfolded for most of the trip here. She still didn't know the layout of most of the city. The harbor was a large, open area with buildings all around it. All the roads leading into it had been barricaded with whatever they could find, and there were distant shouts coming from the city center. Several broken arrows lined the streets, and there was blood and a few bodies scattered around the buildings.

One thing that Anni noticed was how few people there were in the surrounding area. Most of Stonor's men had probably been devoted to defending the harbor or pressing his interests elsewhere in the city.

The harbor itself was surrounded by a large wall that rose straight out of the sea, with a pair of huge, metal gates large enough for a ship to pass through when open. It probably served as a defensive barrier in times of war, or as a breaker during heavy storms.

The gates were closed, as Stonor was probably trying to stop word of his insurrection from reaching Zoltan. Most of the ships in the harbor had been destroyed by the fighting. Several ships were half submerged by the harbor docks.

306

REUNITED

Anni scanned the streets for an opening, but she could see no way out for her or the others. All the barricades blocking the streets had men guarding them, and most were firing arrows over them at an attacking force somewhere beyond the wall.

There was no way out. In all the chaos of the civil war, if the High Council managed to overtake Stonor's defenders, then Anni and the other prisoners would probably get caught in the middle of it.

An arrow sailed over Anni's head and embedded itself in the warehouse behind her, and there was more shouting from the edge of the harbor.

"We need to get out of here!" shouted Ackleman, scanning for a clear route out of the harbor.

Another arrow flew over her head and sliced into the water below with a tiny splash.

"Look out!" shouted a voice.

Anni turned to see a massive piece of rock flying through the air from somewhere else in the city; it crashed into the warehouse they had been in moments before.

The prisoners scattered in all directions.

Seeing no other escape, Anni jumped off the edge of the pier and into the waters below.

The rubble of the warehouse collapsed onto the wharf, destroying several support beams, before splashing into the harbor waters some distance away from Anni.

307

THE BLUE HAIRED GIRL

Unlike the other prisoners, who lived in and around the seas, many of whom were already getting out of the water, Anni had spent her whole life on the plains of the goatlands. She had never even stood in water that was higher than she was.

Anni couldn't swim.

She started to panic, struggling against the rising water, trying in vain to swim but having no idea how. Anni tasted salt as her face dipped below the waves, and she started coughing, only to have more water force its way into her lungs.

She coughed and struggled relentlessly, but the surface was only getting farther and farther away.

The pressure in Anni's chest was growing and the world was starting to go dark.

Suddenly, Anni felt a great force from somewhere underneath her, and air surged into her lungs.

She felt herself land on something hard and flat.

Slowly, Anni's vision cleared, and she found herself lying on the harbor's stone walkway.

An image of a woman snapped into focus.

"Breathe, Anni, breathe," she said, slapping her back, forcing Anni's airway to open.

It was Valentia.

Anni took a few labored breaths.

"S-Stonor…"

"Stonor and his men left this part of the city when we

REUNITED

broke through."

The chairwoman looked a little disheveled—her hair was a mess and her staff had a few blood spots on it—but the fact that she was there was a good sign. The only way the safe house would have let her leave was if the battle was starting to turn in their favor.

All around Anni were piles of rubble, and men wearing yellow and orange uniforms. A few civilians were scattered among them, as well.

As Anni caught her breath, she realized that she was sitting on the cobblestone road alongside the harbor in a few inches of water. The water was quickly receding back toward the harbor and pouring over the edge of the docks, back into the seas below.

The warehouse had been utterly destroyed; pieces of it were scattered along the docks and floating along the water surface.

The dock itself had been heavily damaged, as if some unseen storm had been battering it for hours until it finally submitted. A huge section of the dock had collapsed into a smattering of broken wood planks. Several huge support beams had been snapped in half. They stood pointlessly jutting out of the water, attached to nothing but the seabed.

Whatever had happened to the harbor in the last few moments, it had done an enormous amount of damage.

THE BLUE HAIRED GIRL

It was then that Anni realized there was a man sitting next to her, who was supporting her where she sat.

He had a bald head, a long beard, and birdlike nose.

"Kolten!" spluttered Anni, and she gave the dwarf a hug.

"Are you okay?" asked the dwarf, hugging her back.

Anni took a few more deep breaths; her lungs were finally starting to clear, and the cough reflex was dissipating.

"What happened to you?" asked Anni.

Kolten told her the story, although she had guessed much of it already. The dwarf had, indeed, picked the lock of his jail cell with the wooden fork from his meal tray and escaped with several members of the High Council. They were then able to rally support against Stonor.

"Anni, did you get the message to the brynywyn?" asked Valentia.

Anni told her about losing the letter, and her and Ackleman's capture.

"It's okay, Anni," said Valentia. "Once the council escaped jail, they were able to organize a counterattack. Even without your brynywyn friends, we might be able to stop Stonor."

It was then that Anni noticed just how many fighters had come to the council's aid. There were at least a hundred men, in the harbor alone, who had joined the fight. It seemed that Stonor's plan to arrest the other members of the High Council

310

REUNITED

had been crucial. Without them in custody, Stonor's coup wasn't going as planned.

"So, what do we do now?" asked Anni.

"Anni, you've done brilliantly," said Valentia. "But we'll take it from here. Stonor won't get away with this. I'll have one of my men take you to a safe house until this is all over."

"I'm not going to just sit around while you guys fight!" snapped Anni.

"Anni…" said Valentia.

"No!"

"Anni, she's right," said Kolten. "It's dangerous out here."

"No way! I want to help!"

The idea of just sitting down right now and hoping everything turned out okay seemed ridiculous to Anni. Considering how involved she had been so far, if anyone had proved themselves able to help the war effort, it was Anni.

It was then that Ackleman approached the group and whispered something to Valentia.

In an instant, her face turned from a look of concern to fear.

"Anni," she asked, her eyes wide, "how did you escape from the warehouse guards?"

311

- CHAPTER 27 -
The Lightwrists

Despite an initial refusal to cooperate, Anni soon found herself in another one of the city's hidden safe houses. This one's entrance was in a fake water barrel secured to the outside of one of the warehouses.

The barrel had been enchanted to work just like an ordinary water barrel that the sailors could use every day. Valentia had explained to Anni how it worked. The large water barrel had no lid and would always magically refill itself with clean, fresh drinking water when no one was looking. This ensured that citizens could use it every day if need be, yet it would never be removed or examined too closely, allowing the safe house to hide in plain sight.

THE LIGHTWRISTS

As Anni climbed into the large barrel, she found her feet stayed completely dry as they slid past the water's surface. Her toes did not find the floor of the barrel; instead, they passed right through it and found a ladder into a hidden room under the docks, and probably below the surface of the sea.

Valentia now stood before her at a table, with a stern look on her face.

"Now it all makes sense," said Valentia. "This may be why Blegor is after you."

"What does?"

"Everything, Anni. The bounty on your head, Stonor's interest in you, the warehouse—everything!"

"I don't understand."

"Anni, you're a sorceress."

"Not you too," said Anni, thinking about Stonor's obsession with his idiotic theory. "I am not."

"Anni, you killed a man by burning him to death, less than an hour ago. Of course, you are."

"But I didn't do anything."

"Anni, I've talked to Kolten and Ackleman; they've confirmed it."

"Now I know you're lying," snapped Anni. "Kolten knows I'm not a witch!"

"Anni, I need you to stay calm for me," said Valentia, raising her hand soothingly. "I didn't say witch—I said, a

313

THE BLUE HAIRED GIRL

sorceress."

"Whatever, I'm not one of those either!"

"Anni, Kolten told me about the ashdrake."

"It wasn't me!" Anni shouted. *"It was the thunder elk! Don't you people know what a thunder elk is!? Let me go!"*

For the second time in as few days, Anni found her back pinned up against the ceiling of a room by the purple light from Valentia's crystal staff.

"Anni, I don't want to hurt you! But I can't risk you losing your temper!"

"Let me go!"

There was a sudden cracking sound, and the room gave a short, violent shake, as if it had been kicked by a giant foot from the outside.

Anni collapsed to the floor, flat on her stomach.

Valentia was breathing hard, leaning on the table beside her, and her jaw was tightly clenched.

"Anni, that hurt! You need to calm down!"

"I didn't do anything!" shouted Anni, getting to her feet.

"Anni, you'll kill us both!"

"But—"

"Listen to me, Anni. I've been working with magic since I was younger than you are; I know what we need to do here. But you need to calm down. Take a few deep breaths."

Anni did as she was told, and she felt her heart rate

314

THE LIGHTWRISTS

slowing, and she hoped it would be enough to convince Valentia not to make the room shake again.

"Are you okay, Anni?"

The chairwoman was holding her staff out in front of her defensively.

"I'm sorry, I didn't mean to shout at you."

"It's okay, Anni. You don't know how to control your powers yet."

"What do you mean?"

"Anni, you're a sorceress," she repeated.

"No, I'm not," said Anni.

"You just made the room shake and would have burned me alive now if I hadn't shielded."

"I—I…"

"It's okay, Anni," she said. "It's not your fault."

Anni looked down at her hands, and they were starting to smoke again, like they had in the warehouse.

"Anni, stay calm," she said.

"I don't…"

Valentia made a quick move with her staff and Anni found her arms drawn out in front of her, toward the chairwoman. It felt like each of Anni's arms were being pulled forward by invisible ropes, dragging her toward Valentia.

"Anni, I'm sorry to do this, but this is for your safety and for ours."

315

THE BLUE HAIRED GIRL

A pair of glowing, hoop-like objects emerged from Valentia's staff and floated in midair toward Anni's outstretched arms.

Anni knew exactly what they must have been, and she started fighting furiously against the magic that held her; the room started to shake more violently than before.

The was a bolt of lightning like that of a thunder elk, and both Anni and Valentia were thrown off their feet.

As Anni struggled to come to terms with what had happened to her, she felt something on her arms.

A look of horror crossed Anni's face, as she looked down at the new pair of darkwrists that decorated her hands.

"Good, now, we can talk," said Valentia with a sigh of relief. "Don't worry, Anni. They're not what you think they are."

Anni stared at her.

"You're not my slave."

"But…the darkwrists…"

"Anni, I've spent my entire career trying to abolish slavery; I'm not going to go back on it now. Those are not darkwrists, but they will help."

"What have you done to me?" asked Anni, a little hotly.

"They will help you keep control of your powers."

"My powers…What are they?"

"They're called lightwrists," she said simply, as if knowing the name was of any use at all.

316

THE LIGHTWRISTS

"I don't understand."

"Look closer."

Anni stared down at the hoop-like objects around her wrists. They looked a bit like darkwrists, but they were the wrong color. Instead of the deep black she remembered, these were the color of pure ivory. They felt much friendlier on her wrists; somehow, they reminded Anni of Kolten, like a close friend or a teacher that only wanted to help.

"Anni, darkwrists are designed to control others. Lightwrists, as the name suggests, are sort of the opposite; they're designed to help someone control themselves—or, rather, their magic."

"My...magic..."

"From what I've heard, your powers have been getting stronger and stronger over the last few days. You nearly killed me just now—and don't worry, I'm not angry," she added when she saw Anni's eyes widen apologetically. "It was an accident, I know that. Lightwrists are usually given to children, especially toddlers, who show early-onset magical abilities but are too young to be trained."

"I-I didn't even think I had any powers."

"I know, that is why I stepped away from the war effort to make sure we had this under control," she said with just the slightest hint of indignation. "Untrained magic-users are very dangerous. At the rate your powers were growing, there was no

THE BLUE HAIRED GIRL

time to lose. You already caused a tidal wave and destroyed most of the harbor when you fell in the water. I needed to rein this in."

A tempering feeling emanated from Anni's wrists and flowed up her arms, like warm water was being pumped through her insides from her hands.

Everything was happening so fast. A few hours ago, the idea that she had any magic at all was laughable, but now that seemed a distant memory.

"So, I really am a…"

"Sorceress, yes…Well, when you're trained, you will be. For now, we're just trying to make sure we have this under control."

Anni took a moment and thought back to their journey over the last few weeks.

She had destroyed part of the harbor; blown up that man who had tried to kill her in the warehouse; knocked out the man in the stables; hurled one of Stonor's thugs clear across the street; and survived Stonor's deadly poison without an antidote.

In fact, now that Anni thought of it, she couldn't be entirely sure that the incident with the ashdrake that Stonor was so obsessed with had just been her thunder elk at all; she had never seen one wield that kind of power before or since.

Anni had somehow managed to break the spell of Mareitsia's darkwrists, stolen her mistress's other slave, and stopped Mareitsia from beating her after Blade had ruined her

318

THE LIGHTWRISTS

dress.

Even that old, blind man on the road outside the city had seemed to sense something was amiss with her, though that one might have been a coincidence.

The pattern was too hard to ignore.

But there was still one thing that bothered her.

"I don't understand. If I have magic, then…Mareitsia would be—"

Valentia's face filled with understanding.

"Your former mistress," she said with a nod. "You think, if you had powers, you wouldn't have been a slave."

Anni nodded.

"Your scars," said Valentia, pointing to Anni's wrist with her eyebrows raised.

Anni looked down at her own wrists where, under the ivory-colored lightwrists, deep, red scars encircled them, like large, ugly bracelets.

"Your darkwrists probably kept your powers in check, just like these do. It's a good thing, too; my guess is an enslaved magic-user could be forced to use their powers for their owners. But it sounds to me like your former mistress didn't know you had magic—you didn't even know."

"But, then why did my darkwrists stop working?" asked Anni, thinking back to when she had first rendered her shackles useless.

319

THE BLUE HAIRED GIRL

"I don't know, Anni. It's possible that your powers grew too strong for them to control. They may have been defective, or something may have happened to weaken or break them. We may never know."

"But I thought you knew all about this sort of stuff," said Anni.

Valentia smiled. "Magic is complicated, and the laws that govern it are not well understood. I don't know what happens when magic is kept caged for years by darkwrists and then suddenly released. It's possible no one knows."

Anni touched her hand to her temple in thought, and as she did so, her hand brushed her hair.

"Wait, is this why my hair is blue?"

Valentia nodded.

"Magic can sometimes manifest physically. Sorcerers have been known to sometimes sprout twigs or scales from their bodies. It's *very* rare, but it's possible."

"And is that why Blegor is after me?" asked Anni thoughtfully. "Because I have magic?"

"I don't see how he could know about your magic, any more than we did. Stonor only seems to have picked up on this when he met you in the forest, and there are other sorcerers in Decareia. So I don't see why that would be of interest to him."

"So, I have to wear these from now on?" asked Anni, looking down at the ivory-colored bracelets again, still not quite

THE LIGHTWRISTS

sure about them.

"Just for now. Don't worry. They're not like darkwrists—they won't hurt you," said Valentia, reading Anni's face. "Just be careful with them. They're a lot more delicate than darkwrists, and they will break. Once this is all over, we'll get you on a transport ship to the Republic. Zoltan has some of the best magic trainers in the world. They'll help you learn how to use and, more importantly, how to control your powers. That was where I learned."

"But I don't..."

"Anni, have you forgotten?" asked Valentia. "There's a war on up there, and we're just starting to win it. Those lightwrists will last for a few weeks before they fall off, but for now, they'll help you keep in control. It's not as good as the years of proper training that you will need, but they'll do for now."

"What now?"

"Well, all the other children your age are being evacuated out of the city. Don't worry, Anni. I have no intention of trying to force you to leave with them," she added when she saw Anni was about to protest. "Even with the lightwrists, I'd still rather have you close by, where I can keep an eye on you."

Before Anni could answer, the room filled with light from the world above, outside the safe house.

"I said not to disturb us," said Valentia in an annoyed tone. "This is a dangerous situation."

321

THE BLUE HAIRED GIRL

A young soldier in his early twenties climbed down into the safe house. He was wearing a Yuspiereian uniform and helmet.

"I'm sorry to interrupt, ma'am. But there's been a development. The situation has become more complicated."

"What do you mean? What's Stonor up to?"

"Ma'am, it's not Stonor. There's an army just outside the city gates," said the solider gravely.

Valentia waved her staff through the air, drawing out a perfect circle. A line of magic followed it and traced out a smoke-like image floating in midair.

As Anni stared at it, the smoke began to swirl around until it formed the image of a bird's-eye view of Yuspiereia city. Camped just outside the city wall was a massive force. Although she couldn't make out any detail from this distance, there must have been close to two thousand warriors, and they were taking up positions around the city.

From the magical window's vantage point, the army seemed to be chopping down trees from the nearby forest.

Anni wasn't sure if they were building something or they needed firewood, but it didn't matter. If this army was planning on attacking the city, they had chosen the time well, as all sides had been weakened by Stonor's bid for power.

It would have been difficult for the Yuspiereian guard to fend off a force of that size under normal circumstances; with the

THE LIGHTWRISTS

city in civil war, it was downright impossible.

"This is really not a good time for this," said the chairwoman.

"There's more; they left a message for you, ma'am," he said, holding out a small scroll for Valentia to read. As he did so, Anni noticed his eyes fall on Anni's hair.

The chairwoman opened the scroll, and Anni watched as her eyes moved across the ink symbols written on the parchment. Her eyes narrowed on Anni as she lowered it.

"What's it say?" asked Anni.

"It's from the commander of the army." She read aloud, *"In the name of Blegor of the House of Dragmor, we bid you greetings. Our scouts tell us that your city is in chaos. We are prepared to help either side end the conflict and restore order to the capital, if our demands are met. In the name of Blegor the Cruel, give us the blue-haired girl or we will burn this city to the ground. You have until sunset."*

- CHAPTER 28 -
The Horde

Kolten wrapped his arm around Anni's shoulders in a gesture of protection. She was sitting next to the wall of the safe house and Kolten was holding her close.

He had an ax resting on his lap.

In all the chaos of Stonor's coup, Anni had almost forgotten about Blegor the Cruel.

Ackleman, Valentia, and several members of the High Council stood around the table in the center of the room, discussing their next move.

"Stonor will have received the same message," said Ackleman sternly.

"Shouldn't we send someone to meet with Blegor?"

THE HORDE

asked one of the High Council members that Anni didn't know. "Maybe he is willing to negotiate."

"Blegor doesn't negotiate. He just kills people," said Valentia, turning to him.

"But we should at least discuss the possibility—"

"Don't even think about it!" roared Kolten, pulling Anni closer to him.

The dwarf's face was cold and fiercely protective.

They had been talking for more than an hour; sunset would soon be upon them, and the conversation had gone nowhere.

"Kolten, of course we're not going to do that," said Valentia, "but we need to come up with some kind of a plan."

"I've got a plan for you," said Kolten hotly. "Anni stays here, and that's the end of it!"

"And when Blegor attacks the city?" asked the councilor.

"We're in a safe house; Anni will be fine," said Kolten sharply.

"And what about the rest of the city?"

"I'm sorry, but me and Anni didn't ask to get dragged into this damned war," said the dwarf coldly.

"I'm going to surrender," said Anni simply.

All eyes were upon her.

"Absolutely not," muttered Kolten, with a twitch of his left hand.

THE BLUE HAIRED GIRL

"I'm not going to be responsible for an entire city being destroyed," said Anni.

"Anni, you can't be serious," said Ackleman. "This is Blegor the Cruel we're talking about here."

Anni had given this a great deal of thought, and it was a decision that she had reached entirely on her own. If she tried to hide or run, the horde would attack and destroy the city, and she would end up their prisoner anyway. Even the hidden safe houses wouldn't be able to protect them from the horde forever, if the entire city was destroyed.

If Ackleman was right and Stonor had received the same message, it wouldn't be long before he would be tearing up half the city looking for her. If Stonor managed to capture her and was the one to hand her over to Blegor, the council would be finished.

It didn't really make sense for Blegor to want her dead. He had offered ten thousand golords for her capture. He would have to be really stupid to pay that much for a corpse. It was probably her powers that he wanted, which meant he probably wouldn't kill her. Anni hoped that was the case, anyway.

Even if he did kill her, at the very least, Kolten's remaining darkwrist would be useless without her as his mistress, and he would be free once and for all. Stonor would be defeated, the High Council would be restored, and the war would be over.

It was not a decision that Anni had reached lightly, but it

326

THE HORDE

seemed the honorable thing to do. In a way, it might even make up for her mistake with Valentia and the poison, and at the very least, she would finally have some answers. Although, with a name like Blegor the Cruel, Anni couldn't imagine he would be pleasant.

"I'm the one he wants."

"You're not surrendering to Blegor the Cruel," said Valentia hotly, as if Anni had suggested that goats could fly.

"You can't stop me," said Anni simply.

"Oh, yes, we can," said Ackleman. "Anni, you're outnumbered, and we have Valentia's magic. You're not going anywhere."

The dwarf hugged Anni closer.

"No, you can't," said Anni.

Everyone stared at her.

"Kolten, I order you to help me leave."

The dwarf's eyes opened wide with a cold realization. The defective darkwrist shifted on his hand.

"*No! No! No! No! No!*" shouted the dwarf as he was forced to his feet by the magic of the darkwrist.

"*Ahhhhh!*" he screamed. "*No, Anni! Please! No!*"

"I'm sorry!" sniffed Anni. "I have to! Use your ax."

Everyone took a step back as the dwarf lifted his battle ax, and Valentia readied her staff to stop him.

"Anni, please! I don't want to hurt him!" shouted

327

THE BLUE HAIRED GIRL

Valentia.

"I know, you don't!" sobbed Anni as she started to cry. "But I have to go. Kolten, attack Valentia until I get away."

Kolten's arms shook violently as he resisted the pain of the dark magic with every ounce of strength he could muster. His teeth were gritted, and he started to whimper as he was forced to charge at Valentia.

The chairwoman raised her staff defensively and a blast of purple light burst from its crystal to stop him.

Anni seized her chance and ran toward the entryway of the safe house as Kolten started flailing around, trapped in the beam of magical light, swinging his ax wildly.

Ackleman made a grab for Anni as she clambered up the entrance toward the water barrel. Anni felt the heel of her foot slip out of Ackleman's grasp.

"*Anni! No!*" shouted Kolten's voice from somewhere below her. "*Anni, I—*"

The dwarf's voice vanished the instant that Anni's head popped into the bottom of the water barrel.

Anni clambered out of the barrel and ran down the side of the warehouse; she knew that Ackleman wouldn't be far behind.

There were many of Yuspiereia's soldiers all through the harbor. Some were talking, others eating, and a few were playing cards. Taking a well-deserved rest before the battle resumed. Anni

328

THE HORDE

slipped down an alleyway between two warehouses, until she saw what she was looking for. A ladder that led up to the city wall at the edge of the harbor.

Anni climbed up it.

Although she didn't know the city well, she guessed that the harbor's defensive wall would connect to the city's outer wall, and she could find her way down from there.

It broke Anni's heart to think that the last time she would ever see Kolten, he had been attacking people she cared about on her orders. Kolten was the last person in the world that would ever have allowed Anni to surrender to Blegor, and yet she had forced him to do it anyway. Hopefully, if Anni managed to get far enough away from Kolten, his darkwrist would stop working, or maybe Valentia could figure out how to remove it.

Anni wiped a tear from her eye as she hurried onward.

As she ran, Anni kept peering down over the edge of the city walls. Soon, the water at the base of the city walls turned to sandy beaches, and then to grass as she made her way around the city. Despite the sizable force just outside the gates, the wall battlements remained completely unmanned, as most of the defenders were probably still embroiled in the conflict within the city itself.

Anni suddenly spotted a clear piece of soft-looking ground below the walls.

The city walls of Yuspiereia were perhaps fifty feet high.

THE BLUE HAIRED GIRL

Too high to jump safely, but Anni had formed a plan as she went.

Looking down at the lightwrists that hung from her hands, Anni hoped that they would at least help break her fall. After all, she had used her powers to save her own life several times already, even if she had trouble controlling them. It seemed perfectly reasonable that lightwrists would make her powers perform better. All she needed was to slow her descent a little bit.

The lightwrists warmed slightly, like a friend holding her by the hand, as she jumped.

The pain in her legs was excruciating as she hit the ground at the base of the city wall. The lightwrists had tempered her magic, but in doing so, they had weakened it considerably.

It seemed the lightwrists had slowed her descent enough to prevent any serious injury, though.

These are going to take some getting used to, thought Anni with gritted teeth as she looked at the white bracelets.

A few members of the horde had seen her jump. They would have had to be blind not to. Soon, a pair of ugly hands pulled Anni to her feet, and within moments, she was whisked away from her uneasy landing.

This was the first time Anni had seen a gloknore, and Mareitsia's stories had done them justice.

They were ugly.

The gloknore had bumpy features, covered in dark-gray

THE HORDE

skin. They also had long, tusk-like canine teeth in their upper jaws. They were tall, grotesque-looking, subhuman beasts. Most of them wore armor, and all of them were heavily armed.

Within moments, Anni found herself in the midst of a gloknore camp.

The horde smelled like sweaty men and rotting food, and all around her were tents, campfires, weapons, and piles of supplies. Apparently, the horde was planning to be here quite a while.

Off to one side, a team of gloknore and a few humans worked with several long timbers. One of the men was sharpening the end of a thick tree trunk, while two more men were attaching handles along it lengthwise. This was presumably to attack the city's wooden gates. In addition to the battering ram, a few more were building a huge, triangular, wooden frame and wrapping thick ropes around part of its base, fashioning what looked like a crudely built catapult. There could be no doubt. This army was planning to attack Yuspiereia city, and they were planning on doing it sooner rather than later.

"Where are you taking me?"

"No talk," muttered the one holding her, his speech slurred by his massive, tusk-like teeth.

Several of the gloknore hissed and catcalled at Anni as she was marched through their camp. At the rear of the camp, near the tree line, was a large tent, bigger than all the other ones.

THE BLUE HAIRED GIRL

Anni could only guess this one belonged to Blegor. She was going to meet him at last.

Before her guards reached it, however, the tent opened.

Anni's heart sank as she saw the only person who could possibly make her situation worse.

Stonor looked worse for the wear—his eye was black, and he walked with a slight limp—but his face lit up as soon as he saw Anni.

"See! See! I told you!" he shouted. *"She's here!"*

The tent opened again, and out stepped what could only be the horde commander.

The horde commander was a tall gloknore with no hair at all. He must have been well over six feet tall, and his left tusk was missing. He was holding a live, struggling squirrel in his hand. As he approached Anni, he promptly bit the squirrel's head off and started eating it.

"I delivered her!" shouted Stonor. *"I told you I would!"*

The commander held up a clawed hand to Stonor to silence him, the headless squirrel in his other hand.

There was no way Stonor could have known Anni would be here, but the timing could not have been worse. If Stonor was able to take credit for Anni's surrender, the war would be over. Stonor would finally have more than enough men at his disposal to end the civil war and defeat the High Council, once and for all.

THE HORDE

For a while, it had seemed that Valentia and the other councilors might just be able to win the battle with Stonor's rebels, but if this horde sided with Stonor, they wouldn't stand a chance.

Anni was sure that Stonor wouldn't let there be any mistake this time, either. Valentia was as good as dead, as was Ackleman. If Stonor found out that Kolten was the one who had released the other councilors from jail, and he probably would, Kolten would be murdered too. Probably quite painfully.

Then it occurred to Anni that, thanks to her magical blunder, much of the harbor had been destroyed, making escaping to the sea impossible. The war was, for all intents and purposes, already over. The High Council just didn't know it yet.

The horde commander approached Anni and took another bite of squirrel.

"I have lived up to my end of the bargain," insisted Stonor.

"I didn't come here because of you," snapped Anni, finding her voice.

"She's lying!" shouted Stonor.

The commander ignored them both and reached out his clawed hand and pulled on Anni's hair. Anni fell painfully forward to her knees as the commander gave her blue hair a loud sniff. He then took another bite off of the squirrel and swallowed it with a loud gulp.

THE BLUE HAIRED GIRL

"I've brought you the blue-haired girl, as promised."

He still didn't respond to Stonor, and he grasped Anni's face in his huge, monstrous hand and poked and prodded at her scalp with his long, spider-like fingers, as if trying to figure out if her hair was real or not.

The commander stuffed the rest of the squirrel into his mouth and crunched it down loudly.

"Are you Blegor?" asked Anni weakly.

Several of the horde laughed.

I'll take that as a no, thought Anni.

"What does Blegor want with me?" said Anni, though her voice was muffled by the gloknore's hand.

The horde erupted in spiting laughter.

"You promised to end the war if I delivered the girl," said Stonor.

The gloknore commander sneered and grunted at him in recognition.

"We need to hurry; they've taken back most of—"

The gloknore commander threw Anni to the ground and turned on Stonor.

"We fight," he said, speaking for the first time. His words were slurred and muffled by his one remaining tusk.

"Stonor didn't send me, the High Council did!" shouted Anni.

"I arranged it," said Stonor. "I am on the High Council,

THE HORDE

you see."

"I didn't come here for you!"

The gloknore commander snarled for silence.

"No care who sent," he muttered. "Get reward."

"Yes, yes," nodded Stonor, sounding a little flustered. "The reward for the girl is yours. I just want the city."

"More," he said sharply.

"More?" asked Stonor, puzzled.

"More!" he grunted.

Stonor must have really wanted control of Yuspiereia to risk allying himself with these creatures. They really didn't seem like the type of creatures you would want to associate with. If the commander had wanted to, he could have simply killed Stonor and taken the city for himself and his horde. The horde had come for Anni, and they had her, so they had no more use for Stonor than Stonor had had for Anni.

"Y-You want a bigger reward?" stammered Stonor.

The commander stared at him in contempt and nodded.

"That wasn't part of the deal."

The commander drew a long, jagged, S-shaped sword in one hand and lifted Stonor clear into the air by the front of his robes with the other.

In Anni's opinion, Stonor was being stupid right now. It was obvious to Anni that the commander wanted a greater reward for their help. And Stonor didn't have much bargaining power, at

335

THE BLUE HAIRED GIRL

the moment. All things considered, now was not a good time to get cheap on them.

"A-All right, I can pay more," said Stonor, who seemed to have reached the same conclusion as Anni.

"Fifty thousand more."

"Fifty thousand?!" Stonor said, shocked.

The gloknore commander opened his mouth, about to bite Stonor in the face.

"Okay! Fifty thousand! I-I'll pay it!"

The commander dropped him on his backside.

"I-I just don't have it with me! Once I'm in control of the city, I'll get it for you. I promise!"

"You lie, you die," the commander snorted.

Anni assumed it was a lot of money they were asking for. It was much more than what they were going to get from Blegor for the bounty. But, if Stonor regained control of the city, he could pay them out of the Yuspiereian treasury, or using the money stolen from the people of the city.

"I want to see Blegor," said Anni in a tone that was much braver than she felt.

"Blegor no here," the commander muttered.

Suddenly, there was a loud crack, and the gloknore commander staggered sideways, almost falling over. Anni instinctively looked down at her hands, but they remained quite cool and smokeless. The lightwrists remained on her wrists; it

336

THE HORDE

wasn't her powers.

Something else had happened.

A fist-sized stone had struck the commander's left shoulder, leaving a sizable bruise, and it fell to the ground.

The commander wailed as a second barrage of stones came pelting into the midst of the horde, from the direction of the forest.

Coming from the tree line was the distant sound of music.

"Is that bagpipes?" asked Stonor, who was still on the ground, on his backside.

Before Anni could even ask what bagpipes were, the music was joined by the sound of drums and singing.

It was a song that Anni had heard before.

A thousand years ago or more,
There stood a mighty drake,
A fiery beast, from dark it came,
It burned all in its wake.

The drake laid waste to armies,
They fell before its might,
None could dare to stop the beast,
It set our world alight.

THE BLUE HAIRED GIRL

But then there came a hero,
A brynywyn, you see,
Though tiny in his stature,
He wished all to be free.

He turned his gaze toward the drake,
And said with great suspense,
"Leave this land, I order you,
Or face the consequence!"

The fire drake, he didn't stall,
"You, puny one, are frail,
None can stand before me,
I am beyond the pale."

"Now leave me be to rule my land,
And fear me as you must,
Or I shall use my fire breath,
And turn you all to dust."

Our hero held firm his ground,
With a determined eye,
He drew out his hunting knife,

THE HORDE

And was prepared to die.

Letting fly a mighty throw,
With not a thought to run,
Soon the blade found its mark,
The battle, it was done.

So, remember this, our children,
Even if you're small,
When you stand for what is right,
Anyone can be tall.

The fiery drake is dead now,
And you know the epic tale,
Of the battle of the brynywyn folk,
Now, let's all sip our ale!

The singers were, as before, very out of tune, and the lyrics were still poorly written, at best. But the song conjured up the happy images of a pub and a drunken bartender from the beginning of her journey.

Anni's jaw dropped as the singers emerged from the tree line. Many tiny and lightly armed warriors were assembling near the edge of the camp.

THE BLUE HAIRED GIRL

The brynywyn folk had answered the call.

- CHAPTER 29 -
The Cloudburst

Somehow, someway, the brynywyn had gotten Anni's message, even though she had lost the letter and the elk had taken off without her.

Their forces were few in number, and from what Anni could see, were poorly outfitted, but they stood at the tree line defiantly.

In fact, to have called them an "army" would have been generous. It was clear just from looking, even at this distance, these were not professional soldiers. They wore simple woolen tunics that would offer little, if any, protection from blade or arrow.

They had no archers at all. The force involved in drawing

THE BLUE HAIRED GIRL

a bow might have been too much for their tiny bodies. Instead, at the front of the force were a handful of brynywyn wielding woolen slings that had pelleted the gloknore with stones moments before.

Most of the force were not well armed. It looked as though they had gathered whatever armaments they could find. Some carried hunting knives or wooden clubs; others had hand tools or farm implements; the odd one had a wood cutter's ax.

They were clearly not a battle-hardened force.

A few of the men carried simple shields made from pieces of wood hastily nailed together. Anni noticed that at least one had taken it upon himself to cut out holes in the sides of a watering can, turning it into a crude, ugly, and most-likely useless battle helmet.

Still, despite their having foraged for weapons, every man Anni could see had their precious blue bird embroidered into his tunic. Each insignia was crude, and they didn't match one another. Anni guessed they had probably been stitched by their wives or mothers only days before, but they puffed out their tiny chests, displaying them proudly.

Standing only three feet tall, it was unlikely the brynywyn could even reach high enough on a human-sized gloknore warrior to do any real damage, even if they knew how.

The gloknore horde must have been larger than the entire population of the brynywyn village, leaving the small force

342

THE CLOUDBURST

heavily outnumbered.

Emerging from the shadows of the forest, near the center of the small force, was a gray pony, pulling a wooden war chariot.

Anni couldn't help but notice that this chariot looked suspiciously like the vegetable cart that had tried to sell her carrots and apples in the brynywyn village. It, like the army itself, had been hastily pressed into military service. Someone had nailed wooden stakes to its front and sides to serve as protection for the riders.

In the cart were three brynywyn.

A stout driver to control the pony, a musician that played the bagpipes to the tune of their drinking song, and the third, Anni recognized immediately.

It was Jarabei.

The loud, drunken, and jolly bartender from the Silver Spear Pub. It seemed like an eternity ago that Anni and Kolten had enjoyed the man's hospitality. He was wearing a bright-red traveling cloak and that ridiculous blue-winged helmet that Kolten had struck the bounty hunter with. In his hand, reaching high over his head, was the silver spear itself, that had stood over his pub, displaying a blue flag.

Jarabei hardly looked like a great military commander, and the flag atop his spear had rows of stitches and stains as evidence of its age and past repairs. Yet, there was something oddly impressive about seeing the tattered and frayed blue flag on

343

THE BLUE HAIRED GIRL

the tip of a spear, blowing wildly in the coastal winds.

The driver of the cart gave the reins a quick flick, and the cart left the brynywyn militia standing along the tree line.

Jarabei was waving the flag high over his head as they approached, signaling a parley.

Several dozen spears and swords were pointed at the small vegetable cart and its passengers as it approached the horde and its leader.

The piper continued to play the drinking song, though his breath quivered with fear. Both he and the driver shuffled back further into their seats, placing as much space as possible between themselves and the horde; the cart had come to a stop right outside the commander's tent.

Jarabei himself, however, stood his ground as his gaze shifted back and forth, surveying the army that surrounded Anni, Stonor, and the city. Jarabei held up his hand and the piper stopped playing immediately.

"Who's in charge here?" asked Jarabei calmly.

The leader stepped forward.

"Ah, care for a pint, friend?" he said, offering the commander a mug with a friendly smile, as if he were one of his customers.

Jarabei didn't look drunk—or, at least, certainly not as drunk as when Anni had last seen him. It was nothing short of a miracle that Jarabei's head wasn't already decorating his own

THE CLOUDBURST

spear.

The commander said nothing. He merely glared at Jarabei.

"We're ready to negotiate your surrender," said Jarabei, taking a swig from his tankard.

Cold, maniacal, humorless laughter passed through the horde.

"Hello, Anni," he said, looking down at her. "They treating you okay?"

Anni nodded.

"Give us the girl, and we leave in peace. Otherwise, we attack." Jarabei nodded toward the tree line.

The commander scoffed.

"Go away, pygmies!" shouted Stonor. "This is not your affair!"

Jarabei glanced over at Stonor from the perch atop his cart, with a cold look on his face at the sound of the word "pygmy," but he said nothing to the man.

"How dare you attack us!" barked Stonor.

The commander grunted at Stonor to silence him.

"Well?" asked Jarabei.

The gloknore commander only stared at the brynywyn on the wagon.

"What are the terms of your surrender?" he asked, taking another swig of his tankard.

345

THE BLUE HAIRED GIRL

There was more laughter from throughout the horde.

Jarabei, however, didn't seem fazed by the horde's reaction in the least. The only explanation Anni could think of for Jarabei's impertinence was that he was hoping to bluff their way out of this, or that he really didn't appreciate just how badly the odds were against them—or, worst of all, he really was drunk.

The commander only sneered at him.

"Sorry, I didn't catch that," Jarabei scoffed.

"You're outnumbered," said the commander, speaking to Jarabei for the first time.

"True," said Jarabei, not bothering to bluff, "but we have something you don't have."

The commander cocked his head, with just a hint of curiosity.

"We have right on our side."

Anni couldn't help but let out an involuntary, mirthless laugh along with many of the gloknore warriors.

"If you don't surrender, you're going to wish you had," said Jarabei. "This is your last chance."

"Kill them," muttered the commander.

Jarabei nodded toward the piper. He quickly dropped his bagpipes and placed a second instrument to his lips.

It was a large elk antler, that had been hollowed out to form a highly intricately carved hunting horn.

The brynywyn musician blew the instrument. For such a

THE CLOUDBURST

delicate object, it produced a shockingly loud sound.

The blast was followed by several more horns from the direction of the forest, echoing the first.

A flock of birds from the forest took to the air, as if roused by some great, unseen force, and the gloknore warriors hesitated.

Suddenly, the air turned cold and an icy gust of wind swept across Anni's face, from the direction of the forest. Several of the gloknore's tents billowed in the wind, and a few of them toppled over and collapsed.

Despite the warm, clear summer's day only moments before, out of nowhere, dark-gray clouds filled the skies. Within moments, the sun disappeared, swallowed up by darkness, cloaking the land in shadow as far as the eye could see.

There was a sudden flash of lightning, followed by a booming clap of thunder, emanating from the forest.

Something strange was happening.

"What magic is this?" asked Stonor, as the blackened clouds burst open and a sudden torrential downpour of rain fell on their heads.

Before Anni could react, she felt a hand grab her from somewhere above. Jarabei had reached down and pulled her atop the vegetable cart chariot.

Jarabei was smiling with a serious grin.

"This is going to be rough, Anni!" he grunted, holding

THE BLUE HAIRED GIRL

on to the wagon.

Although no one had explained it to her, Anni realized what must be happening.

She grabbed on to the side of the cart and held on with every ounce of strength she had.

There was only one kind of magic she could think of that could even hope to conjure such a storm.

A magic that only the brynywyn possessed.

There was another blast of a hunting horn, followed by several more.

If a single thunder elk, when roused, deafened a dwarf or took down an ashdrake, then that would mean an entire herd of thunder elk...

"*Hang on, Anni!*" yelled Jarabei as the forest tore itself asunder. "*It's a stampede!*"

The tree line exploded with thunder and lighting, like a river bursting through a dam. A herd of hundreds of furious black thunder elk tore out of the forest, spurred on by the storm they, themselves, had created.

Bolts of lightning struck down from the heavens and passed from one elk to the next. Each footfall brought with it a huge clap of deafening thunder.

The brynywyn had drawn their secret weapon. When charging at a full gallop, a herd of thunder elk moved with the force of a hurricane.

348

THE CLOUDBURST

The stampede collided with the horde square in the center, and the gloknore were completely overrun by the power and sheer number of the magical beasts. Lightning struck the antlers, trees, and soldiers alike. Gusts of wind tore tents to shreds. The thunder, darkness, and rain caused confusion among the ill-prepared invaders.

The furious thunder elk were all around them. The sound was deafening and the flashes of lightning so bright, all Anni could do was cover her face and ears with her arms and wait for the onslaught to end.

Anni had known the thunder elk had magic, but she had never imagined anything like this.

The cart gave a sudden shift, as if one of the elk had struck it with such force that one of its wheels left the ground for a moment, but thankfully, it didn't tip over.

After what seemed like hours, the ringing in Anni's ears subsided, and the flashes slowly dissipated.

Anni opened her eyes.

The herd had kicked up so much water vapor from their storm that it covered the land in a thick mist, and Anni couldn't see much of the battlefield.

As the fog cleared, Anni could see that little was left.

Tents had been ripped to shreds, campfires trampled, and the bodies of gloknore were everywhere, trampled, burned—*annihilated* by the stampede.

THE BLUE HAIRED GIRL

A few stragglers still remained in the destroyed encampment. The males bucked their heads left and right, jolting the warriors that remained. The females let out claps of thunder, stunning any that stood before them and trampling those that dared to stand up to them.

The commander himself had somehow survived the onslaught. It must have been half his warriors that had been wiped out by the brynywyn's stampede. He looked murderous.

Anni noticed his large tent was gone.

As the elk herd approached the city gates, the stampede seemed to lose its power. They slowed down from a gallop to a canter and began scattering into small, clustering groups.

The magical storm they had conjured dissipated as the stampede came to an end. The clouds broke up, and the rain stopped.

But the damage was done. The brynywyn had landed a lucky blow—a sucker punch to the eye of the horde, leaving them shattered.

There came another blow of the musician's horn, and the vegetable-cart-turned-war-chariot faced the destroyed remains of the camp.

Standing as tall as his tiny form would allow, Jarabei held the silver spear high over his head.

"Charge!" he screamed at the top of his lungs, the spear and blue flag slicing through the air. The cart's driver gave a whip

350

THE CLOUDBURST

of the reins, and the pony pulled the cart into the camp at a full gallop, like a distant echo of the thunder elk stampede.

Anni saw some movement at the tree line. Bursting out of the forest behind them were the brynywyn militia, waving their simple weapons with all the fury that the little folk could muster.

Guarding both the left and right flanks of their little army were several dozen or so brynywyn cavalry. They didn't ride ponies, or even thunder elk. Instead, these warriors rode upon rams. Large, big-horned sheep, with each rider carrying a long, wooden spear and shield. With a whistle and click of their mouths, the cavaliers took off after the herd, presumably to rally it again for another charge.

It was truly a sight to behold—an army of tiny, child-sized brynywyn folk being led by a bartender astride a vegetable cart, flanked by big-horned sheep cavalry, with the fading flashes of thunder and lightning cheering them on.

Although they were small, they had played their hand well, and had given themselves a much-needed advantage.

With a final blow of the musician's horn, the brynywyn reached the camp.

The battle had begun.

- CHAPTER 30 -
The Battle for Yuspiereia

The war cart tore through the remains of the camp at a full gallop, Jarabei thrusting his spear left and right. The musician had dropped his horn and was waving a wooden club as the wagon's driver concentrated on controlling the frightened pony that drew the wagon through the camp.

Anni, having no weapon and being too rattled to try her powers, could think of nothing else to do but hold on and try to keep low in the wagon to avoid injury.

Suddenly, a gloknore warrior was thrown across the muddy ground right in front of their wagon, a broken antler jammed into his chest and a barking elk bucking after him.

The pony pulling the wagon panicked. The ground

THE BATTLE FOR YUSPIEREIA

under its hooves was turned up and slick from the thunder elk's stampede, causing the animal to stumble. The pony was unable to regain its footing and collapsed. The cart behind it, pressed on by its own inertia, kept going forward and crushed the poor animal.

Anni was hurled off the wagon, along with Jarabei, the musician, and the driver.

She tasted mud as she landed face first in the wet, turned-up ground.

Anni spat the dirt from her mouth and wiped her eyes as best she could with her filthy sleeve.

The wagon was ruined, its axle snapped by the force of the crash. The pony was dead; its back had been broken by the weight of the out-of-control cart.

Jarabei and the musician, however, were alive and helping the injured driver off the remains of the cart; he appeared to have a broken leg. The musician gave his horn a blow as they moved the driver off the remains of the wagon. Once again, even among all the chaos of the battle, Anni was sure she heard the sound of a horn echoing the first.

Anni looked around her. The storm clouds had gone, and the weather had returned to its normal warm summer day. There were several gloknore bodies around her, and even now, long after the storm had passed, she still heard distant claps of thunder and flashes of light as the gloknore continued to battle

THE BLUE HAIRED GIRL

with the elk stragglers.

Moments later, a brynywyn cavalier emerged from nowhere, his big-horned sheep bleating with enthusiasm. He hopped off his mount and helped Jarabei and the musician lift the wounded driver on to the animal's back.

The brynywyn cavalier chattered something to the ram in a language Anni didn't understand. The animal took off with the injured brynywyn in the direction of the forest, leaving his rider behind.

"Where's he taking him?" asked Anni, looking around furiously for danger.

"Back to camp, in the forest," said the musician. "They'll take care of him."

Before Anni could even think what to do next, the eyes of the brynywyn cavalier fell on Anni's muddy, but still very blue hair.

"Et a quoi! Et a quoi!!" he shouted, pointing at her head, still speaking in a language she didn't understand.

"What?" she asked.

He pointed to his own hair with one hand and to Anni's with his other.

About fifty feet away, Anni saw a pair of gloknore warriors, and one of them pointed toward her with his sword as they broke into a run.

"Quoi! Quoi!" shouted Jarabei. "Yes, it's blue! Now, come

354

THE BATTLE FOR YUSPIEREIA

on!"

Jarabei picked his silver spear out of the muddy ground and led the charge toward the advancing group of gloknore.

The musician held his club high over his head and the cavalier drew a hunting knife from his belt and wielded it like a sword.

Off to her left, Anni spied a dead gloknore nearby with a sword in his hand. The warrior had been burned and trampled by the stampede.

Taking care not to look at the corpse, Anni reached down and pulled the sword out of his hand.

It was extremely heavy, and she could hardly lift it, but she needed a weapon, nonetheless.

As she pulled it out of the corpse's clawed hand, she saw the brynywyn reach the gloknore.

Jarabei thrust his spear at the throat of the nearest; the blow glanced off his armor, but the warrior staggered, all the same.

The musician and the cavalier leaped on the other like lions attacking an elephant. The musician grabbed him by the back and beat him with his club, while the cavalier stabbed at him from below.

Anni, not able to think of anything else to do, lifted the sword to join them. The blade was so heavy and awkward, she couldn't lift it above her waist. The gloknore, it seemed, were

355

THE BLUE HAIRED GIRL

every bit as strong as they appeared.

The one that Jarabei had hit with the spear was gathering himself now.

Anni hurried awkwardly toward him, wielding the heavy blade as best she could.

One look at Anni's blue hair, and the gloknore made a grab for her.

Anni felt the blade being wrenched out of her grasp and an arm start to lift her off the ground.

Before her feet left the mud, the gloknore dropped to the ground, dead.

There was a long, silver spear in his back where Jarabei had thrust it.

The other two brynywyn had felled their foe as well.

"We'll find you a better weapon," said Jarabei, looking at the sword Anni could hardly lift.

Behind a half-destroyed tent, a second group of gloknore had spotted them. Anni's hair was acting like a beacon, drawing attention to them. There must have been closer to ten in this group, far too many for them to fight.

Within moments, they were surrounded. Dozens of swords and arrows were pointing down at Anni and the brynywyn.

Jarabei and his two men took positions around Anni, with spear, knife, and club defending her from all sides.

356

THE BATTLE FOR YUSPIEREIA

"Give us the girl," hissed one of the gloknore.

"Never!" shouted Jarabei, as he thrust his spear forward threateningly to drive them back.

"Then you die," said the gloknore simply, as a few dozen more gloknore appeared around them, with several brynywyn prisoners in tow.

It seemed that, since the stampede had dissipated, the gloknore had rallied their forces. They had been badly crippled by the thunder elk, but they were still the superior fighting force.

The horde had taken the brynywyn's strongest blow and come up standing. The brynywyn folk might have had heart, but they simply didn't have the numbers to defeat the horde.

The gloknore began to advance on the trio of Anni's defenders.

"It's okay, I-I'll go with them."

"The hell you will!" snapped Jarabei in an uncharacteristically sharp tone.

"I was going to go with them anyway."

"Anni, we didn't come all the way out here to lose you now."

"If I go with you," said Anni, ignoring Jarabei's protests, "will you let them go?"

The nearest gloknore sneered but nodded.

"You're *not* going with them!"

"Look around," said Anni. "It's over."

THE BLUE HAIRED GIRL

It was true. The sun was setting over the battlefield, as if even the sun itself knew the gloknore had won the day. The lightning flashes and claps of thunder that had so demolished the gloknore had vanished. The herd had probably scattered, much of their magic spent. The sounds of battle had been replaced with the barking of orders and the distant rattling of chains. Another group of gloknore warriors passed nearby, marching a group of brynywyn toward them. Each had been relieved of their weapons and had their hands on their heads in surrender.

Despite their initial success, the battle had been short-lived. The brynywyn had relied too heavily upon the stampede to destroy the gloknore's forces. Without the powerful thunder elk, the small and lightly armed brynywyn militia were simply outmatched by the battle-hardened gloknore horde.

"Anni, you can't!" said Jarabei.

"Do you have any better ideas?!"

"I'm thinking! I'm thinking!"

Anni sighed and pressed her way out from between Jarabei and her other defenders and approached the nearest gloknore.

"Remember, if I go with you, you need to let them go."

The gloknore warrior said nothing, his eyes only resting on her hair.

"You can take me to Blegor. I won't put up a fight."

One of the gloknore stepped toward her with a pair of

358

metal shackles

Suddenly, there was a distant sound on the air.

It wasn't the thunder elk, but it was coming from the direction of the city.

The gates of Yuspiereia city had opened.

A blast of purple light from the direction of the capital told Anni what must have been happening.

It seemed the gods had given the brynywyn a reprieve for their bravery.

Pouring out of the city gates were men and women, soldiers and civilians alike, charging straight at the gloknore horde.

Leading them at the front was a woman clad in yellow and orange armor, riding through the air on a magic staff like a witch astride a broom.

Valentia grasped the handle of her magic staff with one hand and held a bloody sword in the other, pointing straight at the horde.

"For Freeeeedooooommm!"

The thunder elk were a force to be reckoned with when roused, but they were nothing compared to the greatest weapon that the High Council had drawn against the invaders.

The people of Yuspiereia.

Following the chairwoman looked like the entire population of the city. It seemed everyone had answered the High

THE BLUE HAIRED GIRL

Council's call to put an end to Stonor's coup. They bore down on the horde, making one final push to restore their precious freedom. Even at this distance, there were many faces that Anni recognized.

Kayell the guard had a bandage over his head but led his men at full charge. Ackleman was wearing elaborate plate armor with a purple lion emblazoned on the chest and carrying a crossbow.

There were faces that Anni knew from the marketplace as well. The sweaty, fat man from the meat stand was waving a meat cleaver, the full-bodied prostitute wielded a whip, the tailor held a pair of cloth sheers, and the elf woman was astride a unicorn, with a whole menagerie of creatures at her heels that had come to join the battle.

The brynywyn prisoners had seized on their chance to strike back at the horde that was rounding them up. They struck, bit, scratched, and tackled the gloknore nearest to them and throttled them with their own chains.

The invaders were trapped between the Yuspiereian soldiers on one side and brynywyn militia on the other; even a few thunder elk remained in the fray. A handful of cavaliers who had refused to surrender weaved every which way, their steeds ramming headlong into the foes, while the riders stabbed with their wooden spears.

Jarabei swung and thrust his silver spear into every foe he

THE BATTLE FOR YUSPIEREIA

could reach with it, but always staying at arm's length to Anni.

Valentia threw one magical blast after another from her vantage point upon her staff above the fray, killing anyone who stood in her way. Ackleman let loose bolt after bolt from his repeating crossbow.

Chaos reigned everywhere as the Yuspiereian guard, High Council, and civilians reached the camp.

Spears, swords, arrows, stones, magic, and bolts of lightning flew through the air alongside the shouts and battle cries across the battlefield.

Everywhere Anni looked, the battle seemed to be turning. The brynywyn had rallied when help arrived. Anni saw a pair of brynywyn prisoners on a gloknore's back, strangling him with a pair of chains. A woman wearing High Council robes had mounted a female thunder elk, and she led a group of supporters after a group of fleeing gloknore. A team of brynywyn cavaliers had somehow taken control of the elf woman's battle boar and had managed to steer it toward any that stood in their way, using the beast's ferocity and sheer size to lay waste to nearby enemies.

The horde broke ranks and fled. Some headed into the forest; a few scattered toward the beach; others limped every which way—and all of them were terrified.

Just as it was looking as if they had won the day, Anni saw something out of the corner of her eye.

It was the only person Anni hadn't seen since the battle

361

THE BLUE HAIRED GIRL

began.

How it had happened, Anni had no idea.

Kolten had found himself locked in hand-to-hand combat with the gloknore commander himself. How he had survived the onslaught of the thunder elk and the Yuspiereian counterattack, Anni could not begin to guess.

Kolten and the commander were wrestling on the ground, both of their faces bloody, fighting with their bare hands, their weapons nowhere to be seen.

The commander was easily twice Kolten's size, if not more, but Kolten's strong dwarven limbs made him a formidable opponent.

The commander was lying on top of Kolten. One of his hands was under the dwarf's beard, wrapped tightly around his throat.

Kolten started to twitch as his face turned blue.

Anni didn't know what to do. Her greatest friend was dying right before her eyes.

She felt a sudden pulse from the delicate, white bracelets that hung on her wrists.

There was only one thing Anni could think of doing. She shoved Jarabei out of the way and slipped her fingers under each bracelet, taking a firm grasp of each one as she ran at the commander.

Anni charged with a determination she had felt only

362

THE BATTLE FOR YUSPIEREIA

once before. An eternity ago, when looking down at a wretched black raven in a gypsy wagon.

Time seemed to slow as Anni collided into the gloknore commander. With a great, jerking pull, she snapped off the delicate lightwrists, unleashing her magic.

A massive explosion echoed across the battlefield, and then silence.

- CHAPTER 31 -
The Coward

Anni landed on the ground in a heap, dazed from the force of the explosion.

She must have been thrown thirty feet, and her hair had been badly burned by the out-of-control magic.

As Anni forced herself to her sit up, she saw around her, the battle was well and truly over. The gloknore that remained had either been killed or surrendered, and the Yuspiereian forces were rounding them up.

Sitting next to Anni was the gloknore commander's leg, and that was all. Pieces of him were everywhere; he had been completely destroyed by the force of Anni's magic.

But that means that— thought Anni as she looked

364

THE COWARD

around for her best friend.

Sitting about forty feet away was the hunched-over form of Kolten. His back was to her, and he was hurt, but miraculously, somehow, he had survived.

"Kolten!" she shouted as she forced herself to her feet.

"Over there!" shouted Ackleman, as he emerged from the battle and pointed off toward the forest. "He's getting away!"

Anni turned to see the frightened form of Geldman Stonor. The man had mounted a stray horse and was racing toward the forest at a full gallop.

A single black thunder elk with a pair of glowing antlers emerged from the chaos and raced toward Anni.

The elk knelt down beside Anni, allowing her to mount him as he nodded toward the fleeing man on the horse. How Anni's elk had found her among all the chaos, Anni had no idea, but none of that mattered now.

"But I can't...Kolten..." Anni said to the elk.

"I'm fine!" shouted Kolten over his shoulder, his back still to her. "Don't let that bastard get away!"

Ackleman had reached the dwarf and was helping him to his feet.

Anni looked back toward the forest, and with each passing moment, Stonor was getting farther away.

Anni clambered up on the elk, bareback.

"Anni!" shouted Jarabei. "Catch!"

365

THE BLUE HAIRED GIRL

The brynywyn tossed the long, silver spear to her.

Anni caught it, and with a gentle kick, she and her elk raced after him.

Stonor would have had to be a fool not to realize that the battle was over and his side had lost. The only choice left for the cowardly old man was to flee and to abandon his supporters to face the wrath of the High Council, to save his own worthless hide.

As she pursued him, thoughts of all the man had done flashed through Anni's mind. The people of Yuspiereia had been robbed, killed, raped, and had all manner of other terrible things done to them on Stonor's orders. A city pillaged and burning, a country invaded, countless innocent people dead and dying. All of that suffering had been caused just over this man's lust for power.

You will pay for this, thought Anni as Stonor's horse disappeared into the tree line.

Without a saddle, it was difficult for her to keep her balance and hold the spear at once, but her elk seemed to sense it and adjusted his stride accordingly.

As the battlefield vanished behind her, the sky was swallowed up by the forest canopy. Anni knew Stonor would never get far. He wouldn't dare use the roads, as half the country would be looking for him, and his horse would tire out soon.

As the minutes yielded into hours, night fell over the

THE COWARD

land, but Anni carried on with her pursuit. Her thunder elk moved through the forest with ease. The underbrush was where the thunder elk were in their element; no horse could outrun them on this kind of terrain.

Anni wasn't much of a hunter, but his trail was so clear that a blind man could have tracked Stonor. Hoof prints, horse feces, and even the odd piece of Stonor's clothing laid the trail behind him, and the thunder elk's excellent sense of direction made following him easy. It seemed he was more concerned with putting space between him and the capital, and he wasn't concerned about being followed.

With a shake of her elk's head, the foliage parted, and they found themselves at the top of a familiar, high ridge overlooking a barren, blackened valley.

Standing over a collapsed horse nearly dead from exhaustion, at the very edge of the ridge, was the scowling form of Stonor.

"It's over, Stonor," said Anni.

"I should have killed you in the forest! You blue-haired bitch!" he spat.

"You probably should have," agreed Anni as her elk barked in agreement. "You're coming with us."

"If I go with you, they'll hang me."

"Probably," Anni said.

"I—I can pay you!" he pleaded. "If you just tell them you

THE BLUE HAIRED GIRL

couldn't find me. I—I'll make you rich!"

There was a bolt of lightning from Anni's elk, and it struck the ground before him.

"You're coming with us."

Stonor drew his sword, but with a quick bolt of the elk's lightning, he dropped it.

The man took a step back, toward the ridge.

"Stonor, you're coming with—"

But it was too late. Stonor leaped off the ridge and half stumbled down the hillside into the valley below.

Anni sighed and patted her elk on the neck.

"Let's go get him before he gets himself killed."

Her elk snorted his derision, but he obeyed.

As they reached the floor of the valley, surround by the all-too-familiar blackened dirt, it didn't take long for the rumbling to start.

The ground shook, and soon, spires of flame were shooting up into the air all around them.

It seemed easier to avoid the flame spires while maneuvering over the valley floor this time around. It might have been Anni's elk was getting better at seeing them, or they might have been in a better part of the valley. In either case, Anni's steed moved with much more confidence than he had the last time they entered the valley.

Stonor was running as fast as he could across the valley

THE COWARD

floor, but even on horseback, he couldn't have outrun Anni's elk. He had no chance on foot.

There was a loud rumble, and the valley floor ripped itself open, splitting at the seams as it had several days earlier.

An ugly, black, six-legged ashdrake forced its way out of the valley floor. Several jets of flame erupted from its back. Stonor's escape was cut off; he was trapped between the ashdrake on one side and Anni on the other.

The smell of sulfur filled Anni's nostrils as the beast opened its mouth to devour Stonor.

Anni suddenly felt a strange warmness in her hand as the spear began to glow with power. Without her lightwrists tempering her magic, her powers were at full strength.

Stonor had turned around on the spot and run straight back toward Anni and away from the ashdrake that was bearing down upon him.

Remembering what Jarabei had told her a lifetime ago, and the song that the brynywyn would sing in their pub, Anni lifted the silver spear and concentrated on the ashdrake's center eye.

With her powers guiding the blade, she hurled it through the air with all her might.

It sailed through the air, straight at ashdrake's largest eye.

"Now!" shouted Anni.

Her elk let out the greatest bolt of lightning he had ever

THE BLUE HAIRED GIRL

mustered.

The bolt struck the spear's shaft just as it pierced the surface of the beast's center eye.

The ashdrake let out a roar of rage and convulsed violently. Flames shot out of his back erratically; every limb twitched as the lightning reached the monster's brain.

Then, after a moment or two of convulsing, the beast moved no more.

Anni's thunder elk let out a bark of fury, as if to taunt his defeated enemy, as they rounded on Stonor.

At first, Anni thought he had gotten away, as he was not immediately visible, but as the dust settled, Anni saw he was lying on the ground a short distance away.

Anni climbed off her elk and looked down at the man.

Yeah, he's breathing, she thought, slightly disappointed at seeing his chest rising and falling gently.

Oddly enough, there was not a scratch on him.

Anni patted her elk affectionately, a half-smile on her face.

Stonor had fainted.

- CHAPTER 32 -
The Brynywyn's Secret

Anni opened her eyes and found herself lying in a warm, comfortable bed. She was instantly reminded of the safe houses. But this was not like any safe house Anni had ever visited. It wasn't underground; it was far too bright.

Light poured in from an open window and bathed the room in the light of a warm summer morning.

Anni sat up in her bed and found herself in a white-painted room with long curtains hanging by the head of her bed. Her clothes had been neatly folded and stacked on the floor.

Anni's hands showed signs of minor burns, and they stung a little, but the pain was little more than a minor annoyance.

THE BLUE HAIRED GIRL

Her wrists had been fitted with a fresh pair of ivory-colored lightwrists, since she had broken off her old pair.

Anni climbed out of bed and approached the window.

She was standing in a high tower, looking down at the Yuspiereian capital. The morning sun lit the whole city, and she saw signs of life returning to it below.

From her vantage point, Anni could see down into the Yuspiereian marketplace, and though it looked smaller than it had before, there were undoubtedly shops opening up again for their morning business.

There was no sign of the brynywyn, the thunder elk, or the horde.

"Oh, you're awake?" said a voice.

There was a woman in the room with her. She wore a white apron and had a white headband on her head, with a reflective metal disk on her forehead.

"Where's Kolten?" asked Anni, suddenly remembering why she had removed her lightwrists—which, in retrospect, was probably not the smartest decision.

"He's alive," she said simply. "Now, back to bed."

"I want to see him!" snapped Anni.

"Not right now. He needs rest, and so do you."

"But I—"

"Bed, now," snapped the woman, pointing Anni back to her bed. "I need to examine you."

372

THE BRYNYWYN'S SECRET

Anni begrudgingly returned to her bed and allowed the woman to examine her.

The doctor checked Anni's pulse, and she placed one end of a long, stick-like object against Anni's chest. She placed the other end in her ear.

"Good, good, very good."

"Where's Kolten?"

"He's in another part of the hospital; his injuries were a lot worse than yours."

Anni neither knew nor cared what a hospital was.

"Where is he?"

"I've already told you," she said. "He's being looked after."

Anni was about to protest, when the door opened.

Standing in the doorway was a tall man with a very gentle face.

"Hello, Anni," said Ackleman brightly. "How are you feeling?"

"Where's Kolten?"

"She won't stop asking about him," said the doctor.

"I'll take you to see him as soon as I can, Anni. I promise. He'll be fine," he added when he saw she was about to protest.

"What happened to rest of the gloknore, and all the brynywyn?"

THE BLUE HAIRED GIRL

"The gloknore army fled into the woods once their commander was killed. Kayell and his men are rounding them all up. As for the brynywyn, most of them survived the battle. We've moved most of the wounded to the hospital."

"Awake, is she?" asked a familiar voice.

It was Jarabei, and he wasn't alone.

Standing beside him was his nephew, Tycron.

"You're alive!"

Jarabei had to climb up on to Anni's bed in order to hug her, as did Tycron.

"Takes more than a few uglies to kill us," said Tycron.

"Where's Stonor?" asked Anni.

"A prison cell," said Ackleman lazily. "Where he belongs."

They chatted for a while about the battle and the thunder elk, until Ackleman cleared his throat. "You know, I have a question," said Ackleman, looking at Jarabei. "Why did you come?"

Jarabei stared at him, looking a little indignant.

"Don't get me wrong," said Ackleman quickly, "I'm glad you did; you saved all our lives. But why? From what I've heard, you only just met Anni. Why would you all risk your lives for her?"

"I'm surprised they didn't tell you," Tycron said, looking at Ackleman.

THE BRYNYWYN'S SECRET

"Who?" asked Ackleman.

"The Republic of Zoltan," said Jarabei.

"What's the Republic got to do with any of this?" asked Anni.

Jarabei hesitated, and then nodded to his nephew.

"Anni, we haven't been entirely honest with you," said Tycron.

"What do you mean?"

"Anni, a few years ago, a man from Zoltan came into our village," said Jarabei. "He said that the Republic was looking to build an elected council for Yuspiereia. The man said to us they were looking for friends in the Southern Continent that would help support a democratic government."

"That does sound like something the Senate would do," Ackleman beamed.

"The man told us that if the High Council ever needed our help, we should help them, and if we did, the Senate would be in our debt," said Tycron.

"And when a country as good and as powerful as Zoltan asks for a favor, you don't refuse." Jarabei smiled broadly.

"The Senate knew the power of the thunder elk," said Tycron with a hint of pride. "So, we were the Republic's secret weapon."

"Then, a few weeks ago, the blue-haired girl with the bounty on her head showed up at our village," explained Tycron.

375

THE BLUE HAIRED GIRL

"We knew you were going to the capital, and then a huge horde of gloknore warriors was tearing up the countryside, heading that way too."

"Then this arrived at our village," said Jarabei.

Jarabei smiled as he reached into his pocket and pulled out a flask. Anni was about to ask what he meant, when he pulled a second object out of his pocket. It seemed the flask had only been in the way.

Sitting on the brynywyn leader's open palm was a tuft of sky-blue hair from Anni's own head.

Anni touched the place on her head where Stonor's thugs had cut it.

It was all too clear what had happened. When her thunder elk had realized that Stonor's men weren't going to let her go, he must have grabbed the blue hair off the floor in his mouth and headed for the brynywyn village. When Jarabei had seen it, he had known she was in trouble.

The thunder elk continued to impress.

"When Tempest arrived at our village, he was so upset that he nearly set fire to my pub," said Jarabei. "Wasn't hard to figure out what must have been happening."

"When who arrived?" asked Anni.

"Tempest, your elk," replied Tycron. "Didn't I tell you his name?"

Anni shook her head.

376

THE BRYNYWYN'S SECRET

"I wonder why the Senate didn't tell me about this?" asked Ackleman thoughtfully. "Overseeing the new government is why I'm here."

"It was for security reasons," said Tycron. "Only the chairwoman knew about us. If Stonor had found out, he would have destroyed our village long ago."

Anni thought back to when she had awoken in the safe house. Valentia hadn't said much about the brynywyn when Anni had thought of calling them, but she probably hadn't wanted to breach security.

"So, should you really be telling us about all this?" asked Ackleman slowly.

"No point in trying to keep the secret anymore; the whole world knows whose side we're on now," said Jarabei.

"Why didn't you tell me this? I can keep a secret," said Anni quickly to the two brynywyn sitting on her bed. "Me and Kolten were in your pub all night, and you didn't say anything about you having connections with Zoltan."

Jarabei smiled.

"Security, Anni. We were planning on bringing you to the capital ourselves, but those men showed up in the pub before we got the chance. There was a *big* debate about that in the pub that night, after Tycron found you. But, at first, we weren't sure if you were the girl Blegor was after."

"I wonder why Blegor was after me?" asked Anni, though

THE BLUE HAIRED GIRL

she was certain no one present knew the answer.

"Why Blegor is *still* after you," corrected Ackleman. "He's doubled the reward for the blue-haired girl since the battle ended."

There was a brief silence, with Anni looking annoyed.

"We're trying to find out what he wants with you," said Ackleman at the look of mild frustration on Anni's face as she learned that the reason for Blegor's interest would likely have to remain a mystery for the time being.

"You feeling up to getting out of here for a while?" asked Ackleman kindly.

The doctor threw him a cold look.

"She'll be fine," said Ackleman in a reassuring tone. "We'll bring her right back. She probably wants to see Kolten."

"*Yes!*" shouted Anni, climbing out of bed.

"The dwarf is in intensive care," said the doctor sharply. "You won't be able to visit him."

"We know," said Ackleman. "I just came from there. You won't be able to speak to him; he's unconscious. But you can *see* him."

"I want to!" said Anni. "*She* said I couldn't go!"

The doctor ignored this obvious insult and busied herself with one of the other beds.

"Let's go!" shouted Anni, already leading them toward the door. She stopped when she saw that Ackleman and the

THE BRYNYWYN'S SECRET

brynywyn hadn't moved.

"Anni, you do know what happened to him, don't you?"

"He's alive, right?!"

"Yes, Anni, but—"

"Then I don't care; I want to see him!"

"Anni, are you sure—"

"Yes!"

Ackleman and Jarabei exchanged cold looks, and Tycron stared uncomfortably out the window.

"All right, Anni," said Ackleman calmly. "If you're sure you're ready for this."

"Come on! Where is he?!"

Ackleman led the way out of the hospital room and down a long hallway, with Anni and the brynywyn at his side.

There seemed to be something wrong. There was clearly something that neither Ackleman nor the brynywyn seemed to know how to tell her.

Finally, they reached a large glass window in one of the hallway walls. The brynywyn were both too short to see over it, but they made no complaint. Anni, however, was tall enough so her chin touched the bottom of the windowsill.

Lying on one of the beds and sleeping peacefully was the bearded face and birdlike nose of Kolten the dwarf. His face was heavily bruised, and his beard had been cut short.

Anni's hand covered her mouth in shock as she saw

379

THE BLUE HAIRED GIRL

Kolten's left arm. All that remained of the dwarf's hand was a white-bandaged stump at the end of his wrist. The darkwrist was nowhere to be seen.

It seemed that Anni's magical explosion and proximity to the dwarf's malfunctioning darkwrist had finally broken the spell. The sheer force of Anni's out-of-control magic had destroyed the last remaining bracelet, and the dwarf's hand along with it.

Kolten Citrane was free of the darkwrists at last.

- CHAPTER 33 -
The Skystag

Anni sat in her room in the inn, sitting under the window with an open book in front of her. Her private tutor had left her with a new assignment only minutes before.

There was a series of letters written in the book that she needed to work with before their next lesson.

In the book was a series of pictures with words written under them; each word had its first letter underlined.

"L...is for lion," she said to herself. *"L-l-l-l...lion."* Anni had been working on her letters for almost a week now, and she still didn't have them all memorized yet. It was hard—there were dozens of them, and they were hard to remember. Anni had gotten very frustrated with her tutor yesterday when they started talking about the difference between the letters "C" and "K."

381

THE BLUE HAIRED GIRL

Anni was still quite convinced there was no difference between them.

It was made worse because she suspected the book she was learning from was made for babies. The drawings in it all looked cute and cuddly, even though some of them were of ferocious beasts like lions and dragons.

Over the years, Kolten had tried to teach Anni how to read and write, but it was impossible because, as long as Anni had been with her mistress, Mareitsia had never owned any books. In fact, Anni wasn't entirely sure that Mareitsia even knew how to read, herself. There was only so far they had been able to get drawing letters in the dirt and trying to spell them out loud after Mareitsia had passed out; as kind as Kolten was, he wasn't much of a teacher.

But as hard as reading was, Anni found writing the letters was downright infuriating. She had always known that when someone read or wrote something, they went across the page from left to right.

This had never mattered, as she had never used a quill before. But once she tried, she noticed that her writing tended to smear as she dragged her hand left to right across the letters she had just written.

It seemed that Anni was left-handed.

She had always known that she preferred to use her left hand, but it had never made a difference before, as most of her

THE SKYSTAG

life she had only needed to build fires, clean the wagon, and cook meals; Kolten had always done everything that involved using serious tools.

When it came to writing, though, the hand she used seemed to matter a great deal. Every time she finished writing out a few letters, the edge of her hand would be covered in ink that was hard to wash off, and the letters she had written would be smudged across the page.

Although her tutor always insisted that she was doing well, Anni couldn't help but feel stupid trying to learn from a book that was written for toddlers, and she couldn't even write a few letters without messing up the whole page.

Reading was hard, and writing was harder.

Kolten still hadn't left the hospital yet. Ackleman had since explained to Anni that a hospital was a place where healers cared for people who were sick or hurt. Given how badly Kolten had been injured, it was probably a good place for him to be.

Anni had gone to visit him every day, but he still hadn't woken up yet. The healers had given him a powerful sleeping potion so he could rest until his wound healed enough to make the pain bearable.

Anni had no idea what she would say to Kolten. It was her fault he had lost his hand. If she hadn't removed her lightwrists, he wouldn't have gotten hurt. As tough as Kolten was, even he couldn't regrow limbs. Would he ever forgive her? How

383

THE BLUE HAIRED GIRL

could Anni even hope to explain to him that she had been trying to help him, and that it was all a mistake?

There was a knock at the door.

Anni pressed her books aside and opened the door.

It was Ackleman.

"How's the studying going?"

Anni wanted to say, "Fine," but it would have been a lie.

Ackleman seemed to read the look on her face, and he smiled.

"It will get easier."

"It's hard."

"I know it is. You feel like taking a break?"

Anni nodded, looking forward to getting away from her books for a while.

"But my hair…"

"Anni, you saved the whole country; no one is going to bother you. Come on."

Anni put on her new shoes, left her hair uncovered for a change, and followed Ackleman out of the inn.

Soon, she and Ackleman reached the marketplace. It was still buzzing with activity, though it was far less busy than it had been before Stonor's insurrection, and it was filled with a somber mood. Many of the stalls were empty or closed, having been destroyed or pillaged by Stonor's thugs. Still, the place showed clear signs of returning to normal.

384

THE SKYSTAG

There were the sounds of bartering and haggling all around them, and the occasional sound of arguing. As Anni walked through the stalls with Ackleman at her side, many people glanced down at her hair, but no one bothered her. In fact, a few people actually thanked her for what she had done for them. It seemed no one was interested in the reward for her capture; at least, not at the moment.

Soon, the sound of music reached Anni's ears. She recognized the sound of the instrument, as they had heard it days before. However, the music was different...more lonely, slower, and much more melancholy. When they rounded a corner, Anni could see why. The once-proud musical group now had only a single member remaining. Only the older woman with the dented, metal, bowl-like instrument was sitting in their stall.

The guitar and pair of flutes lay on the ground untouched, surrounded by fresh-cut flowers honoring their lost owners, as the woman sang a sad-sounding tune in a foreign language.

The tailor's tent was closed, and his assistant, the young human girl, was cleaning the place up as best she could. Her face showed signs of having cried recently, and the tailor himself was nowhere to be found.

The brothel had been closed and was entirely empty; where the prostitutes were, Anni couldn't begin to guess.

The smell of cooking meat filled Anni's nostrils. The

THE BLUE HAIRED GIRL

sweaty, fat man that Anni had seen join Yuspiereia's final push stood before his grill, looking very lonely.

The man turned to Anni as she and Ackleman walked by and offered Anni another free taste; he was crying.

"You lost someone?" asked Ackleman quietly.

The man nodded. "My son," he sniffed.

Ackleman patted the fat man on the shoulder consolingly. Anni couldn't help herself; she reached out and gave him a hug, which the man returned gratefully. She even bought one of his pieces of meat on a stick, using some money Ackleman had given her, and she paid the man more then he asked for.

Soon, they reached the edge of the marketplace, and Ackleman gestured for Anni to follow him. They walked through the capital, and saw the fires had been put out, but much of the city had been destroyed by the fighting.

Anni was going to ask where they were going, when they reached the city's main gate, and Ackleman led out into the field surrounding the city.

The battlefield had been cleared of bodies, and most of the tents and half-built siege weapons had been hauled off, presumably to be destroyed. The only sign of the battle that had transpired was the turned-up ground caused by the thunder elk's charge.

Near the tree line, the herd of thunder elk ate grass under the watchful eye of the brynywyn masters.

THE SKYSTAG

Anni and Ackleman walked toward the herd, and she could see most of the brynywyn were huddled together in a tight-knit group by the tree line. Only the cavaliers on their rams were away from the huddle as they kept the thunder elk in check.

Tycron and Jarabei stood at the edge of the huddle, and like everyone else in the city, they had sad looks on their faces.

As Anni approached, she saw why.

Lying on the vegetable cart were several tiny bodies. The brynywyn had suffered some casualties of their own. Close to ten little bodies filled the vegetable cart.

Anni's hand darted to her mouth as she saw the lifeless face of the white-mustached Sheppard. It was the old brynywyn guard who had stopped her and Kolten at the gate of the brynywyn village after they first escaped from Mareitsia. His tunic had a puncture hole in it about the size of an arrow, right where his heart was. His mustache had been neatly combed, and his eyes had been pulled shut, as if he were still asleep at his post.

"Is this really what victory looks like?" sniffed Anni, looking down at Sheppard.

Ackleman shook his head. "No, this is the price of freedom."

Jarabei raised his tankard, as did the other brynywyn, as they toasted the deaths of their friends.

"My friends," said Jarabei. "Today, we say goodbye to the bravest of us all: those who gave their lives to defend their

THE BLUE HAIRED GIRL

brothers and sisters and safeguard the freedom of this land."

Jarabei recited the names of each and every brynywyn that had not survived the battle, and he spoke with a strong yet doleful voice. Anni guessed that Jarabei knew each and every one of the dead brynywyn personally, because he recited their names from memory.

They gave one final, tear-filled rendition of their song about the brynywyn and the drake. With a whip of the reins, the repaired vegetable cart and its new pony began to move into the forest with a contingent of armed brynywyn honor guards escorting it back to their village, where they could bury their fallen comrades.

"I'm sorry for your loss," said Ackleman, looking down at Jarabei.

Jarabei nodded. "When we get home, we will have a formal goodbye at the Silver Spear. You're both welcome."

"We can't. We have duties here," said Ackleman. "And so do you."

Jarabei looked up at Ackleman curiously.

Ackleman produced a piece of parchment from his pocket and handed it to Jarabei.

"The High Council wants to meet with you before you leave."

Jarabei read the letter and nodded up at Ackleman.

"There is one more thing," said Jarabei, turning to Anni.

THE SKYSTAG

"What?"

"There's someone that I would like you to meet."

"Who?"

"You'll never believe it unless you see it."

Jarabei tapped one of the brynywyn that Anni didn't know on the shoulder and the man shouted something in a foreign language.

"It's the hill-folk," said Jarabei. "They don't speak the common tongue."

One of the brynywyn riding on his ram came to them. His ram let out a bleat of welcome. The brynywyn rider gestured for them to follow him.

"The hill-folk aren't from our village. They live in the mountains, but no one herds the thunder elk better than they do," Jarabei explained as they followed the rider. "When we heard of what was happening in the capital, we sent riders to gather all the help we could find, and the hill-folk came to help. About half of this herd is theirs."

The rider stopped when they reached the edge of the forest and hopped off his mount. Lying on the ground just before the tree line was a familiar black female elk. It could only have been Kolten's steed. Standing beside her was Anni's elk, Tempest.

Anni approached him and gave him a pet on his side.

"Good boy, Tempest."

He licked her affectionately as she used his name for the

THE BLUE HAIRED GIRL

first time.

"Icy," said Jarabei, looking at the female, "we just want to have a look."

The female elk looked a little unsure about all these people around, but she stood up, moved a bit to one side, and lay back down again.

Curled up on the ground beside its mother, and snoring contently, was a tiny thunder elk calf. Anni saw it was male, and Tempest looked every bit the proud father.

Now, Anni understood why the female had been ill when she had seen her in the stables. It also made sense why Tempest had been so fiercely protective of her.

She had been pregnant.

This thunder elk calf was different from any of the other ones. On either side of his ribcage, just behind his shoulders, was a pair of folded-up, black, feathered wings like a bird.

"It only happens once every few centuries," said Jarabei. "There called skystags."

"It's impossible," said Ackleman.

"Yet, there it is," chuckled Jarabei. "He'll need a name."

Jarabei looked to Anni. "Anni, what should we name him?"

Anni looked down at the magnificent winged creature.

Suddenly, the calf gave out a little cough. The tiny bumps on his head, where the antlers would be, sparked like the

390

THE SKYSTAG

passing of a static shock. Tempest held his head even higher with pride.

"Well…" said Anni thoughtfully. "How about Bolt?"

Anni looked down at the cute little calf, and he almost seemed to smile at her as she said his name. His mother pulled him in close, and Tempest got in between them and the calf, as if he had decided they had looked at his son enough for one day.

As Anni turned back to Ackleman, she saw one of the Yuspiereian guards walk up to him and whisper something to him.

Ackleman nodded and then he turned to Anni.

"Kolten's awake."

- CHAPTER 34 -
Forgiveness

As Anni and Ackleman walked toward the hospital, he had tried a few times to engage her in conversation, but she didn't feel much like talking. Anni couldn't help but wonder if she would be going to Zoltan by herself now if, indeed, she was still going at all.

Anni had been both hoping for and utterly dreading the moment when Kolten finally awoke from his sleep. The dwarf was the only father she had ever known. The last time she had spoken to him, Anni had ordered him to attack their friends, and it was all her fault that he had lost his hand.

How could Kolten ever forgive her?

Would he even speak to her? At least, let her explain that

FORGIVENESS

it was an accident. She had been trying to save him from the gloknore commander.

"You know, Anni, it really wasn't your fault," said Ackleman, trying to engage Anni in conversation.

"Yes, it was," muttered Anni. "I never should have taken off those lightwrists. Valentia warned me about that."

Ackleman patted Anni on the shoulder kindly as they rounded the corner toward the hospital. A pair of Yuspiereian guards were at the entrance, but they made no attempt to stop them from entering the building.

Soon, they found themselves at the hallway with the large windows.

Suddenly, Anni heard some shouting in a familiar, rough voice.

"Will you get off me! I'm fine!"

Ackleman pushed open the door and Anni saw him.

Kolten was fending off one of the nurses with his remaining hand. It looked like he was refusing to take his medicine.

"I told you, I'm f—" Kolten's voice failed him as his eyes found Anni.

Anni started to cry again at the sight of the bandaged stump that was all that remained of Kolten's left hand.

Without another word, Kolten knocked the nurse aside and leaped out of the bed. Before Anni knew it, she was being

393

THE BLUE HAIRED GIRL

hugged tightly in his powerful dwarven arms.

"*Don't you ever, ever scare me like that again!*" shouted Kolten, holding her close. "*Blegor could have killed you!*"

"I'm so sorry!" Anni cried. "It's all my fault you got hurt."

"I'm just glad you're okay," said Kolten, holding her tighter.

"Kolten, I didn't mean to!"

The dwarf pulled back from Anni and looked her square in the eye.

"What, you mean *this*?" he said, holding up his stump in disbelief. "Anni, I'm just glad you're safe."

"Please, forgive me, Kolten," Anni cried. "I'll do anything."

Kolten chuckled.

"You know, Anni, I owe you a lot. I wouldn't have survived with Mareitsia if it hadn't been for you," said Kolten.

"But you always tried to protect me from her."

"Anni, you're the strongest person I've ever known. You wore the darkwrists every day of your life and yet you never once stopped hoping for freedom. Before Mareitsia bought you, I had given up. I thought I would die a slave, working for that old hag. I'm not a brave man, Anni. Mareitsia scared the hell out of me. But once you came into my life, you gave me a courage that I never knew I had. You gave me the strength to hang on.

FORGIVENESS

Compared to that, as far as I'm concerned, my hand doesn't even matter. I owe you everything, Anni, and more."

"So, you'll forgive me?"

Kolten smiled.

"There's nothing to forgive. It was an accident; I know you didn't mean to. I don't consider you to be *like* my daughter, Anni. You *are* my daughter. I love you, and nothing in this world could ever change that."

Anni hugged the dwarf again.

"I love you too, Kolten. You're better than a father."

Anni let out a tearful laugh and held the dwarf as tightly as she could; she never wanted to let go.

More than a week had passed since Kolten had awoken in the hospital, but they still hadn't released him yet.

Now, Anni stood in the High Council chamber, in the circle of light she had been in more than a week before. Valentia had returned to her place in the highest of all the seats, and she was smiling, the crystal in her staff glowing brightly.

Ackleman gave Anni a wink from the shadows.

Most of the High Council had survived Stonor's purge, taking refuge in the safe houses like Valentia had done. Anni made a mental note to thank someone from the Republic for building them, if she ever got the chance to see Zoltan.

"Anni, we are in your debt," said Valentia. "You saved all our lives and you saved our democracy."

395

THE BLUE HAIRED GIRL

"I didn't do much," said Anni earnestly. "It was the brynywyn, mostly."

Every hand went into the air from the other councilors wanting to speak. Valentia tapped her staff and the window above Ackleman opened.

"Thank you, Chairwoman," said Ackleman politely. "I would like to remind the witness that she called for the reinforcements that saved the country, freed several prisoners from unlawful confinement, captured a dangerous terrorist, and saved the chairwoman from an assassination attempt. That sounds like she did quite a lot to me."

When he said it like that, it sounded a lot more impressive than it actually was. The last part, especially, as it was Anni herself who had been the would-be assassin in the first place. Oddly enough, no one bothered to mention that part.

"The council," said Valentia after Ackleman sat down, "has decided you are deserving of a reward for all you have done for this country."

"I don't need anything," said Anni simply.

"The council makes the decisions around here, Anni," said Valentia with a half-smile.

The only thing that Anni wanted was the same thing she had always wanted. The thing that had led her to battle whole armies and fight monsters. Something she would happily risk her life for all over again, even for just a chance to attain.

FORGIVENESS

Anni wanted to be free.

When she told the council this, they didn't seem to understand how important it was to her; a few of them even chuckled. They acted as if freedom were something that she already had. Worse still, they acted like everyone always had it, as if it couldn't be taken away at a moment's notice.

Anni knew better than anyone in that chamber that that was not the case. Freedom was not a birthright. It was a rare and precious thing. Delicate and easily lost, if not properly cared for. It was worth more to her than all the gold, jewels, power, and prestige in all of Decareia.

Several councilors glossed over her request and made suggestions for how to properly honor her and Kolten. They suggested everything from a statue of the two of them in the city square to handing over Stonor's lands to Anni and Kolten. None of which sounded even remotely of interest to Anni.

In the end, she asked only for passage across the Great Sea to Zoltan for her and Kolten; Ackleman agreed to escort them both there personally on his way home.

"Summon Stonor," said Valentia simply. "Let's get this over with."

As Anni descended down the long, spiral staircase toward the ground floor of the round building, part of her wanted to stay and watch what would happen to Stonor when they dragged him into the chamber, to watch him beg for mercy, but she decided

397

THE BLUE HAIRED GIRL

against it.

Stonor wasn't worth the time.

After a few days, Anni found herself down at the harbor.

Much of the damage that Anni's tidal wave had caused
had been repaired. Anni did, however, notice that the water
barrel that she knew hid the secret safe house remained
untouched and as inconspicuous as ever.

The warm summer wind and spray of the sea filled
Anni's lungs, and she couldn't stop grinning.

Kolten had finally been released from the hospital, and
he stood beside her. The stump that was all that was left of
Kolten's hand was still heavily bandaged, but it seemed to be
healing nicely.

The dwarf had been talking lately about building some
kind of clockwork, mechanical prosthetic when they reached the
Republic, and had, at one point, even jokingly asked Anni if she
could "give him a hand with it."

The dwarf was not known for his sense of humor.

But Kolten's spirits were higher than Anni had ever seen
them. He had even combed and neatly styled his short beard,
much of it having been burned off by the explosion. It now lay in
short but tidy dreadlocks-style braids for the occasion. He wore a
dwarf-sized traveling cloak, with the hood drawn up over his bald
head.

As a reward for his bravery, the High Council had

398

FORGIVENESS

offered Kolten anything he wanted. Not surprisingly, Kolten was not much for rewards or statues in his honor; he preferred something more practical. Instead, he had chosen a full assortment of new workman's tools of the highest quality, along with a chest of gold that was already on board the ship. Both of these would help him and Anni build new lives in the Republic of Zoltan.

She and Kolten stopped before the gangway of the Republic ship *The Seagull* as it was ready to depart. The harbor gates were open, and before them was nothing but the vast waters of the Great Sea.

"Come on, you slugs! Look alive, passengers coming aboard!" bellowed a strangers voice from the ship above.

Jarabei, Tycron, and Ackleman were waiting for them on the harbor pier. Even Valentia had taken the time out of her busy schedule to see them off. The chairwoman's crystal staff glowed blue with the bittersweet occasion.

Anni wore a lovely pale-blue dress that made her hair look less striking and more like a deliberate fashion statement. For the first time in her whole life, Anni had a full change of clothes and a whole chest full of personal belongings that were hers and hers alone.

Valentia had even paid for Anni to see a proper hairdresser for the first time. The tufts of blue hair she had lost to the dagger and the explosion had forced her to have it cut short,

399

THE BLUE HAIRED GIRL

but still, it looked nice. Like she was wearing a sky-blue hat.

"Now, Anni," said Valentia, handing Anni a new book. "You promised that you would practice. You'll need to know how to read in Zoltan."

"I will," said Anni earnestly.

In the weeks since the civil war had ended, Anni's reading had been progressing slowly. She still had a hard time with a few letters, but she was improving. It had been wonderful seeing Kolten's face light up the first time Anni was able to write the dwarf's name. Although her tutor had pointed out that the name *Kolten* didn't start with a "C," the dwarf had insisted that he liked it better that way.

Jarabei was completely sober, and his tiny chest was puffed up so proudly, it made it impossible for anyone to miss the over-sized, golden badge that was pinned over his heart.

It was a golden anchor, stitched to yellow and orange velvet, and at the top of the anchor was an inscription.

The Yuspiereian Medal of Bravery.

"I wish you could stay," said Tycron, who wore a lesser badge himself.

"There's a price on my head. Zoltan is the safest place for me," sniffed Anni. "You should come with us!"

"Our place is here," replied Valentia. "Stonor did a lot of damage. There's a great deal of work to be done. Yuspiereia needs all the help she can get."

400

FORGIVENESS

Kolten sniffed a little but hid it with a cough.

"The Republic is leaving the country in the best of hands," said Ackleman, shaking Valentia's hand.

Jarabei burst into sobs, his bushy mustache dripping with tears. He threw himself into an awkward hug around Kolten, who immediately tried to fight him off.

"Oi! Watch the arm!"

Anni gave out a tearful chuckle.

"Th-The brynywyn folk will f-find a way to stop Blegor!" sobbed Jarabei. "Then you can c-come back!"

The only thing Anni had ever wanted in her whole life was to be free and leave Yuspiereia behind her. Now, all she could do was dream of the day she would return. She had made such good friends here, it was hard to imagine never seeing them again.

Anni hugged Jarabei, Tycron, and Valentia each in turn.

Kayell, the reinstated captain of the Yuspiereian guard, approached with several other uniformed men.

They were escorting the bruised and heavily chained form of Stonor to a nearby ship.

"Hello, Stonor," said Valentia brightly. "As you may know, the High Council has voted to have you permanently banished from Yuspiereia. And the Senate has requested we hand you over to them."

Stonor said nothing.

401

THE BLUE HAIRED GIRL

"By the way, we're currently in the process of selling off your lands and holdings. The money will go to repair the damage you did."

Stonor twitched slightly but still said nothing.

"You had better hope your ship sinks," muttered Kayell quietly. "You'll wish it had, by the time the Senate gets through with you."

"You were right about one thing, Stonor," said Valentia, and Stonor eyed her darkly. "Yuspiereia will always be a democracy, as long as I am alive."

"Hey, what's that over there?" shouted Kolten, pointing off in one direction.

The moment Anni turned to see what the dwarf was pointing at, she heard a loud crunching sound.

Kolten was shaking his one remaining fist painfully, as Stonor spat out a tooth.

They all burst out laughing.

Kayell looked down at the dwarf disapprovingly, but even he couldn't hide a smile. His men took their prisoner down the pier, to where a high-security prison ship was waiting.

"All aboard for the Republic!" shouted a voice. "We sail with the tide!"

"That's us," said Ackleman, turning toward the gangway.

Anni gave one final hug to all three of them, and followed Ackleman aboard.

402

FORGIVENESS

As the ship started to move, there was a burst of light from Valentia's crystal, and the ship's sails filled with favorable winds. As a final parting gift, the chairwoman had given them fair winds to speed them on their journey.

Anni looked down at her friends and waved desperately to them, her blue hair lit brightly in the morning sun as the ship headed toward the horizon.

Anni wiped the tears from her eyes and turned toward Kolten.

His rough exterior and birdlike nose almost glowed as he beamed at her with a proud, father-like smile.

Anni hugged Kolten tightly, tears pouring down her cheeks.

The dwarf held her close, his bandaged stump on the small of her back.

"It's okay, Anni," sniffed Kolten, and a single tear rolled down his birdlike nose. "It's over. We're finally free."

The End.

EPILOGUE

The Golairian warlord, Blegor of the House of Dragmor, sat upon his throne of silver, finishing the meal that his chef had prepared for him.

He was a tall, muscular gloknore, and had a deep, scar etched across his face, from his right eye to his left cheek. A pair of huge, tusk-like canine teeth jutted from his top jaw and slurred his speech slightly. His head and neck were shaved into a mohawk, and the hair went all the way down his spine, stopping just above his buttocks.

Blegor, or Blegor the Cruel, Blegor the Hated, Blegor the Vile, Blegor the Evil—he was known by many names. He was one of the most powerful warlords, controlling the largest land parcel in all of Golairia.

EPILOGUE

His lands were inhabited mostly by fellow gloknore, humans, and a few scattered dwarven camps, and most of the inhabitants were either slaves or slave owners. He had taken his throne from a dark wizard that he had murdered years before. Both he and his predecessor had found that the easiest way to keep his people in check was to keep them in chains.

As Blegor picked remnants of the meal from his teeth with his finger-claw, he found a small piece of bone had lodged itself near his left tusk, and he sat there poking and prodding around his tooth, trying to free it.

After a moment or two, the piece of bone came free, and he spat it on to the floor.

The chef had been warned not to prepare meals that could get lodged in his teeth. Blegor made a note to have one of the chef's fingers cut off to help him remember.

He could hear, in the work yard outside his castle, the familiar sounds of the iron forges, broken by the frequent sound of a horsewhip and the occasional scream. Blegor knew these sounds well—they were the sounds of profit. Human, gloknore, dwarf, elf, it didn't matter…they all could be broken by the whip.

On the table by his throne sat a printed letter with a purple lion insignia at the top. Blegor didn't know why he was keeping it. He had read the letter several times, and each time he had, he had nearly thrown it into the fire in disgust.

Greetings, Blegor of the House of Dragmor… The Republic

THE BLUE HAIRED GIRL

of Zoltan has received reports of various types of humanoid rights violations within your borders…We received no response to our other inquiries…The Senate respectfully requests that you allow a commission to be appointed to assess the accuracy of these reports…killings, institutionalized slavery, mass rape, possible genocide…failure to do so may result in further actions taken against your administration…Economic sanctions…

This was not the first letter he had received from the Republic, but it was the first one he had read all the way through and had, for some reason, chosen to keep. It seemed the Senate was simply refusing to mind their own business.

Although he had received letters from them in the past, they had never threatened sanctions before. That could cause him some problems, as many of the goods the slaves produced were sold in the Republic.

He heard the sudden sound of a particularly loud whip, followed by a scream, coming from the work yard.

What went on outside the borders of the Republic was not of their concern.

They're just jealous that we found a better way to run things out here, he thought as he read the letter again.

There was a sudden knock on the throne room door.

"What is it?!" snapped Blegor.

"Sorry to bother you, Master," said one of the guards as he poked his head in the throne room nervously. "But she's finally calmed down."

EPILOGUE

"The old hag?!"

"Yes, Master. I asked them to wait so you could interrogate her yourself."

About time! The old woman's been babbling like a lunatic for weeks.

All thoughts of the Senate, its commission, and its economic sanctions vanished from his mind instantly.

He got up from his throne and followed the guards down the hall to the dungeon.

As he entered the prison, the smells of feces, death, and misery assaulted his senses, but he took no notice. The cells on either side of the passage were all overcrowded with men, women, and even children.

On the far wall of the dungeon was a tiny cage. It was only three feet deep and three feet wide, and about four feet high. Any prisoner locked up in it was unable to do anything but sit on the floor.

Locked in the cage was a busty woman; both her hands were shackled to the walls. She was probably in her early- to mid-fifties, but her time as a prisoner had aged her considerably.

The woman was awake and recoiled slightly when Blegor entered.

"Get her," he ordered.

The guard unlocked the tiny cage and pulled the woman out, dumping her in a chair in the middle of the room.

"Who are you?" demanded Blegor.

407

THE BLUE HAIRED GIRL

The woman didn't answer; her gaze darted toward the dungeon door.

"You're not going anywhere," shouted one of the guards, seeing what she was looking at.

"I-I didn't do anything," she stammered.

"Your name!" snapped Blegor.

She opened her mouth and closed it again.

"Now!"

"M-Mareitsia! Th-That was my horse! I didn't steal it!"

"I'm not interested in your damned horse," snapped Blegor. "I want to know about the girl with the blue hair."

There was a short pause.

"If I tell you, you'll let me go?"

There was scatted laughter around the room; even some of the prisoners chuckled ironically.

Blegor turned toward the fire pit on the side of the room. The guards held their captive firmly by each shoulder.

Blegor removed a red-hot iron from the fire and held it in front of Mareitsia's face.

"This is not a negotiation."

The prisoner struggled with her captors as best as her tired limbs could manage, but they would not let her arms free.

Blegor lowered the iron down slowly toward the woman's leg, and she let out a scream of agony as the tip made contact with her flesh.

"She was my slave! I bought her years ago! Her, and my

EPILOGUE

dwarf!"

"When did you buy her?"

"I can't remember!"

The hot iron was pressed against her again.

"Ahhhhh!"

"When?!"

"Eight or ten years ago!" Mareitsia screamed.

"How old would the girl be today?" asked Blegor, holding up the red-hot piece of metal.

"M-Maybe eleven or twelve."

That's the right age, thought Blegor.

"And where is she now?"

"I don't know!"

The smoldering piece of metal was pressed against her flesh again, this time on her stomach.

"Ahhhhh! I don't know!"

"Then where do you suspect? If she was your slave for all those years, you must have some idea where she would go."

The torture continued for several more minutes, until finally, Mareitsia let out the coughing croak of, "Zoltan."

"She was heading to Zoltan?" He lowered the hot poker.

The woman nodded and explained about a pair of defective darkwrists, using as few words as she possibly could to get the point across.

Blegor hesitated. He knew she must be telling the truth, but he still didn't like it.

409

THE BLUE HAIRED GIRL

It would make sense for her to head to Zoltan; it would be far away from here.

Blegor gestured for the woman to be thrown aside. One of the guards fondled her breasts unnecessarily as he did so.

Blegor soon found himself back in his throne room, pacing back and forth as thoughts and possibilities flew through his head, and he began to argue with himself in his own mind.

*My mercenary horde was defeated at the gates of…*said one part of his mind. *She blew up one of my best, so she must have…*

*It's got to be her…*said another thought.

"Zoltan! Damn it!" he shouted out loud, nearly stomping his foot in frustration.

I've already doubled the reward for her, he thought. *Even Zoltan has to have people that would take that offer. But I can't really count on that.*

He sat down on his throne for a moment in quiet contemplation. The letter from the Senate was still sitting on his table.

The Republic of Zoltan was on the other side of the world, where people were different. If she was escaping slavery, Zoltan would be the logical place to go. It was a place that Blegor had never visited, although privately, he often wondered what it would be like to see it. The huge sea towers, the great bridges and canals, the capital city of Zed. The Zoltanian National Guard, and the rest of the Republic's impressive army.

If the blue-haired girl was there, she would likely be safe.

EPILOGUE

It would be difficult for anyone to touch her.

"I need to come up with a plan," said Blegor out loud, massaging his temples.

For there was nothing in all Decareia that the mighty warlord, Blegor the Cruel, feared more than the blue-haired girl who had haunted his nightmares for the past eight years.

WANT TO FIND OUT WHAT HAPPENS?

Check out our website at www.thezoltanchronicles.com. There you will find links to other books in the series. You can also access our Facebook, Twitter, and YouTube channel for official Zoltan Chronicles content.

Also, if you enjoyed this book, please consider taking a few minutes to give us an honest review on amazon. Scan the QR code below or search for The Blue Haired Girl on Amazon to post an amazon review.

Manufactured by Amazon.ca
Bolton, ON